HEAL

PIPER SCOTT

 LOVELIGHT

First LoveLight Press electronic publication: December 2017
http://lovelightpress.com

Heal is set in the USA, and as such uses American English throughout.

PROLOGUE

GABRIEL

The dreams always started the same.

The bed shifted. Gabriel opened his eyes to a darkened room, but he didn't need to see to know that someone was rising out of bed beside him. Drowsy confusion led him to lift his head, and he blinked a few times in rapid succession to clear the sleep from his eyes. In the shadows, a grainy gray shape emerged.

Humanoid. Masculine. Familiar.

Gabriel settled back into the sheets and rolled over to take up the space where the figure had slumbered. The residual body heat left in their blankets warmed his skin, and the smell of the figure's cologne—marine mineral notes with earthy, mossy overtones—partnered with the scent of alpha and soothed Gabriel's soul.

Home.

"Garrison?" Gabriel's voice cracked from disuse. He pulled the sheets closer to his body and looked through the darkness at the form freshly risen from the bed. "Come back to sleep. It's not time to get up yet."

There was no reply.

The figure standing at the bedside stepped away, putting distance between himself and Gabriel.

"Garrison?" Gabriel asked again. He sat up, body protesting. It was too early to be awake. He'd worked long into the night, his hair still damp from his last shower of the evening. If he pretended, he couldn't smell the lingering traces of his last john. "Don't go."

Gabriel's eyes were blurred from sleep, and he blinked several times to distinguish the figure in greater detail. He stood facing away from the bed—proud shoulders, a sensible haircut, body not overly athletic, but still toned enough that Gabriel enjoyed every solid muscle and each hard line. He was nude. Gabriel allowed himself to trace the outline of his body and drink it in.

Safety. Adoration. Comfort.

He was in love, and he knew he'd feel that way forever. Garrison Baylor was his soulmate, and Gabriel wanted more than anything to prove it to him.

"Come back to bed. Please?" Gabriel scooted over to close the distance Garrison had put between them. "Please, Garrison? We can make love, or, um, you know, whatever you want..."

There was no response.

Frowning, Gabriel swung his legs over the side of the bed. The soles of his bare feet met the cold wooden floor, and a tremble ran up his spine that he couldn't shake. A hazy part of Gabriel's brain told him it was summer, but the floor was freezing. This disconnect worried him, and for a moment, he remained seated on the edge of the bed while he tried to get over the strange rift between what he knew and what he felt. His gaze parted from Garrison, and he didn't notice him move across the room until the squeak of the doorknob brought him to lift his head and refocus.

Garrison was leaving.

He was leaving again.

But this time, he was leaving when Gabriel was awake and willing to offer his body.

He was leaving to bed another boy.

2

Impulse brought Gabriel to his feet, but his sleep-weakened knees weren't ready to support his weight. He stumbled as he stood, barely catching himself on the bed. A shrill gasp broke from his lips on the way down, and once he was steady, he took a second to regain his breath before trying to stand again. No matter what he did, his legs were uncooperative, unresponsive, and sluggish, like Gabriel's brain was only intermittently in control of his body.

"Don't go!" Gabriel cried through the darkness, but his voice came as nothing more than a whimper. "Don't leave me! Don't go. Don't go to him..."

Garrison pulled the door open. The darkness of the room gave way to the light of the hallway beyond it, and the sudden brightness blinded Gabriel. He squeezed his eyes shut and ducked his head, but the spots in his vision didn't go away. In desperation, he covered his face with his hand and counted down from five, trying his best to remain calm in the face of crisis.

A floorboard creaked in the hallway. The sound of heavy footsteps approached. Carefully Gabriel parted his fingers, allowing a modest amount of light to reach his eyes. This time, the light didn't blind him—it allowed him to see.

What he saw made his heart stop.

Standing in the doorway was another man—a man whose presence alone made Gabriel tumble onto the bed and crawl backward, seeking salvation. He wanted to run, to hide, to do *something*, but his feet couldn't find purchase on the bed, and his arms moved like he'd submerged them in a tub of syrup, if they obeyed him at all.

"Do you want him?" Garrison asked the man. "He's one of the finest omegas you'll ever get your hands on. Pliant. Subservient. *Broken.*"

I'm not broken, Gabriel wanted to whisper, but his jaw wouldn't move. *I love you, Garrison. I* love *you. There's nothing broken about that.*

"I want him," the man replied. Those ugly words were curled with disgusting self-indulgence. They made Gabriel want to

3

scream. "Can I take him? Right here? Tangle him up in those sheets and make him mine?"

No. Gabriel squeezed his eyes shut. His body had abandoned him, leaving him trapped in his mind. *This is my bed with Garrison. We're supposed to be together. I don't want you here.*

Nothing he thought did any good. Gabriel was caught on the bed like a mouse in a glue trap—stuck, helpless, and afraid.

Why was Garrison doing this to him? He'd been good and done everything Garrison had told him to do. He'd bedded every man Garrison had asked without complaint, because Garrison had told him that if he did, eventually they'd have enough money to get married. Why couldn't they just be together?

It wasn't fair.

The man beyond the doorway moved past Garrison, entering the darkness. Gabriel's heart raced as he approached the bed, and it nearly burst when the man's knees sank into the mattress. Gabriel smelled him on the air—like wood and leather, and beneath that, the putrid scent of an alpha whose soul was rotting.

As the man moved across the bed, straddling Gabriel inch by inch, Garrison left through the open door. Gabriel lifted his head and tried to cry out for him, but words refused to come. He knew that if Garrison closed that door, he'd never see him again. He *knew* it.

So why was Garrison going? Why was he leaving Gabriel with someone he didn't want? Why was he letting this happen?

If Gabriel could just get up from the bed, if he could move his legs, if he could do *something,* then maybe they could still be together. Maybe he could follow Garrison wherever he wanted to go.

But he couldn't move. He couldn't talk. He could barely breathe.

Garrison closed the door behind him. The room was plunged in darkness once more, and Gabriel felt the weight of the man without a name pushing him down into the mattress.

The dreams always started the same, and they always ended the same, too—as nightmares.

───────────

Gabriel woke up screaming. Mouth dry, throat sore, and heart pounding, he struggled against the thin blankets on his bed only to find that he was trapped in them. The scream of terror turned into one of anguish, and he struggled to roll to the side, but his body refused to let him.

"Gabriel?" a familiar but distant voice asked. "Gabriel, you've got to come back to us. Come back down from wherever you are and come back to us. It was a dream. It was all a dream. You're *safe*."

Only Gabriel didn't feel safe at all. He hadn't felt safe since the bust on The White Lotus brothel had robbed him of his home—and of Garrison.

"Gabriel!" the voice said again, firmer this time. "Gabriel, come back down. Come back to us."

But Gabriel couldn't. He didn't want to. All he wanted to do was go back to when he had been safe, and loved, and cared for. Before he'd come to Stonecrest Omega Rehabilitation Center, before he'd been taken from the brothel during the bust and kept unjustly by the man with no name, he'd been with Garrison, and that time had been the happiest of his life.

He wanted to go back.

"Gabriel?"

Gabriel focused and found himself in his closet-sized private room at Stonecrest, light streaming through the singular window as Counselor Kendrick held him by the shoulders. The concern on the counselor's face should have made Gabriel feel cared for, but instead, it made him feel worse.

Broken.

He wasn't broken. Not really. Not in any way that counted.

Love broke men. It made them weak. Gabriel didn't get why

5

none of the counselors here understood that. He hadn't been shaped into something he wasn't—he'd been formed into the man he was, and Garrison had been the one who'd molded him from useless putty into a creature of exquisite beauty. He'd taken Gabriel when he was still bumbling and confused, unsure of his sexuality, unsure of his body, unsure of *everything,* and he'd shown Gabriel the world. But now that world was small and gray, and Gabriel longed to see color again.

Gabriel blinked away tears. He was alone.

Blinking didn't do anything to keep the tears at bay. They rolled down his cheeks in silence until Gabriel's nose blocked and he had to breathe through his mouth. It was a mistake. The air hitched in his throat and turned into an ugly, shuddering sob.

All he wanted was to get to Garrison, and he'd *failed*. He'd let his brother, Adrian, put him in this place, thinking that he might be able to figure out a way to get back to the man he loved, but instead, he'd languished. The things the counselors tried to teach him weren't meant for people like him—he wasn't broken by circumstance, he was broken by love, and that was different. So different.

"Gabriel?" Counselor Kendrick tried again. His hands tightened on Gabriel's shoulders, the pressure reassuring instead of overbearing. "Where are you, Gabriel?"

"Lost," Gabriel said through a rattling sob. "I'm lost, and I don't want to be here anymore."

"Gabriel?" Counselor Kendrick's tone became worried. "What are you saying?"

Gabriel let loose with one last ugly wail that shook his chest and hurt his lungs, but he couldn't hold back the truth any longer. "I want to call my brother. I want to go home."

1

CEDRIC

"So, Mr. Langston..." Sterling didn't glance at the papers in front of him, some of which Cedric knew were his resume and cover letter. "I'm not going to waste your time with questions meant to psychoanalyze you. What I want to know more than anything else is why, after five years away from The Shepherd, you've decided to come back to vie for a managerial position?"

To sit across from Aurora's one and only Sterling Holt, owner and manager of kink club The Shepherd, was an honor. Cedric smoothed his hands down his thighs, cognizant of his posture, and looked Sterling in the eye. He hadn't come so far to waste this opportunity. If Sterling remembered him from his short-lived membership at The Shepherd, Cedric took it as a good sign. There was silent trust already established between them—a relationship that other candidates might not have, if only he could explain his way around his long absence.

That wouldn't be difficult. There was a reason why he hadn't come back to the club, and if Sterling didn't understand it, it was his loss.

"Vie isn't the right word for it." Cedric held himself with his back aligned but his shoulders loose. His posture conveyed confidence, but hinted at familiarity he hoped would help ingratiate himself with Sterling. Age didn't mean anything—all that mattered was that he appeared to be in control when speaking with men in positions of power. And Cedric was in control. His genes had already taken care of half the work—now all he needed was to make sure he sold himself as the total package. "Vie would suggest that I'm on a level playing field with your other skilled candidates. The truth is, I'm not—I'm ahead of the competition."

A playful glint sparked in Sterling's eyes, accompanied by a charmed, upward curl of his lips. "Oh?"

"Not only was I a regular member of The Shepherd who maintained excellent standing for a year-long period, but since my departure, I've aligned my life in ways that have strengthened my appreciation of the community. As is listed on my resume, I—"

Sterling folded his arms on the desk and leaned forward an almost imperceptible amount. The light in his eyes changed from playful to paternal. Cedric wasn't sure whether he should be humbled or humiliated. Sterling was almost twice his age, after all. A look like that could easily be patronizing. But Cedric's gut told him that Sterling's intentions were nothing but pure.

"Forget about the resume, and forget about all the canned interview responses you've been practicing in front of the mirror in preparation for today. I want to hear about your life from *you*. Tell me about what you do, and tell me why you're passionate about it."

The request swelled like a balloon in Cedric's chest, its presence not stemming from fear or anxiety, but from pride. Of all people, Sterling wanted to hear about what he'd done with his life. It was an interview, sure, but the kindness in Sterling's words and the quiet domination he exuded resonated with Cedric. He fed off Sterling's vibe and mirrored it. If Sterling wanted to be approached as an equal, then it was what Cedric would do. Age separated them, but there was no reason to disparage himself simply because his experiences were limited by time. Cedric had done a lot of growing in the last five years. It was time to show off who he'd become.

He would make Sterling understand his truth.

"I'm a professional Dom." Cedric kept his posture straight but his shoulders relaxed. He met Sterling's eyes when he spoke, staring down those pools of blue to make it clear that he wasn't afraid. The prestige Sterling held over him would not divide them. Cedric was worthy. "Over the last four years, I've made a name for myself in the kink community as a professional, dependable, and courteous service provider. I deliver release from the pressure of modern life for men and women both, of any genetic variation, but I specialize in omega services."

"Why omegas?" Sterling's eyes showed mild interest sharpened by something Cedric couldn't quite put his finger on. Engagement? Curiosity? Whatever it was, it left him feeling eager to continue to explain himself.

The answer came easily. "Because omegas deserve release just as much as anyone else. The men and women who seek my services give their all in competitive fields, and strive to maintain positions of authority. Alphas and betas in high-pressure jobs have been the ones who traditionally seek submission, but there is a stigma around omegas seeking the same—as though if they go after what they really want, it makes them weak, or that giving in to the pleasures of submission is inextricably linked to their biological drive. In my opinion, the truth is far more nuanced than that."

It was as if he'd flipped a switch in his head. The words he spoke were formal and structured, but they rolled from his tongue like he was chatting with an old friend. Sterling had invited him to open up, and so Cedric had—but that was no excuse to get sloppy. He was professional in what he did, and he was determined to show Sterling as much.

Sterling's interest didn't lessen. "Explain."

"Omegas are like anyone else." Cedric spoke with conviction, and he spoke with truth. He'd stood by his ideals since his eyes had

9

been opened at The Shepherd almost seven years ago, and he wasn't about to back down from them now. "No matter what society or the media says, I fully support the Omega Rights Movement. These are intelligent, dependable, and hardworking men and women who deserve to be treated the same way anyone else is treated. They work the same high-pressure jobs, suffer from the same stresses, and work toward the same hopes and dreams that we do. So why not offer them the same kind of release?" Cedric searched Sterling's face for signs that he wanted to interrupt, but he found none. With Sterling's unspoken permission, he kept talking. "Professional Doms and Dominatrixes have offered private services for alphas looking for release from their stressful lives since forever, but who has stepped in to fill the need of omegas looking for the same relief? It's not about genetics, and it's not about a sense of natural superiority... what I do, I do because they deserve it."

"And how do you know that you're not overstepping your boundaries?" Sterling asked.

Cedric got the impression that this wasn't part of the job interview anymore. The professional slant in Sterling's voice, once so prominent, was gone.

It didn't matter. Cedric sat up a little straighter, made sure to meet Sterling's eyes, and replied with sincerity. "I know because I'm not afraid to ask."

The statement hung heavily between them, thickening the air as it set the tone for the rest of the interview. Cedric refused to look away from Sterling's gaze. The interview made him nervous, but he wasn't afraid. He would not compromise on his beliefs, even if it meant he had to pass up the job that would change his life.

Even if it meant he had to dishonor her.

Sterling arched a brow thoughtfully. "I'm curious as to how—"

The office door flew open. The doorknob struck the wall guard with a metallic *chank* that made Cedric jump. His eyes had been trained on Sterling—he hadn't been expecting the interruption.

Sterling, however, looked unperturbed. When he spoke, he did so with affection laced with controlled exasperation. "Welcome home, Adrian. I wasn't expecting you back so soon. I'm in the middle of an interview."

A young man stormed into the room, his dark gray suit and formal white shirt only made less casual by the infant he cradled against his chest. Done up in a pink onesie spotted with little yellow ducks, she curled her fingers around her father's collar and tugged. Short, downy blond hair covered her head. But it wasn't the sudden appearance of the man or the strange contrast of business-professional against paternal that widened Cedric's eyes—it was his identity. "*Adrian?*"

None other than Adrian Lowe stopped in his tracks and diverted his attention from Sterling to Cedric. The hardened look on Adrian's face softened with confusion. He squinted at Cedric, brows knit together, like he wasn't sure that Cedric was real.

To be fair, Cedric wasn't sure that what he was seeing was real, either. The last time he'd seen Adrian Lowe was right before they'd graduated high school. There'd been rumors in their group of friends about the tragedy the Lowe family had been through during the summer break between high school and college, but Cedric had never been involved enough in Adrian's life to concern himself with the details. To see him now, a baby clutched to his chest, standing in Sterling's private office above The Shepherd, was a shock Cedric hadn't braced himself for.

Adrian spent a long moment looking at Cedric, then flicked his gaze back to Sterling. He squared his shoulders. Irritation read clearly on his face, and Cedric couldn't help but feel like it was meant to be directed at him.

"We need to talk," Adrian said.

"I'm in the middle of an interview, Adrian. You'll have to wait."

"We need to talk *now*." Adrian stepped forward, coming to stand beside Cedric. At such close proximity, Cedric could pick up just a hint of the omega he remembered from high school. There was no doubt about it—it *was* Adrian Lowe. "It's about Gabriel."

The atmosphere changed. Like a blackout curtain pulled across a southern-facing window, the room was robbed of its light. Sterling's professionally playful expression faded, and he eased up from his chair with thinly veiled urgency that Cedric wagered would have looked like fear had Sterling not been in such tight control of himself. When Sterling met his eyes again, his expression was drawn and his emotions were masked. "I'm sorry, Mr. Langston. Would you excuse me for a moment?"

"Of course." There was no other answer. Whatever was happening was serious, and Cedric was in no position to pin Sterling to an interview when it was clear he was needed elsewhere. Burning bridges with Sterling Holt was a bad, *bad* idea if Cedric wanted to remain an integral part of Aurora's kink community— and if he still wanted a shot at the job he was interviewing for. "I'll wait here. Take your time."

Sterling and Adrian exited the room, leaving Cedric to process what he'd just seen. It was ludicrous to think the eighteen-year-old Adrian Lowe he remembered from high school would be the same person after half a decade, but to think that Adrian's life would have shaped up in such a way that they'd meet again in Sterling's office? Cedric still couldn't believe it.

With a heavy outward sigh, Cedric settled in his chair and tilted his head back until it couldn't go back any farther. The ceiling was plain and white, offering little distraction. He let his eyes drift out of focus while he came off his interview high.

While he wished Sterling and Adrian the best, he knew that the interruption likely meant he'd be overlooked for the job. Whatever emergency was going on would distract Sterling from their interview, and Cedric would fade from his mind and be disregarded as a qualified candidate when he sat down to make his choice. Cedric did his best to accept that reality for what it was. The faster he moved on from the loss, the faster he'd be able to bounce back. It wasn't that he was hurting for money, but the lateral move from professional Dom to manager at The Shepherd was too good an opportunity to pass up. The connections alone were worth it.

What it would have meant to Brittany sweetened the deal that much more.

Minutes passed. There was arguing in the hall—one-sided, by the sounds of it. The only raised voice Cedric heard was Adrian's, but he was silenced following a heavy thud that vibrated through the office wall. Cedric lifted his head and turned in his chair to look at the door, an eyebrow raised. No further noise followed.

Five more minutes passed. There were footsteps down the hall, and then the door was opened once more. Adrian stepped through the doorway with partially lidded eyes and ruddy lips, his hair mussed. His blown-out pupils paired with the dreamy look on his face hinted that he was teetering on the edge of subspace. He no longer held his baby daughter to his chest. Sterling entered behind him, the baby cradled in his arm. She cooed and tugged at his jacket, but in that moment, Sterling's eyes were only for Adrian. If Cedric had ever doubted the validity of their relationship, he no longer did. The chemistry between them burned red-hot, and the Dom emerging from inside Sterling fitted the starry-eyed submissive Adrian had melted into to a T.

"I apologize for the interruption." Sterling took his seat, careful not to disturb his daughter. Adrian stood behind him—he did his best to look firm, but the faraway, relaxed look in his eyes betrayed him. "I'll be blunt. Due to personal circumstance, the position I was looking to fill is momentarily closed while we adjust to a new family dynamic."

Cedric's heart sank. He knew to expect as much, but to hear it from Sterling so firmly and directly? It hurt.

But Sterling didn't stop there. He met Cedric's eyes, and the uptick in Cedric's heartbeat and the way his breath jammed in his throat spoke for his excitement before it resonated inside of him. The intensity in Sterling's gaze pinned him, but Cedric met it and returned it. He would not allow himself to come across as meek.

Not now. He'd left submission behind five years ago, and nothing could make him go back.

"Another position, however, has opened up." Sterling adjusted the baby in his arms, keeping her cradled protectively to his chest. Her presence did not detract from the stern, immovable force that was Sterling. Even with a pink-onesie-clad infant, Sterling commanded respect. "...One which I believe you would be a prime candidate for, and one which may serve as a test, of sorts, to determine if you're a proper fit for the management position once it does open back up."

"All right." Cedric pressed his lips together. "I'm listening."

"I want to see what kind of a Dom you really are." Sterling looked into his eyes, but his gaze didn't stop there—it pierced Cedric deep, as if Sterling was looking to pluck out the truth from his very soul. "I want to see your work ethic in action. I'd like to hire you on twenty-four seven to care for an omega who is desperately in need of release from the life he's been brought to lead."

"Twenty-four seven?" Cedric's fingers tightened against his palm, well out of Sterling's line of sight.

"Full-time domination." Sterling's expression did not waver. "Paid, of course. You will not be asked to overstep any of your limits or boundaries, nor will you be restricted as to what you can or cannot do, so long as you believe it is in the best interest of the submissive."

Adrian planted his hands on Sterling's desk and leaned forward, subspace blown to pieces as his eyes narrowed and his lips scowled. "But if you touch my brother, I will personally see to it that you will *never* touch him, or any other omega, ever again."

Gabriel.

They wanted him to dominate Gabriel Lowe.

Cedric's gaze locked with Adrian's, and his eyes narrowed. "It's not your decision whether the domination is sexual or not."

The room went silent. The tick of the clock hanging on the wall filled the emptiness, but Cedric barely heard it. His eyes stayed locked on Adrian's. Back in high school, Adrian had barely been a blip on his radar, but Cedric remembered him well enough. After he'd gone into heat, he'd changed—become bolder and more outspoken, like he had a point to prove, and no one would keep him from proving it. Cedric would not allow himself to be spoken over, and he would not allow his potential submissive to suffer at Adrian's hands, either, whether that submissive was Adrian's brother or not.

It was Gabriel's decision whether Cedric lay his hands on him. Adrian would not speak for him.

Eventually, Adrian scowled and dropped his gaze. He set his hand on the back of Sterling's chair, eyes narrowed and directed to the side, like he was insulted.

Cedric returned his attention to Sterling. "For how long?"

"However long it takes." Sterling set a hand on his daughter's back, but his eyes did not leave Cedric. "A few months at most, if I had to guess. The problem with Gabriel is that he--"

Adrian's hand moved to squeeze Sterling's shoulder, and Sterling stopped what he was saying and shook his head. Cedric looked between them curiously, but he didn't push for further information. Whatever it was they wanted to tell him about Gabriel, he would find out on his own.

"I can't take the job unless I meet him. I need to know it's what he wants." Consent and communication, above all else, were essential if an arrangement like that was going to work. Power was always in the hands of the submissive—Cedric only ever satisfied their needs. He never forced a client to do anything they weren't one hundred percent certain they wanted. Sterling, of all people, should have known that. "A full-time arrangement isn't something you take lightly. I need to know that he trusts me, and I need to know I can trust him to express himself."

Adrian pushed off the desk and crossed his arms over his chest. Sterling, however, smiled. "That response leads me to believe that you're the right man for the job. I'd be glad to arrange a meeting. Something casual. Are you available tomorrow afternoon?"

"Anytime after three."

"You'll meet me at the doors of the club at three-thirty tomorrow." Sterling rose from his desk slowly, careful not to disturb the child he cradled in his arm. "We'll introduce the two of you and make sure that the fit is right, and from there, we'll finalize the details."

"Tomorrow at three-thirty." Cedric followed Sterling to his feet and held out his hand. The gesture was returned. Sterling's grip was firm, and the hardened glint in his eyes promised that what he asked wasn't some kind of elaborate joke.

"It's been a pleasure, Mr. Langston." Sterling released his hand, leaving Cedric on his own to process the unexpected turn of events. "We'll see you then."

2

GABRIEL

The spare bedroom was gone. Gabriel leaned against the doorway and looked across the room in silence, stunned into inaction. Melancholy crept down his throat and into his stomach, tingling and unwelcome. No matter what thoughts he tried to cling to, the awful feelings it brought wouldn't go away.

The room he'd used to call his own was an office now. Sterling's desk, chair, and filing cabinets occupied the space where Gabriel's bed used to be. Not that it was *really* his bed, but in the few months he'd lived with Sterling and Adrian, Gabriel had grown fond of the blankets and the downy mattress. He'd liked the sleek, modern dresser across the room, glamorous with its dark finish and meticulously polished surface. He'd even liked the coat hangers in the closet, with their velvet covering.

Now all of it was gone.

"We turned Sterling's office into Lilian's nursery," Adrian explained softly from behind Gabriel's shoulder. He set a hand between Gabriel's shoulder blades. "Sterling moved his office into the guest bedroom, and we've put the furniture that was in it into storage. We're planning a move in the next few years, anyway—sometime before Lilian starts kindergarten."

"Where can I sleep?" Gabriel couldn't speak any louder than a near-whisper. The way his throat tightened convinced him that if he tried to raise his voice, he'd start to cry. The last two years had been nothing but change, and after having stability for such a long time while at The White Lotus, he hated it. "I know you w-weren't expecting me, but..."

"We had the foresight to invest in a sleeper sofa." Adrian's thumb worked in small circles against Gabriel's back, but it didn't help Gabriel feel any better. "It's comfy. We have spare pillows and blankets, the same ones that you used when you were staying in the old guest bedroom. You'll like it."

The sleeper sofa didn't make a difference. Not really. Gabriel had slept on the floor, and sometimes, when he'd been very bad, he'd been forced to sleep while standing. Comfort didn't matter to him as much as Adrian's perception of him did, and it was obvious from how Adrian had done away with the guest bedroom that he didn't think very highly of him at all.

Adrian and Sterling hadn't expected him to come back. They'd had their baby, they'd remodeled their penthouse, and they'd worked him out of their lives. They'd expected him to recover and succeed.

He'd failed them.

A part of him, a dark, twisted part, whispered that if his plan had worked, he would have been failing them, anyway. If he'd found a way to get to Garrison, Adrian would have been disappointed and worried, even more than he was now. But if his plan had worked, another voice murmured, then at least he would have been happy. At least he wouldn't have become a burden on his brother. Adrian's life was about Sterling now, and Gabriel's return threatened to ruin it.

"You don't have to worry about privacy," Adrian promised. "We've got some screens we can put up, so you'll have walls between us and you. You only need to come out when you want to. We won't bother you."

Gabriel's fingers curled upward until he found the sleeve of his sweater. He picked and pulled at the hem nervously. Fundamentally, he knew that what Adrian said was true, but it didn't help him get over his rising anxiety.

"Lilian is quiet. Once or twice a week, she gets a little fussy, but for the most part she's a well-behaved baby. I don't think you'll have to worry about her waking you up in the middle of the night. And if you'd like, we can move her crib into our room, so you won't hear her at all."

The slow, steady thud of Gabriel's heart managed to rattle his ribcage. He blinked a few times in rapid succession, then took a deep breath and let it all out in an attempt to relieve some of the pressure building up inside.

"Besides," Adrian murmured, leaning a little closer like what he had to say was a secret, "I've got something I want to talk to you about. It might not matter if there isn't a room with a door or if Lilian is fussy at night much longer. Let's go sit, okay? We should talk about it now, before we get distracted."

The declaration pulled Gabriel out of his head, and he found the strength to turn and look at his brother. The last nine months hadn't changed Adrian physically all that much—his face had matured a little, his stubble thicker and his eyes more wary than they'd been before, but his hair was still the same golden-brown Gabriel remembered, and his eyes the same gray-blue that Gabriel had always wished he shared. What was different was how he held himself, like he had something to look forward to instead of something he constantly had to tolerate.

It was purpose. Life. A family.

Gabriel's stomach twisted. He'd lost his purpose the day he'd been pried away from Garrison, and now it felt like he was never going to get it back.

"Come." Adrian was firm, but not overbearing. With a gentle application of pressure, he guided Gabriel from the doorway back into the living room. The leather couch Gabriel remembered from his last visit had been moved—in fact, all the furniture had been rearranged. Everything was different in small, unsettling ways.

The new sleeper sofa was in a divided part of the living room, separated from the modern furniture Sterling kept by a long, folding screen divider with frosted glass panels. The not-a-room was tiny, but it was cozy, and Gabriel eyed the blankets and pillows already laid out in anticipation of his arrival. Sterling hadn't been in the car when Adrian had picked him up and checked him out of therapy, so Gabriel assumed it was his handiwork.

He wondered if Adrian resented him a little for it. Sterling was Adrian's alpha, not his, and yet here he was, making a home for Gabriel when Gabriel had no claims on him.

"Sit. Make yourself comfortable." Adrian nodded toward the couch. His hand left Gabriel's back. "Do you want anything from the kitchen?"

"No, thank you." All Gabriel wanted was the familiar blankets on the couch.

"I'm going to bring you water anyway."

Adrian left. When he did, Gabriel checked over his shoulder to make sure he wasn't being watched, then sidled up to the couch and gingerly selected one of the blankets left on top of it. Guiltily, he wrapped himself up in it like a silkworm spinning his cocoon, then sank down and curled up to stare at the ceiling.

There had to be a way to get to Garrison. All he had to do was consider his circumstances and reflect on what he knew so far. The last he'd heard, Garrison had been arrested after the police had stormed their brothel and had been found guilty of crimes Gabriel couldn't hope to understand. Lucian—one of the boys Garrison had brought into their brothel—had a new alpha, and that alpha had worked to make sure Garrison was behind bars for good. For a while, Gabriel had been furious that Lucian had allowed something like that to happen to the man who'd given everything to take care of them, but the longer he sat and thought about it, the more he appreciated what Lucian's alpha had done. Behind bars, he knew exactly where Garrison was. If he could do something bad enough that he could get arrested, too, then he'd be sent to jail just like Garrison. In jail together, he wouldn't have to feel so lonely anymore. Neither of them would.

As he pondered his next steps, Adrian came back from the kitchen with a glass of water and a frosted martini glass with a single olive. Gabriel sat up and let the blankets fall so he could accept the water Adrian offered. Adrian stepped up onto the couch and lowered himself gracefully so he sat cross-legged at Gabriel's feet.

"What are you drinking?" Gabriel asked. It occurred to him that he'd had a birthday in Stonecrest, and he was now legally able to drink. Another unwelcome change. He wished he could shrink farther into the blankets and hide his nose behind the fabric, but his new position made that impossible.

"Vodka martini. Sterling drives me up the wall with his gin and tonics." Adrian plucked the tiny plastic skewer with the olive and waved it at Gabriel. "You're old enough to drink now. We should go out sometime. You want the olive?"

"Yes," Gabriel mumbled. The olive traded hands, then found its way between his lips. When it was gone, he frowned and let his gaze come to rest on Adrian's shoulder, right by the crook of his neck. It was less intimidating than looking him in the eye. "But that's not what you wanted to talk to me about, is it?"

"No. It's not." Adrian cradled the martini glass in one hand, its stem dipping down between his middle and ring fingers. Slowly, he tilted the glass this way and that, but never enough so that the clear liquid inside spilled over the rim. "We need to talk about what you're going to do to get better."

More than ever, Gabriel wanted to burrow under the blankets and never come out. Getting better meant that Adrian thought he was broken, but that wasn't the case at all. Gabriel wasn't broken—he was lovesick and stuck in a situation he didn't want to be in. There was a difference.

21

"It's okay that Stonecrest didn't work out." Adrian took a sip of his drink, then frowned and lowered it to his lap. The rounded bottom dangled by his thigh, not quite brushing it, but close. "Not everyone heals in the same way. That's fine. I'm not angry at you for that. If anything, I should have pulled you out sooner. Six months without results is a long time, but nine months? That's my fault, and you have my sincere apologies."

"You shouldn't have to feel sorry." Gabriel looked away from Adrian to watch as he tapped his tiny plastic skewer against the rim of his glass. The delicate bell-like noise was a kind distraction, and it allowed him to focus on something other than his brother's body language. Adrian said one thing, but the tension in his posture screamed disappointment, and Gabriel didn't want to think about it. The truth was, he'd fought against his therapists with everything he had. He'd actively resisted treatment and done everything in his power to shut down his therapy sessions.

He wasn't broken. All he needed was to get back to Garrison.

"Well, I do... but not for anything you did. The thing is, I have a solution... I just need you to trust me."

The tone of Adrian's voice wasn't right, like he was reluctant to share his master plan. Gabriel glanced up from his glass and dared to look at Adrian's face, but what he saw only confused him further. There was concern there, yes, but there was disinclination as well. It stretched his lips thin and turned his face more serious than it should have.

"Adrian?" Gabriel asked uncertainly.

Adrian took another drink, deeper this time, then set the glass down and ran the back of his arm across his lips. He sat up straighter, furrowed his brow, then tightened his shoulders in a way that convinced Gabriel that what he had to say next would be difficult.

It was.

Adrian closed his eyes, let his shoulders drop, then spoke the words that would shape the rest of Gabriel's life. "We want to give you to someone, Gabriel—someone who can help you in a way that Stonecrest never could. If therapy isn't helping, we have no choice but to try something else."

"Who?" Gabriel asked as his lungs shrank and every muscle in his body wound tense with apprehension.

Adrian closed his eyes and shook his head. "We're entrusting you to an alpha."

3

GABRIEL

The bottom dropped out of Gabriel's stomach, and the abyss he found waiting beyond it stretched into infinity. The glass in his hand was suddenly too cold, its weeping condensation too wet. A chill ran down his spine, and for a second, it felt like the same clammy beads of water that clung to the glass had adhered to his body. "You... what?"

"We want to give you a new alpha." Adrian tightened one of his hands into a fist, then relaxed it. The movement drew Gabriel's attention, but it did nothing to yank him out of his free fall. The world spun, and the first pangs of nausea tightened his throat and flooded his mouth with saliva.

A new alpha?

No.

He couldn't.

"You're sad Garrison is gone, aren't you?" Adrian was looking at him—Gabriel felt the intensity of his stare—but he couldn't bring himself to meet his gaze. "You can't mourn forever, Gabriel. Garrison isn't coming back. It's time to move on."

No.

Gabriel squeezed his eyes shut, as if blackening out the world might make Adrian and his awful statement disappear, too. It didn't, and it wasn't until cold water from his glass splashed over Gabriel's trembling hand that he realized that closing his eyes was making things worse. Desperate to find relief, he opened his eyes and thrust the glass at the tiny end table set up beside the couch. Water spilled over the rim and soaked the table, but he didn't care. In that moment, his world was falling apart—ruining the finish of his brother's furniture came second to his own welling despair.

He belonged to Garrison. He was Garrison's property. If Garrison found out he was with another alpha, bad things would happen. Bad, *bad* things. All Gabriel wanted was to be *good*.

"We're going to give you to someone." Adrian reached forward and gripped Gabriel's knee through the blanket, likely in an attempt to be reassuring, but Gabriel didn't want to be touched. Panic poisoned his thoughts and left him breathless. It speared his lungs, thousands of minuscule pinpricks strong, and made each breath he tried to take painful to draw in.

No.

He wouldn't. He couldn't.

Adrian couldn't make him.

Gabriel jerked away from Adrian, but his legs were tangled up in the blanket, and he tumbled to the floor. The hardwood bit into his palms, and the force of his ungraceful impact sent searing pain through his knees, but panic numbed him to external stimuli.

He needed to run.

Like a startled rabbit, Gabriel kicked the blankets back and scampered across the floor. He'd left his shoes by the door, and his socks slipped against the smooth wood and made traction difficult, so he depended on his palms to guide him as he darted forward blindly. There were two ways out of Sterling's penthouse—one that led to the fire escape down the back of Sterling's building, and one into the club Sterling owned. Gabriel had never been to the club before, but he felt like maybe if he could break for it—if he could lose himself in somewhere he'd never been before—no one would know where to look. Adrian would never find him, and he could figure out a way to be with Garrison all on his own.

He wouldn't be owned by another alpha. It was bad enough the man without a name had kept him against his will after the bust on The White Lotus, keeping him from finding Garrison before Garrison was imprisoned. Gabriel would not allow himself to belong to anyone else again.

"Gabriel!" Adrian shouted, but compared to the rushing in Gabriel's ears, it came across as a whimper.

If he could get across the room and around the corner, down the short hall that led to the soundproof door barricading Sterling's living space from the club, he'd be free. He wouldn't have to make Garrison angry. He could be *good*.

There were footsteps behind him, hurried, close to frantic. They spurred Gabriel onward, and he took the corner half-raised from the floor while skidding on his socks. The door was close, and it was unlocked. All he'd need to do was twist the handle and wrench it open, and from there, he'd let fate take him where it would.

His hand closed around the doorknob, but the knob wouldn't twist. In the fraction of a second it took him to realize the knob was jammed, Gabriel looked up with wide, pleading eyes. Desperate, he pulled the door with as much force as he could.

To his surprise, it flew open.

Someone stumbled in from the other side, their hand wrapped around the outside knob. Gabriel shrieked as the blur of human-shaped weight hit him. They toppled to the floor together, Gabriel effectively pinned beneath the individual's body weight.

Three things made themselves obvious right away, and not even Gabriel's fear-driven mind could chase them off.

The first was that the stranger was an alpha—the scent was subtle, but the notes it bore were powerful and heady.

The second was that the stranger was male—the rugged cut of his jaw and the barely-there stubble that shaded his skin gave him away.

The third? The third made Gabriel's pounding heart skip a beat and stole the air from his already choked lungs.

The third was that the stranger's eyes were pale green, but his pupils were ringed with a rich brown that radiated outward like the rays of the sun. They were the most stunning eyes Gabriel had ever seen.

"You're a flighty little thing, aren't you, Gabriel?" the stranger asked, making no attempt to remove himself from where he'd fallen. Even if he had, Gabriel wouldn't have been able to get up. Those green eyes pinned him in place, and the shock of hearing his name from the stranger's lips ensnared him.

"Who are you?" Gabriel managed to whisper, but his voice was so hoarse and his words were so broken that he wasn't sure the stranger understood.

He had.

The response came naturally, flowing like stream water over smooth pebbles, as if it could wash Gabriel of his sins from the inside out. The magnitude of the reply thrilled him, seeping through his clothes and waterlogging his soul until his mind was choked for thoughts like lungs burning for air.

The stranger looked at him, those green eyes playful and engaged, and said words Gabriel would never forget.

"You will call me Sir."

4

CEDRIC

Hello, Rabbit. What's going on behind those terrified eyes?

Cedric rose from where he'd fallen, careful not to put any pressure on the omega beneath him. Gabriel was on his back, eyes wide, more gorgeous than Cedric ever could have hoped. The frumpy teen hiding his body beneath billowing hoodies had grown into a stunning young man no longer ashamed of who he was.

Tight jeans that hugged his thighs. A fitted shirt beneath a sweater that had ridden up his flat stomach. Pretty flushed cheeks a charming shade of pink...

Cedric was taken by him.

He offered his hand to Gabriel, and after a moment's hesitation, Gabriel acquiesced. The touch of his palm against Cedric's as he accepted Cedric's help shot sparks down his arm and weakened his grip, and Cedric squeezed a little tighter than he needed to in a bid to combat it. The touch startled him, and as soon as Gabriel was on his feet, he broke the contact between them and pushed his hands into the back pockets of his pants. His right hand—the one he'd used to help Gabriel up—found his wallet, and he played with the corner of the thin, soft leather.

It was okay to feel this way. It wasn't like attraction to someone new was a *bad* thing. There were plenty of men who'd caught his eye, and plenty of women, too, but Gabriel?

There was something different about him.

Something different in the way he moved, even if that movement was just to climb to his feet or angle his head downward to dip his gaze and broadcast his subservience. Grace. Elegance. *Something.* Cedric couldn't quite put his finger on it, but there it was, refusing to stare him in the face, just an arm's length away.

And it was his.

All his.

He'd be damned if he backed out now.

"I see you two are already acquainted." Sterling stepped around Cedric and came to stand by Adrian, who'd just skidded around the corner and come to a sudden stop in the hall. Sterling set a hand on the small of Adrian's back and guided Adrian to his side. The fear in Adrian's eyes was obvious to Cedric even in his peripheral vision —whatever had happened to send Gabriel running for the door had rattled him.

And it had rattled Gabriel, too.

Cedric saw it in the startling ocean blues of Gabriel's eyes as clearly as he saw it drain the color from his face. The wonder that had once blown Gabriel's pupils wide and lifted his brows while he lay stunned on the floor simmered into nothing, but Cedric remembered the look. His heart wouldn't let him forget. Golden-brown hair, long enough to tug, framed Gabriel's face. It was just messy enough that it was adorable. The cut of his jaw was delicate, and the bridge of his nose was refined, but his face lacked the severity that Adrian's boasted. The gentleness he embodied, from his feminine face to the slender, willowy build of his frame, was almost too perfect to be real.

If Cedric wasn't careful, he knew that a boy like this would undo him. Piece by piece, he'd dismantle the carefully established boundaries Cedric had put in place and leave him flayed open like a frog on a dissection table, all of his vulnerabilities exposed. He'd lose himself to those eyes, distract himself with the fullness of Gabriel's lips, and then—

"Gabriel?" Sterling asked. His voice tore Cedric from his thoughts so suddenly that Cedric nearly jumped. "Do you know who this is?"

Gabriel didn't lift his head, but his gaze did flicker upward, as if he was curious. He looked at Cedric nervously from beneath his lashes, then glanced back down before he spoke. His shoulders pinched closer to his neck. "Yes. That's... Sir."

Fuck.

Cedric's cock started to stiffen, and he pushed his hands forward in a bid to bunch the fabric by his fly to hide his erection. A short distance away, Adrian's brows knitted together. The panic in his eyes was sharpened by irritation. It looked like he was about to cut loose with a scathing remark, but before he could speak, Sterling tugged him closer. "That's right. He's yours for now, if you like him, at least until we figure out what our next step is. Right, Adrian?"

There was a dynamic at play between Sterling and Adrian that Cedric didn't understand, but he let it go. With Gabriel standing in front of him, he couldn't keep focused on much else for all that long, anyway. How could he? Gabriel wouldn't meet his eyes, but it only made Cedric want to know more.

He was already so submissive. What else could Sterling and Adrian want from him?

"Gabriel knows Cedric from high school," Adrian said stiffly. The conflicted look on his face remained. "Cedric and I hung out with the same crowd. You remember him, don't you, Gabriel? Cedric Langston?"

Gabriel looked up again, only just enough so he could look at Cedric from beneath his eyelashes. For a second, Gabriel watched him. A second was all it took. Cedric swallowed the lump rising in his throat and tried to ignore the way his heart fluttered.

Sex was sex, but emotion? He didn't get emotionally attached to his clients. No pretty faces had ever made his heart skip a beat like Gabriel did.

Gabriel nuzzled against his own shoulder, bunched up so tightly from his nerves that he was stick-skinny. It looked like he badly wanted to be touched, to be held, and to be directed—and the urge to step in and fill that role for him was overwhelming.

Fuck.

"I remember," Gabriel whispered.

"Then you know that there's nothing to worry about." Adrian locked eyes with Cedric. "Because if he does *anything* to you that you don't want him to do, then he'll have to answer to me."

Gabriel folded his arms over his chest protectively, his hands braced on either arm. Cedric remained where he was, studying, learning, and trying his hardest to get over the knee-jerk reaction to step in and make things right.

"We wanted to let you take some time to get to know Cedric in a safe setting," Sterling said. "He's here for you."

Gabriel wouldn't look up anymore. He shifted his weight from foot to foot, his slender hips swaying slightly. Cedric bit down on his lip as he watched. Whatever witchcraft Gabriel was using, it was working like a charm. He fidgeted with the sleeve of his sweater and rubbed the heel of one foot nervously against the other. "I don't..."

"You don't what?" Adrian asked, keeping his tone soft and light.

Before Gabriel could answer, the distant cry of an infant ended their conversation. Sterling lifted his chin and dropped his hand from Adrian's back. He kissed Adrian on the top of the head. "I'll get her. Can I leave you here with Cedric and Gabriel?"

"Yeah. Sure." Adrian's eyes narrowed as he looked in Cedric's direction. "I've got this."

Sterling took his leave, and Cedric found himself alone with the

Lowe brothers. Physically, their shared heritage was obvious. Gabriel was a touch more slender and delicate—classically beautiful—while the years had hardened Adrian and lent him subtle touches of masculinity, but there was no mistaking them for anything but brothers. But where Gabriel was meek and quick to try to hide himself from everything and everyone, Adrian did not back down. He took a step forward and planted himself in front of Gabriel, shielding him behind his shoulder and looking Cedric dead in the eyes. "Before I let the two of you talk, I have to lay down some ground rules."

Cedric wiped the emotion from his face and kept his hands in his pockets, hoping against hope that Adrian wouldn't catch the scent of his arousal in the air, or spot the semi he was doing his best to conceal. "I'll listen, but you have to understand that what you want will never be more important to me than what Gabriel wants."

Adrian's eyes narrowed. "Gabriel is my brother, and he's a Lowe. You *will* treat him with respect."

"Of course." The casual way Cedric spoke seemed to set Adrian off. He scowled and took a small step forward, so Cedric added, "I hadn't planned anything but."

"If I hear that you are mistreating him, or that you're using him, I will *end* you." Adrian stepped away to stand at Gabriel's side. He reached out and set a hand on the small of Gabriel's back to direct him forward. "We might be giving him to you for now, but you need to remember that when it comes down to it, he belongs to *us*."

The intensity in Adrian's voice was in total juxtaposition with the way Gabriel dodged his gaze. The Lowe brothers may have looked similar, but when it came to personality, they were entirely different. To break a man like Adrian, Cedric could understand. But Gabriel? Gabriel was quiet and compliant. Gentle to a fault. Why was this a job Sterling thought only he could do? Any Dom could bend Gabriel to his will with little effort.

There had to be something more.

Gabriel took a few, rushed steps forward at Adrian's insistence.

His fingers curled up to pick and pull at the sleeve of his sweater. Without looking up from his feet, he attempted conversation. "Hello, Sir."

He might as well have punched Cedric in the gut for how those two simple words struck him. The headspace he needed to slip into was hard to get to when every little thing Gabriel did distracted him so much. Cedric did as best he could to get there regardless. "Hello, Gabriel."

There was a tiny noise as air hitched in Gabriel's throat. If Cedric hadn't been so focused on him, he never would have heard it. Everything Gabriel did was timid—Cedric would need to pay close attention to his body language to make sure he didn't overstep any boundaries.

Adrian was starting to prickle—Cedric saw it in the way he broadened his shoulders and stood up straighter—so Cedric directed the conversation toward action. "Let's go somewhere we can sit. There's no need to keep standing in the hallway."

"Great idea." Sterling had returned with his daughter. She'd quieted down, her eyes closed as she nursed on a bottle. Tiny hands wrapped around the plastic, helping Sterling hold it in place. "The living room is just around the corner. Gabriel, if you would direct your guest, it would be appreciated."

Cedric met Sterling's eyes to find Sterling looking directly at him, resolute. It wasn't disappointment he found lurking behind Sterling's blues, but permission. Permission that didn't matter. No matter how Sterling urged him to take immediate control, Cedric couldn't. Consent was more important to him than landing a job. He would push gently, but if Gabriel didn't want him, he wouldn't go through with it, no matter what Sterling wanted.

A niggling part of his mind told him that this was all a test to see how far he'd be willing to compromise his morals in order to land a job. Cedric hoped he wasn't too far from the truth. Sterling was a gentleman Dom, and one of the most patient and understanding men in the community. It was uncharacteristic of him to push for something so obviously wrong.

Cedric didn't have much longer to think on the issue. Gabriel, who stood before him, took a half-step forward and lifted his head just enough to meet Cedric's gaze. All the air in Cedric's lungs found its way out, and he exhaled slowly and steadily even as his body screamed for him to take a breath. Gabriel bit down on his bottom lip, then glanced to the side and nodded in the direction of the hallway. "Will you please come with me, Sir?"

"Yes." There was no way he could say anything but that. Cedric's mouth spoke on autopilot, his tongue navigating a word that should have been familiar like it was his first attempt at speaking another language. The delivery was flawless, but the sensation was strange. Cedric chased it out of his mouth by following it up with a few more words. "Of course."

Gabriel's gaze lingered on him for a second longer than it should have, and in that second, Cedric felt the intensity of their sudden chemistry tighten in his chest and plunge down his spine like water rushing down a cliff face. The physical attraction was there, and it was stronger than any Cedric had felt in years, but no matter how hard it struck, he could not let it win.

This was a job. Gabriel was a client. Cedric would care for him in whatever ways Gabriel needed, but to get his emotions involved?

It couldn't happen.

Gabriel reached forward and took his hand. The skin-to-skin contact shot sparks down Cedric's arm and jolted him from his thoughts to ground him in the moment.

He was in Sterling's penthouse, in the hallway, holding hands with the young omega he was meant to dominate for the next several months.

The same omega who looked at him with shy blue eyes that hid pain.

The same omega who made him feel things he'd thought he'd never feel again.

35

Cedric swallowed hard and returned Gabriel's gaze. It wasn't met for long. Gabriel glanced away, frightened, and just like that, led the way.

Hello, Rabbit. It's time to let me in.

Cedric followed him down the hall in silence.

5

CEDRIC

Around the corner from the hallway was Sterling's living room. Dark wood paired with luxurious leather and strategically placed track lighting to create a space both masculine and tastefully brooding. Gabriel led Cedric to one of the leather couches before letting go of his hand. Gabriel sat on the couch, knees together and elbows tucked in. The attempt to make himself as small as possible worked—pressed into the arm of the couch like he was, he was barely there.

Adrian, who'd followed along behind them, took the spot right next to Gabriel. Sterling stood not all that far behind Cedric, rocking his daughter slowly in one arm. It looked like this was how the conversation was going to go. Cedric didn't mind—in fact, he was grateful. Sitting next to Gabriel would have proved too great a distraction, and right now, he needed to keep his head in the game.

Cedric opened his mouth to speak, but as he did, Gabriel surprised him by taking initiative. "Why are you doing this to me?"

The question wasn't directed at him, but the content was. Cedric would not stand by and allow his image to be negatively impacted by false understandings. "I'm not doing anything to you. I won't do anything until I know that you want this, too."

Gabriel and Adrian looked at him in unison. Two sets of eyes, blue and gray, searched his face for different things. Adrian looked for motive, his lips tight with distrust and his eyes narrowed with suspicion. But Gabriel? Gabriel looked at him in confusion, like the thought that he could turn Cedric down had never crossed his mind before. The confusion was brief, and it blipped out of existence the second Gabriel ducked his head and crossed his arms over his stomach like he was sick. Cedric wished he could have held that gaze a little longer.

"Cedric is here to take care of you, Gabriel. He can provide you with the care that you need." Sterling spoke with calm conviction. "Now that you've left Stonecrest, you need structure that Adrian and I can't hope to provide you with. You need a caretaker—someone who will see to it that your needs are met, and who will encourage you to live your life to its fullest potential. Cedric will help you if you let him. The choice, ultimately, belongs to you."

Gabriel stared at his lap. Eventually, he uncrossed his arms and ran his hands nervously down his thighs. Then, with a tiny sigh that sounded loud in the silence of the room, he looked up at Sterling. The emotion in Gabriel's eyes was muted, as if he wasn't there anymore. "... Okay."

It wasn't right. Consent didn't work like that. Cedric looked between Gabriel and Sterling, judging the dynamic between them. He didn't know much about Gabriel's past—just that he'd gone missing during the summer after Cedric had graduated—but by that point, Cedric was already college-bound, and he'd fallen out of touch with his old group of friends. Now he wished he'd looked into what had happened that summer instead of letting it fall by the wayside.

What was going on in Gabriel's head? What experiences had shaped him into the timid young man who tried his best to meld with the couch and disappear? The confusion in Gabriel's eyes when Cedric had been kind toward him was abnormal. No person should have to think that others were out to hurt him first and foremost. The world was a dark place, but it wasn't that cruel. Cedric had seen suffering, but even when life had taken what he held closest to his heart, he still hadn't lost faith in others.

Not like Gabriel had.

The tiny "okay" that Gabriel had given Sterling wasn't good enough for him. If Cedric was going to do this job, he needed to know that he was doing it right—and that meant that he needed an answer from Gabriel directly, no matter how timid Gabriel was.

Determination clenched in Cedric's chest, as cautious as it was concerned. It rounded itself off with softness, seeping through his core and rushing through his veins. It swelled with urgency, ballooning until he couldn't ignore it anymore. It pushed him to take action, and so he did.

Propelled by instinct, he closed the short distance between himself and Gabriel. All eyes turned to him, but Gabriel's were the only ones that mattered.

Cedric dropped to a knee at Gabriel's feet, careful not to touch him. The tension in the room rose, but Gabriel's stunned wide eyes grounded Cedric in the moment. There was nothing holding Cedric back any longer—not even the startling attraction he felt for Gabriel made a difference anymore. No one else could tell him what he needed to know. If he didn't take initiative, there would be no resolution.

His omega would consent to the treatment he was about to receive. Cedric would not have it any other way.

"Gabriel." Cedric's voice did not waver. He let the utterance hang between them, hoping it would drag Gabriel down from his panic like an anchor through open water. "I need you to understand that everything I do, I do out of respect for you. If you don't want this—if you don't think it's right, or if you feel like you're being taken advantage of—we will call it off right now, no questions asked. I need to know that I'm doing this for *you,* not for anyone else."

Gabriel's eyes stayed on him, lidded now instead of wide with shock. He bit down on his bottom lip and shifted his thighs. "For me, Sir?"

"For you," Cedric promised. He refused to look away. "All for you, Gabriel. Every last action, and every last word."

No one moved. No one spoke. The air between them sizzled—Cedric couldn't deny it any more than he could deny the air he breathed. Gabriel may have been a job, but Cedric meant every word.

It didn't come down to attraction. It didn't come down to how fast his heart beat, or how hard his dick was. It was a matter of making sure that a young man who didn't seem to have much agency got the care he deserved.

"I..." Gabriel looked nervously off to the side, then stared at his thighs again. Cedric could still see the blues of his irises through his lashes. "I... need to think, is that... is that okay, Sir?"

"Yes." Cedric did not move from where he knelt. Since Gabriel did not feel comfortable, he would keep a lower, submissive position in order to boost his confidence. Whatever answer he received, he needed it to be said out of sincerity, not out of fear. "It's a big decision to make. You can take your time."

"Thank you." Gabriel's voice was so small that it was barely there, but with a single flick of his eyes, he stole a glance at Cedric that made Cedric's heart skip a beat. "I need to... I need to go think alone, okay?"

"Of course." Reality was restored, and Cedric realized they weren't alone in the room—Sterling stood behind him, a silent, protective force, and Adrian sat next to Gabriel on the couch, his expression unreadable. This was their penthouse, Cedric remembered. They had the final say. "As long as it's fine with Sterling and Adrian."

"It's more than fine." Sterling's footsteps approached, and Cedric felt the air move behind him as Sterling stood close. "Think about your options, Gabriel. If this isn't the path you want, then we *will* find another for you."

40

Gabriel said nothing, but he nodded. Careful not to step on Cedric, he picked himself up from the couch with cat-like grace from the couch and slunk toward the far hallway. Cedric rose from the floor and watched him go, uncertain how to feel. He'd put himself on the line standing up for Gabriel like that, but was it worth it? Gabriel didn't make the answer obvious.

A door shut down the hall, breaking the tension. Cedric exhaled slowly. What was done, was done. The decision was in Gabriel's hands now, and all Cedric could do was trust he'd make the choice truest to his heart.

6

GABRIEL

There was no space in the house for him anymore—no place with a door that could close and lock like Gabriel wanted—so he fled to the bathroom. The door clicked into place behind him, and he twisted the lock shut before anyone could tell him to come out and quit being so bad.

No one understood. No one *could* understand.

Gabriel didn't want to be bad, but Sir?

Sir made it very, very tempting.

Miserable, Gabriel crossed the room and sank into the bathtub. His clothed legs stretched out across the white porcelain, and for a while, he stared at his knees. Knobby. Slender. Unappealing. They still stung from minutes ago, when he'd fallen to the floor in an attempt to escape from Adrian.

Escaping never made things better—it had only ever made things worse. He should have known. Garrison had taught him that lesson five long years ago.

Garrison.

With a groan, Gabriel tucked his knees to his chest and curled up on himself against the edge of the tub. Sir's green eyes had distracted Gabriel from what mattered, and that was wrong of him.

43

His first priority in all things was to return to the man he belonged to—and no matter what Sterling and Adrian said, he did *not* belong to Sir.

Sir, with his green eyes and dark, dark hair that made Gabriel think night couldn't even compare. Sir, who looked so *different* from all the other alphas Gabriel had serviced in The White Lotus and met casually after coming to stay with Adrian and Sterling. Sir, whose bottom lip was pierced on each side with two tiny black balls that caught the light and somehow made him look even more handsome. Sir, who'd looked at him with kindness, like he deserved respect.

Gabriel shivered and tightened his arms around his knees. Arousal stirred inside of him, unwanted but undeniable. The way Sir looked at him made him feel like... well. To be honest, Gabriel didn't know. The last thing he wanted to think about was how another man made him feel, because he didn't belong to any other man—he belonged to Garrison.

But Garrison was lost. Gone. In trouble with the law. And Gabriel wasn't going to get anywhere if he stayed in Adrian's penthouse, in the tiny not-a-room with no privacy. If he wanted to get out and find Garrison, he'd have to be brave. He'd have to break rules.

He'd have to be bad so he could be good.

There was conversation going on in the other room. The sound of Sterling's voice was a hum in the air, dark and melodic, always sure of itself. Sir's voice followed, a different brand of dominant, but certain in the things it said. It was sleek gunmetal—dark, but nuanced. It shone against the voices it accompanied, distinguished and unyielding. For a little while longer, it was a voice Gabriel would listen to.

He could do that.

It was a good voice.

With a deep, grounding breath, Gabriel let go of his knees and rose from the tub. His legs trembled, and as he walked, he shook them out to try to regain himself. As long as he was with Adrian, nothing bad would happen. He'd seen the narrowed look in Adrian's eyes when Sterling had brought Sir into the penthouse, and he knew that no matter what Sterling said, Adrian wouldn't let Sir hurt him. Where Gabriel was weak, Adrian was strong. If Gabriel needed to ask for help, Adrian would be there to help him.

There was nothing to be worried about.

Gabriel unlocked the bathroom door and made his way down the hall. The door to Sterling's old office was left open, and as he passed, he glimpsed the crib Lilian slept in. For a second, he came to a stop and observed the empty room from the doorway.

A mobile hung over Lilian's crib. It spun slowly, entertaining no one. The room's walls were covered with drawings—not Lilian's, but some other child's. Gabriel didn't know if Sterling had other children or not, but he assumed so, just by looking at the decor. On the wall was a collage featuring photos of Adrian, Sterling, and Lilian all together.

Adrian, graduating college with his degree in business.

Adrian, moments before his first day of work as a division director with Sterling and Lilian there by his side.

Adrian, crying in that very room as Sterling proposed...

Gabriel frowned and looked away. The room reminded him of all the things he wanted but that he'd never been allowed to have. He'd given his body away for Garrison more times than he could count, but no matter how many times he'd been good, Garrison had always told him the same thing.

We're not going to have a baby yet, Gabriel. You're too beautiful to swell with life. You need to be patient and wait.

Gabriel had never understood the connection between his beauty and his ability to bear Garrison a child, but he hated it. Every time Garrison gave him contraceptives, he felt that much more unloved. Garrison was old—well into his fifties—and Gabriel knew that they wouldn't have much longer to make a family before Garrison was too old to properly care for his children. He hadn't been expecting the bust at The White Lotus, but when it had happened, it had almost felt like fate. They'd put off having a family for too long, and now the universe was dividing them for their sins.

...And it had given the baby Gabriel wanted to his brother instead.

But soon, it wouldn't matter. Gabriel would march back into the living room, present himself obediently to Sir, and tell Sir that he was ready to be taken away. Sir expected him to be meek—which he was—but he didn't know Gabriel like Adrian did, and he was already too kind to lock Gabriel in a room at night, or barricade the doors with combination locks like the man without a name had after he'd taken Gabriel from The White Lotus. He wouldn't chain Gabriel to the bed, or bind his hands behind his back so they were useless all day until he was supervised again. As soon as they were on their own, Gabriel would find the perfect moment, and then he'd escape. No one would be there to stop him.

He'd figure out a way to get to jail, and he'd reunite with Garrison.

They'd finally be a family.

Heat spread across his cheeks. He opened his eyes to observe the nursery, imagining the future. One day, he'd have a room like that for his own baby. He'd be a good father. He was compassionate, and quiet, and nurturing. But what he was most excited for was how much more Garrison would love him once he proved his devotion. A baby would be the glue that Gabriel had never managed to be on his own.

A baby would make Garrison stay.

No more late-night visits to other omegas under his employ. No more anyone else.

Gabriel would be Garrison's, and Garrison would be Gabriel's, and they would be *happy*.

Given enough time, Adrian would come to like Garrison, too, Gabriel knew. It didn't matter what Adrian thought of him now—

46

when he saw how Garrison made him happy, he would come around. If that happened, Gabriel could show Adrian and Sterling how a real relationship between an alpha and an omega was supposed to work, and then maybe they could all get along. No one would have to hurt anymore. It was the happily ever after Gabriel had always wanted, and now that The White Lotus was no more, it was within his grasp. Garrison would come to his senses, Sir would leave, and Adrian would finally understand.

The future would be *perfect*—but only if Gabriel had the courage to step into the living room and treat Sir like Sir wanted to be treated. He'd have to be brave for just a little while longer. For Garrison, it wasn't much to ask.

Faith in his plan renewed, Gabriel left Lilian's doorway and went to join the others in the living room.

He could do this.

He would do this.

For *him*.

7

CEDRIC

"This isn't going to work." Adrian stood in front of the couch, his arms crossed. He glared through Cedric at Sterling, who stood by Cedric's shoulder. "I know that he needs help, and I know that traditional therapy isn't getting him there, but... but this? Sterling, I love you, but you are *insane*."

"Cedric is a professional, Adrian."

"And I could call myself a professional Dom, too, if I decided to charge you to ride on my dick when we play." Adrian's lips were tight with anger, but he kept his voice level. No matter how respectful his tone, the words stung, and Cedric refused to let them pass him by without comment.

"I understand that you're under a lot of stress right now, and that Gabriel is your younger brother, but what he decides to do with his life is none of your business." Adrian's wrath turned on Cedric, but Cedric didn't let it intimidate him. No matter how much Adrian wanted to shelter his brother, he couldn't keep Gabriel under his thumb forever. "I was invited here to meet an omega who might be interested in my services. Whether or not you think you think my profession is valid doesn't change that."

"You don't understand who Gabriel is," Adrian hissed back.

"You don't understand the pain he's gone through, or the burdens he's shouldering."

Cedric didn't flinch. "But I will, so long as he gives me the chance."

Before the conversation could grow any more charged, Sterling stepped between them. "I vetted him before the interview, Adrian. I understand your concern, but I promise you, you're worrying for nothing. Cedric is a professional who's spent his career specializing in omega services. He understands omega needs better than any other man out there."

"And the counselors at Stonecrest know omegas, too, and look how well that turned out." Adrian shook his head. "I know that he needs help, but we need to think of something else. We can't leave him with…" Adrian's gaze flicked to Cedric, and he trailed off.

"With me?" Cedric asked softly.

There was no response.

It wasn't Cedric's place to assure Adrian that he was the right man for the job. The best course of action for Gabriel's care wasn't up for him to decide, but he'd been asked to take this job, and he would not let his competence be thrown into question. The more he listened, the more he understood that Gabriel wasn't like his typical clients. The pain in his eyes and the fear in his posture led Cedric to believe that he was damaged, and to hear he'd spent time at Stonecrest confirmed it. Omegas who went through rehabilitation considered themselves lesser, and while Cedric wasn't sure he could change Gabriel's mindset, he was certain that he could inflate his self-confidence and guide him to a headspace where growth was possible. "I know that I'm not a mental health professional, and I understand that you're concerned for Gabriel's well-being while under my care." Cedric looked between Adrian and Sterling, reading their body language. Adrian was on edge, as always—it looked like time didn't change everything—but Sterling's posture was loose and open. He was the one who'd invited Cedric here, after all. It was natural that he'd be receptive to what

Cedric had to say. "Now that I understand the situation a little better, I understand your concerns... but I want you to know that I'm not blowing smoke up your ass when I tell you that I *want* to do this."

"Why?" Adrian's eyes narrowed, and he stepped forward. He was slender and lithe, almost twink-like, but his personality made him seem bigger than he was. "We haven't spoken since our senior year in high school. You don't owe my family any debt, and it's not like we're friends. We hung around in the same group of people, that's all. So why is this so important to you? You're looking to use him, aren't you? To make him into some kind of..." Adrian ended the thought prematurely and shook his head in disgust. "There's got to be something that's made you agree to this, and I want to know what it is."

Out of the corner of his eye, Cedric watched Sterling. Adrian was, he assumed, Sterling's partner, and Cedric didn't want to push too hard or upset either of them. "I just want to help him, that's all."

"Bullshit!" Adrian raised his voice, then glanced toward Sterling and the baby in his arms and shook his head. When he spoke next, it was with low-simmering rage. "People don't just help people like that. Not... not when it comes to a situation like this. You want Gabriel on your own because you see an opportunity. I want you to tell me exactly what it is you're planning."

"If you want to know, I'll tell you." Cedric had nothing to hide. He dug his hands into his pockets and relaxed his shoulders. "What I plan for Gabriel is simple. Submission."

"That's it?" Adrian crossed his arms and stood a little taller, as if by doing so, he could intimidate Cedric into telling the truth. "That's all you have to say?"

"What more do I need to say?" Cedric allowed himself to smile. He kept the things he said simple and understated, but he hoped that Adrian would see the intent behind his words. "I'm not here to hurt him. Sterling hired me to do a job, and I take what I do seriously. This is my career, and Sterling has the power to make me or break me. I'm not going to throw away everything I've worked so hard for so I can screw the Lowe family over."

Adrian didn't look convinced. "I don't believe you."

"Then you're welcome to watch." Cedric shrugged. "I don't care what kind of check-ins you want to arrange, or what kind of scenarios you want me to satisfy, as long as I'm able to do my job and do it well. For the next few months, as long as Gabriel consents to it, *I* will be the only one caring for Gabriel, and he will listen to my word. That's all."

"I do consent," a tiny voice said from the hall. Cedric looked over his shoulder to find Gabriel leaning against the wall, one ankle crossed over the other. His head was bowed, and the golden-brown hair that crowned his head fell in front of his lowered eyes. "I want to go with Sir."

All conversation stopped. All eyes looked at the tiny omega in the hallway. With his refined features and his girlish grace, he looked younger than he was, but to Cedric, no matter his age or his status, his word was law.

"When will I go?" Gabriel asked. He looked up shyly, dodging Cedric's eyes to look at Adrian. "I just got home, but... home isn't home anymore. Everything is different. I don't want to get comfortable here only to be uprooted again."

"Of course not." Adrian swept into action, abandoning Cedric to fall into place at Gabriel's side. "If you want to go, then you can go. Sterling and Cedric are going to get the details set up, and then that'll be that."

The dynamic shifted. Adrian's anger and distrust was swept aside, dispelled by Gabriel's presence. Cedric took note of it and stored the detail away in his memory—knowing who Gabriel was closest with might help him understand where he was coming from, and getting into Gabriel's head was key if he was to do what was being asked of him.

As Cedric watched, Sterling set a hand on his shoulder. He leaned forward and spoke into Cedric's ear so as not to interrupt

Adrian and Gabriel. "Adrian loves to argue, but at his core, it's because he's frightened. His brother means the world to him, and he doesn't know you in the way I do."

"What way is that?" Cedric asked. In front of him, Gabriel latched onto Adrian and hugged him tightly. He looked at him from over Adrian's shoulder, and for a second, their eyes met. The lingering look sent shivers down Cedric's spine.

"I think you know the answer to that better than you're letting on." Sterling's hand dropped from his shoulder, and when he spoke again, volume had returned to his voice. "Since Gabriel's in agreement, arrangements will need to be made. Cedric, if you could follow me into my office, we'll take care of finalizing the details. I've had a contract drafted by my legal team, and you'll need to read over it and discuss any addenda with me before we put ink to paper."

"Right. Of course." Cedric looked away from Gabriel to watch as Sterling passed him. When he looked back, Gabriel's eyes were closed, and he'd tucked himself against Adrian's chest. A pang of regret struck. In the small, intimate interactions between them, Cedric got a glimpse into who Gabriel was. Losing an opportunity like that stung, like he'd turned Gabriel away when he'd needed him the most.

But there would be other chances and other opportunities to make things right. Once the terms were set and the contract was signed, Gabriel's care would be his responsibility.

Cedric would see those sad, distant eyes fill up with wonder again.

8

GABRIEL

G abriel felt small in the passenger seat of Sir's Toyota Camry. He pushed himself against the door and gazed out the window as the scenery passed him by. Tall, imposing buildings gave way to quieter urban streets, until they emerged in a sleepy part of Aurora that Gabriel wasn't familiar with. Somewhere west of the city, he knew. By the looks of it, it was on the outskirts of downtown—the monolithic buildings were still visible on the skyline—but it lacked the hustle and bustle of busy downtown streets. If he was being honest with himself, though, Gabriel barely noticed the change—he was too busy stealing peeks at Sir whenever he was sure his attention was devoted to the road.

Dark hair. Rugged features and a handsome chin that complemented a smooth, kind face. A body that was muscular, but that was still slender and agile enough to be lithe. Piercings...

Gabriel's eyes traced the tiny rounded tops of Sir's snakebite piercings, then traveled to the three helix piercings in succession down the ridge of his right ear. There was an earring through Sir's lobe, thicker in diameter than normal earrings were meant to be, and sleek black. It curled into itself like a fiddlehead, its tail jutting forward from beneath Sir's lobe, and its rounded tip left to curl so that it barely brushed his ear.

"Are you interested in body modification, Gabriel?" Sir asked abruptly, his eyes set dead ahead.

Gabriel's cheeks burned with embarrassment. All this time, he'd been sure Sir's attention was on the road. "I-I'm sorry, Sir."

"For what?"

"For staring."

Sir chuckled. "If it bothered me, I would have let you know. Don't apologize unless I tell you that you've made a mistake."

"Yes, Sir." Gabriel sank into his seat and looked out the window as his pulse raced and his instincts urged him to run. He couldn't. Not yet. He'd have to be good until he had a solid plan in place.

A beat of silence passed, during which Sir made a turn. The air was fresher here, and it didn't take Gabriel long to figure out why— a natural preserve bordered the street, filled with old, deciduous trees whose leaves were starting to turn vibrant fall shades as the crisp air threatened to give way to winter. The burgundy and crimson and orange spotting the otherwise green foliage put Gabriel's mind to rest, and some of his anxiety slipped away.

It was peaceful here.

Even though they were near the chaos of the city, he didn't hear a single siren. No traffic rushed by them, and no horns blared. They crossed paths with a few other motorists on the way down the street, but the urgency Gabriel associated with city driving was gone. Apart from one time when he was only eleven, when the Lowe family had left Aurora to vacation in a resort in the Caribbean, Gabriel had never known quiet like this. It spoke to some deep, dormant part of him that lifted its head like an old dog who'd heard his master's car roll down the driveway.

This place, wherever it was, was *good*.

He tried not to think about the fact that he could feel that way when Garrison wasn't around. The counselors at Stonecrest had done their best to tell him that he was independent, but Gabriel didn't believe them. Without Garrison there to put his life in order, nothing was good.

Nothing but this forest, and Sir.

"You know," Sir said as he flicked on his turn signal and pulled into a driveway opposite the preserve, "You never answered my question. Are you interested in body modification?"

"No, sir," Gabriel murmured. It wasn't the truth, but it was a safe answer. He knew not to burden those around him with unnecessary detail.

The truth was, Gabriel had never considered body modification before. Not seriously, at least. Sometimes, Garrison had taken some of the boys to be tattooed or pierced when they'd been good enough to deserve it. The end results were pretty, but Gabriel didn't see the point of going through pain for something that he'd likely grow tired of over time. Sir's piercings were nice, and they suited him, but Gabriel couldn't imagine he'd ever look pretty with metal puncturing his skin. It would make him too red, too swollen, and too bold. The more he faded away into the background, the better.

But maybe having something shiny and unique might be nice. It had crossed Gabriel's mind more than once that maybe the reason Garrison hadn't devoted himself to their relationship was because Gabriel was so boring and plain.

"That's a shame." Sir brought the car to a stop inside a carport. A cheerfully white side door awaited their arrival no more than a few feet away. "While we're unpacking, tell me about some of the things you like. I want to get to know you better."

"There isn't very much to tell, Sir." Gabriel undid his seatbelt, but waited for permission before opening the door. Until he knew exactly how hard Sir intended to be on him, he would not push his limits.

Sir had turned at the hip to face him, one arm rested on top of the steering wheel. He lifted a brow in a playful way and let the beginning of a grin lift the corner of his lips. It was a charming look, but no matter how it made Gabriel feel, he reminded himself that his time with Sir was only temporary. Temptation would not win. "Then tell you what... I want you to lie to me."

"L-lie?" Gabriel stared holes through the thighs of his jeans, not sure whether to be alarmed or excited.

"Yup. Lie to me." Sir swung the car door open and stepped out. He bent at the waist to look in at Gabriel, and Gabriel tried not to think about the kindness in Sir's green eyes. "Come up with another life for yourself. Imagine you're... I don't know. Imagine you're Adrian. Pretend that you have all his likes and dislikes, and then tell me what you like."

"Oh." Gabriel tried to hold back a laugh, but he was only partially successful—it slipped into his words as he replied. "Adrian doesn't like anything or anyone, except for maybe me, and Sterling, and Lilian."

"Shit, you're right. Bad example." Sir stepped back and set his hand on the car door, like he was getting ready to close it. "I guess you'll just have to pretend that you're someone else—someone that you know. Can you think of anyone?"

"Yes, Sir," Gabriel said with a nod.

"Then come on out and help me unpack. I want to get you settled before it gets too late. We don't have much daylight left."

Was that permission to leave the car? Gabriel thought so. He set his hand on the handle, glanced at Sir to make sure he was doing the right thing, then swung the door open. Once he'd exited the vehicle, he closed the door as politely as he could and followed Sir to the trunk. It had already been popped, and Sir eased it open with a single hand.

It occurred to Gabriel that he was expected to talk, but he had no idea who to talk about. The friends he'd kept at The White Lotus hadn't been the kind he'd spent much time getting to know on a personal level, and the individuals he'd met at Stonecrest he hadn't paid much attention to. The only person Gabriel knew was

Garrison, but what was it that Garrison liked? Gabriel thought he should know, but he couldn't come up with anything.

Sir hefted his duffel bag from the trunk and tucked it over his shoulder. It was heavy, but he made it look feather light. Gabriel examined him for a moment, then remembered himself and looked away. "I... I like to have sex."

Sir almost dropped the duffel bag. "Excuse me?"

Molten lava didn't compare to the heat that radiated from Gabriel's cheeks. "You asked me to pretend to be someone else, Sir."

"Right." Sir adjusted the bag on his shoulder and rubbed his mouth. "I did. Keep going. You just took me by surprise, is all."

Was there a hint of color in Sir's cheeks? Gabriel picked up his backpack from where it had been laid in the trunk and swung it over his shoulder. "And I like to meet new people. In fact, I know so many people that sometimes I don't even remember their names."

Sir shut the trunk. The heavy *thunk* startled Gabriel, and he took a few steps back for safety.

"How many people do you know?" Sir led the way to the cheerful white door.

Gabriel followed. "I don't know... seventy-five, maybe? Probably more."

"You must be popular, then." Sir slotted a key into the lock. With a turn of his wrist, it clicked, and he pushed the door open. "Are they all your friends?"

"No." Gabriel didn't want to play this game anymore. He didn't want to think about who those people were to Garrison.

"If they're not your friends, then who are they?"

Gabriel came to a stop in the carport. He knew that he should follow Sir through the door and obey his command, but he couldn't. His mind spun, remembering the sleepless nights when Garrison left him alone in bed, and the times he'd walked into Garrison's office to find other boys sitting on his lap.

All because Gabriel wasn't attractive enough, exciting enough, or engaging enough.

Garrison's favorite, Seth, and the way Garrison had made eyes at him. The lust in his eyes when he took Seth's heat was never the same as when he was with Gabriel. But Garrison had promised that they'd make a family. He'd told Gabriel that he *loved* him.

"Gabriel?"

Words betrayed him. Gabriel's vocal cords clamped, and his jaw locked. He backed away from the door, only stopping when his thighs smacked the side of the car. His backpack squished, caught between his weight and the vehicle, but he couldn't bring himself to worry about whether his toiletries leaked or not. The whole world was closing in on him, and as it did, it pushed the air out of Gabriel's lungs and left him struggling to breathe.

"Gabriel." Sir stepped down from the stoop and crossed the carport, but Gabriel couldn't bring himself to face him. Sir would be angry he disobeyed. He would punish Gabriel for falling short of expectation, and then he would force Gabriel to tell him what he didn't want to say. "Hey. What's going on with you?"

Gabriel's gaze darted to the side. The carport was tidy, and the driveway was a straight shot to the road. Across the street was the preserve and all the beautiful trees with their green and orange and red leaves. If he could make it—

Sir came too close, and Gabriel knew he didn't have time to plan anymore. He bolted from the car and ran for the street. It wasn't supposed to happen this way, but he couldn't be good like he'd thought he would be able to. He'd thought Sir would want to use his body, but otherwise leave him be. Clearly, that wasn't the case, and Gabriel couldn't handle it.

He couldn't take kindness from a stranger when he'd never been offered it by the man he loved.

A shout of surprise pierced his eardrums, but Gabriel drowned it out beneath the sound of his canvas shoes striking the asphalt. He made it to the sidewalk when a slow-moving car brought him to a sudden stop. Its windows were heavily tinted, but the driver's side window was rolled down, and the man inside stared at Gabriel as he drove by.

Gabriel stared back.

He knew that face and the twisted, smug expression on it. He could almost smell the leather and wood on the air.

And the rot.

He didn't want to run anymore.

9

CEDRIC

Instinct consumed him, and Cedric ran. The duffel bag slapped against his side with every impact of his shoe against the asphalt, and his lungs and muscles screamed in protest for going from zero to sixty on the drop of a dime, but Cedric ignored them. There was no other alternative.

He would not lose Gabriel.

Gabriel came to a sudden stop on the edge of the sidewalk, halted by a slow-moving car that passed on the other side of the street. Cedric didn't waste the opportunity. He seized Gabriel by the shoulder and spun him around with more force than he needed to —Gabriel's body was unexpectedly pliant. The dazed expression on his face and the looseness in his limbs spoke for him—he wasn't planning on running anymore.

"What are you doing?" Cedric demanded. He was out of breath, but he did his best to hide it from his voice. Now more than ever, he needed to be a source of strength. "Gabriel!"

Gabriel's eyes were distant, like his body was still on Earth, but his mind was lost somewhere in the cosmos. He was pale by nature, but the kind of pale he was in that moment wasn't healthy. Cedric tightened his hand and resisted the urge to shake him. What the hell was he thinking? "Gabriel!"

"I'm on the sidewalk," Gabriel murmured, unprovoked. "On the sidewalk in front of a bungalow across from a forest."

"No." Cedric's hands left Gabriel's shoulders. He cupped his face instead, forcing Gabriel to look at him. "You're *home*."

Gabriel blinked a few times, and the light came back to his eyes. A sadness softened his features, like he'd lost all hope. Then, like he was guilty of a crime Cedric didn't understand, he lowered his gaze and let his shoulders droop. The deflation brought Cedric down from his fear. He ran one thumb over Gabriel's cheek to soothe him, then dropped his hands and swept Gabriel up into a tight hug. Gabriel squeaked. He was trembling. The movement was imperceptible to the eye, but impossible to miss when he was pressed tight against Cedric's chest.

"I'm sorry, Sir," Gabriel whispered. The sound was so small that it was almost entirely absorbed by the cotton of Cedric's shirt. "That was wrong of me to do."

"Yeah, it was." Cedric didn't let him go. Until his pulse slowed and his fear waned, he needed to know that Gabriel wasn't going anywhere. "You know there will be consequences, right?"

"I do."

"Then let's go inside, okay?" Cedric looked over Gabriel's shoulder at the street, now empty. What the hell had just happened? It bothered him that he might never know. "We'll put your belongings away, and then we'll talk about what just happened, and what you're going to do to fix it."

There was no verbal response, but Gabriel nodded against his chest. He didn't cling to Cedric—he didn't even hug him—but Cedric got the feeling that without physical contact, Gabriel would fall apart. No matter how stressed Cedric was from what had just transpired, he needed to push past his burdensome fear in order to put Gabriel first. As wired as Cedric was, Gabriel was in a place a thousand times worse. The glossed-over look in his eyes wasn't normal. It was like Gabriel had lost himself amongst the wreckage of his past, and what remained was fragmented in such a way that it needed an external source to hold it together.

Cedric was that source.

With a deep, grounding breath and slow, purposeful movements, Cedric ended the hug.

He took Gabriel home.

10

GABRIEL

Through the cheerful white door was an eat-in kitchen. The wooden floor was glossy and the baseboards were neat, white trim against stone-gray painted walls. Gabriel accompanied Sir through the kitchen and into the living room, remarking upon the double glass doors leading out into a screened-in sun room—but the stunning layout and the pristine condition of the building did not distract him from his troubles. Not even Sir's hand, broad and confident on the small of his back, was enough to make him forget.

The man without a name was outside. He'd looked Gabriel in the eyes, and he'd smiled that cruel, twisted smile that made Gabriel feel dirty all over. It was the kind of smile that said, *I've found you,* and that scared Gabriel more than the thought of never being with Garrison again.

There was nothing good about the man without a name. He'd taken Gabriel from The White Lotus and demanded Gabriel be his when it was obvious Gabriel still belonged to Garrison. Those times had been so dark that Gabriel had mostly blocked them out, but he still remembered what the man without a name looked like.

He saw him in his nightmares every time he closed his eyes.

If the man without a name knew where he was, Gabriel needed to act fast. The longer he stayed in this place, the more likely it was that he would be in danger. The last thing he wanted was to go back with *him*, locked up and imprisoned, degraded and abused. This time, there would be no escape. The man without a name wouldn't make the same mistake twice, and Gabriel would be stuck forever.

That couldn't happen.

Sir brought Gabriel through the house to a bedroom. The space was small, and it was a little musty, but it wasn't uncomfortable. The single bed was the focal point of the room, a dust sheet drawn over it to keep it pristine. The wood floor looked recently polished, and the old wood dresser pushed against the wall was dust-free. A door at the back of the room, not far from the bed, led out to the screened-in sun room. A thick curtain was hung above it, drawn to the side for the moment so that the dying light of day could illuminate the room.

Sir dropped the duffel bag on the dust sheet, then turned to face Gabriel. Gabriel set his backpack on the floor by the door and lowered his head as a sign of submission.

"This is your room," Sir explained. He gestured to the bed. "This is where you will sleep."

"Yes, Sir."

"Generally, you will have free run of the house, except for my bedroom. You will be able to take what you want from the fridge and from the freezer. You may help yourself to the glasses in the cabinet and to any plates and silverware you find, but you will make sure that whatever you use is cleaned and returned to where you found it once you've finished with it."

"Yes, Sir." Gabriel glanced at the glass door leading to the sun room. Each of the panels sparkled in the setting sun, so clean that he would have thought they weren't there if it hadn't been for the way they shone.

"When you are in good standing, you are also permitted to use the television and any electronics you want. If you aren't sure how to work something, you need to ask me. Do not attempt to figure it out on your own."

"Yes, Sir." Gabriel paused, and something curious curled inside of him until it was wound so tight he had to let it spring from his lips. "You said in good standing, Sir. Does that mean that I'm not allowed to use those things right now?"

"Not now. You've been bad, Gabriel. You will not run from me again."

Gabriel glanced off to the side and folded his arms across his chest uneasily, waiting for the other shoe to drop. The punishment didn't fit the crime. If all Sir was doing was taking away his television privileges, he was lucky. During his time at The White Lotus, he hadn't been allowed to watch television at all, and he'd only caught glimpses of the odd program here and there when the man without a name demanded his presence in the living room. Sir should have taken away something precious to punish him—his blankets, or his bed, or his clothes. Losing access to electronics didn't make Gabriel feel like he was being punished at all.

"You are not to leave the house under any circumstance unless I have given you permission." Sir closed some of the distance between them, and Gabriel looked up curiously through his lashes as he did. He didn't dare lift his chin. "You will be in bed by no later than eleven every night, and up before nine every day."

"Yes, Sir."

"And Gabriel?" Sir stood before him now, and Gabriel glanced back down at the floor. He observed the toes of Sir's shoes and focused on his breathing.

"Yes, Sir?"

Sir reached out. He curled a finger under Gabriel's chin and lifted his head until they gazed into each other's eyes. Gabriel's heart pounded against his ribcage in a desperate bid to escape, but for once, Gabriel didn't feel like running for safer ground. The way his heart beat wasn't bad. It was...

His eyes lidded, and he nuzzled against Sir's hand as warmth spread through him. The first touches of arousal swirled low and swept him up, and he parted his lips as though he was expecting a kiss. The air he breathed sparked in his lungs, and Gabriel fought against the urge to reach out and touch Sir in the sensual ways that he knew would make them both feel good.

Touching a man wasn't supposed to feel this way. It had never been like this before—not even with Garrison. Sir had to be playing some kind of trick in order to make Gabriel want to stay. If that was the case, Gabriel didn't mind—at least not for right now. Touch was good. Touch was *nice*. After the encounter he'd just had on the street, he needed to feel someone else there.

Through partially lidded eyes, he watched Sir's lips part. The tiny metal balls beneath them shone in the light. When he spoke, the sound of his voice was soothing in a way Gabriel had never heard before, and his words danced upon Gabriel's lips. "I want you to speak freely. I want you to be able to express what's on your mind."

Gabriel didn't know what to say, so he said nothing at all. Instead, he closed his eyes and let the weight of Sir's hand beneath his chin lull him into a sense of security.

He'd done a bad thing by running away, but Sir wasn't punishing him. Not really. Television was a privilege, not a right, and Gabriel was much more used to having his rights removed than anything else. But Sir hadn't lifted a hand against him in anger, and not once had he raised his voice. If anything, Gabriel felt rewarded. Sir's touch was a treat, and he indulged in it for as long as he was willing to share it.

"Is that all, Sir?" Gabriel asked. He knew he couldn't let silence stretch between them forever, as much as he wanted it to. If he never moved, and if he never spoke, maybe Sir would never stop touching him. What would it be like to feel this good forever?

"For now, yes." Sir's hand dropped, and the spell he'd cast over Gabriel came to an end. Gabriel's rapidly beating heart slowed back to normal, and the tingling in his lungs stopped. He tucked his hands behind his back and lowered his gaze, but did not lower his head.

"Since you have nothing else to do, I'd like you to come with me to the kitchen so we can make dinner together."

"Cooking?" Gabriel let a smile stretch his lips, and he looked up at Sir timidly, still expecting that at any second, Sir might change his mind and punish Gabriel for his disobedience. "Really?"

"Well, we've got to eat, don't we?"

"I love cooking."

Sir caught his eye and smiled back, and Gabriel's insides did a strange flip, the kind he'd sometimes experienced as a child when he'd ridden his bike far too fast down a hill. Flustered, he looked away.

"Is that the real you speaking, or whoever you're pretending to be?"

"It's me," Gabriel whispered, shy to admit it. He knew that he could have lied and that Sir never would have known any better, but doing that felt cheap. Sir had been nice to Gabriel when Gabriel had deserved his wrath, and so Gabriel thought it would be good of him to be nice to Sir in return. It didn't mean that he was betraying Garrison... not really. Not at all. One day soon, he'd plan his escape, but until then, there was no point in starving himself of what felt nice. And Sir? Sir felt nice. "I love cooking. It used to be something I'd do when I was... away."

"Then let's see what you've learned." Sir gestured toward the door with a nod of his head, and Gabriel found himself obeying his word without a second thought. "Maybe you can teach me a thing or two."

The quiet delight Gabriel took in thinking that he, of all people, could teach Sir anything turned his tiny smile into a near-grin, and he bowed his head to hide his enjoyment. He stepped to the side to allow Sir passage through the room, then followed him out the door to the kitchen.

11

CEDRIC

The blade passed close to Gabriel's knuckles, each chop slicing the potato he held into thin medallions. The pieces wilted onto the cutting board, and Gabriel left them where they fell.

He finished one potato and moved on to the next.

The confidence with which he wielded the knife was uncanny, and for a while, Cedric only watched. It was his first peek at who Gabriel could be if he only stopped doubting himself. *This* was the omega Cedric wanted to see emerge from Gabriel's psyche. Whatever had happened to make Gabriel hide him away from the world was a crime, and Cedric resolved to make what was wrong right.

"Who taught you to cook?" Cedric asked. He leaned against the counter, listening to the sharp side of the knife hit the cutting board in rapid succession.

"I did, Sir," Gabriel admitted in a timid, but pleased voice. "Sometimes if I didn't cook, then... then none of us would eat."

Cedric studied Gabriel's face to search for meaning, but all he found was guarded disappointment. Eyes on the potato, posture deflated and meek, it looked like Gabriel was trying to disappear into himself.

The Lowe family wasn't poor. Cedric knew there was a difference between having money and being cared for, but there was no excuse why any of the Lowe children would go hungry. Rumor had it that the Lowe estate had its own staff—groundskeepers, maids, and chefs included. Had it all been a lie?

Cedric let it go. Gabriel wasn't ready to be pushed. "What's your favorite food?"

The knife stopped. Gabriel set it on the counter and pushed the end of the potato to the corner of the cutting board, leaving the medallions in a heap in the middle of it. "I like saltine crackers."

"Saltines?" Cedric raised an eyebrow.

A smile troubled Gabriel's face—Cedric couldn't describe it any other way. What should have been joyous fell flat and lacked energy, like Gabriel was forcing himself to believe that he was happy. The smile was a sham, and Cedric saw right through it.

"When I was living away from my family, sometimes when... when I was good, I'd be given them as treats."

The statement was innocent, but it scurried down Cedric's spine like a centipede on the run. He resisted a shudder and rested against the counter as Gabriel scooped the slices into his hands and nudged the sink's tap with his elbow. Cold water rained down from the faucet, which Gabriel used to wash the starch from the potatoes.

There'd been a time in Cedric's life when simple pleasures like that spoke to him on a higher level. The gift didn't matter half as much as the giver, and beyond that, the circumstances behind the gesture were most important of all. When he was Gabriel's age, Brittany had shown him it was true. Under her command, even pain had been a gift.

But Cedric didn't get the impression that Gabriel's statement had come from the same place.

"You know..." Cedric moved from the counter to stand behind Gabriel at the sink. He came close, allowing his groin to meet Gabriel's ass and his chest to meet his back. With deliberate intention, Cedric traced the fingers of one hand up along Gabriel's hip and to the subtle inward curve of his waist. If Gabriel gasped, the rushing water drowned it out. Sparks ignited old emotions desiccated by time, and Cedric let them burn inside of him, aware that he was playing a dangerous game.

Cedric leaned closer, letting his lips brush the back of Gabriel's ear. "...I'm sure we can arrange for better treats if you're good."

Some of the medallions tumbled from Gabriel's hands. Cedric cupped his beneath Gabriel's, letting the water rush between their fingers as he held his omega's hands still.

Timid Rabbit...

"Would you like that?"

The tiny noise Gabriel made was neither affirmative or negative, and when he spoke, his voice was a touch more frantic than it usually was. "M-my hands are cold, Sir. May I please stop the water?"

"Are the potatoes ready?"

"Y-yes."

"Then you may." Cedric nuzzled the back of Gabriel's head, letting his soft blond hairs meet his cheek. Then, sure to take his time, he turned off the tap and took a step back. Gabriel hurried from the sink to the counter and dumped the potato slices on the clean cloth Cedric had laid out for him. Without a word, Gabriel made haste to pat them dry, as though if he worked frantically enough, he could forget what had just happened.

If he felt anywhere close to the chemistry that Cedric did, Cedric knew he wouldn't forget.

Every now and then, Gabriel glanced over his shoulder in Cedric's direction. Each time he saw Cedric looking back, he looked away and tightened his shoulders, like he expected to be hit. There'd been a time in Cedric's life when he'd relinquished his power to another, and he knew what it felt like to be aggressively pursued—to have greedy eyes devour his body, and to be the object

75

of the heinous appetites of men—but that meant he understood what Gabriel was feeling, too.

He'd never forget the way she'd made him feel nervous knots of excitement in his stomach, and in her honor, Cedric sought to gift another the same delight.

More than anything, he wanted Gabriel to know what true submission was.

Gabriel dumped the potatoes onto a baking sheet, then drizzled them with the olive oil Cedric had brought out. As he sprinkled them with salt and pepper, Cedric put himself in Gabriel's shoes. When he'd met Brittany, he'd made the choice to fall to his knees before her and to obey her every word. There'd been no doubt in his heart and no desperation in his soul—he'd given her his agency because it was what he'd wanted, and he'd thrived off the attention he'd received not only from her, but from the men in The Shepherd who'd lusted after an alpha so sure of himself that he wasn't afraid to embrace submission.

It wasn't the same story for Gabriel.

Until Cedric knew his narrative, he'd operate with caution. The fledgling relationship they now shared needed to be nurtured, and Cedric wouldn't rush it. He wasn't acquainted with Gabriel very well, but no matter what kind of a person Gabriel was, he deserved better than that. No matter what it took, Cedric would meet his needs in any way he could. He would find the confident omega who'd been so certain with the knife, and he'd coax him out of hiding.

Gabriel slid the baking sheet into the preheated oven and dusted off his hands, then looked nervously over his shoulder at Cedric. Chicken was already cooking on the stove, and there were peas in the freezer waiting to be heated. Dinner wouldn't be long.

"Everything is cooking now, apart from the peas," Gabriel said, bowing his head. "Does that please you, Sir?"

Cedric came to stand in front of him. He lifted Gabriel's head with a single hand and ran his thumb across his lips. "You please me, Gabriel."

Gabriel's cheeks turned pink, and his eyelids fluttered. "Thank you, Sir."

No matter how Sterling inflated the importance of the job, Cedric's task was simple. He'd teach Gabriel what it was like to be valued.

No more saltines.

GABRIEL

The dishes slid beneath the suds, sinking to the depths of the sink. Gabriel watched them disappear, but it wasn't long before his attention was diverted.

Sir was back.

The force of his presence made itself known to Gabriel before his body did, but when it did come, it was bold. Sir's arms slipped around his waist like they'd always been together—like Sir actually thought Gabriel was worth his time. Then, in a low voice against the back of Gabriel's ear that made him shiver with delight, Sir spoke. "Dinner was delicious."

No matter which way he twisted his thoughts, he couldn't find a reply. Gabriel opened his mouth, but the gesture was futile. No words came.

"It's been a long time since anyone's cooked for me," Sir admitted. As he spoke, his hands began to wander inward, tracing over Gabriel's hip to arrive low on his stomach, near his groin. "I'd forgotten how nice it is. You please me, Rabbit."

Rabbit.

Sir's hands stroked the flattened part of Gabriel's stomach that would one day swell with child. Fingertips like magic, palms treating him to wonder Gabriel had never known, made a tiny gasp spill from between his lips. His cock started to harden.

"R-Rabbit, Sir?" Gabriel asked. Arousal changed the sound of his voice, but he couldn't hide it. Sir drove him crazy.

"Do you like it?" Sir grinned against his ear—Gabriel felt his lips stretch in amusement. "My flighty, beautiful, timid Rabbit. I promise, no foxes will come. I'll keep you safe."

The vow stunned Gabriel. He closed his eyes and let go of his last inhibitions.

Sex was different than this—whatever this was. Sex was selfish, primal, and empty. When men groped him, Gabriel was always able to shut his brain off. There was no engagement in sex. No pleasure.

But with a few words and the gentle touch of Sir's hands upon Gabriel's stomach, Gabriel's balls ached, and his cock begged for attention.

"I like it, Sir," Gabriel whispered. He couldn't do anything else. "Thank you."

"Don't thank me," Sir whispered back. He traced his teeth along the ridge of Gabriel's ear, and the hot words he spoke next were made for Gabriel and Gabriel alone. "This is your reward for pleasing me. Enjoy it. Be *selfish*."

The hands low on Gabriel's stomach slipped downward, and Sir cupped Gabriel's clothed cock. With a startled gasp, Gabriel pushed into Sir's hand and rubbed himself shamelessly into his palm.

"You're already so hard," Sir whispered, like it was a compliment. "Oh, Rabbit, what am I going to do with you?"

Sir's fingers slid back up to undo the button of Gabriel's jeans, and Gabriel squirmed as he undid the fly beneath, too. Sir's broad hand slipped through the opening it had made and toyed with the thick elastic of Gabriel's briefs while his other hand continued to cup and squeeze Gabriel's erection from outside his pants.

"I like you," Sir whispered. His words were silk, smooth and sleek in ways that Gabriel never wanted to lose. "I want to know that you like me, too."

"I like you, Sir," Gabriel uttered. Never had he said something as true. There was no more guilt. "I like you very much."

"Good."

Sir's hand slipped below the elastic, allowing his fingertips to brush the head of Gabriel's stiff cock. With a needy cry, the air left Gabriel's lungs. It didn't matter. Sir gave him everything he needed.

"When is the last time someone touched you like this?" Sir asked, his voice a teasing presence against the back of Gabriel's ear. His hand slipped down and wrapped around Gabriel's shaft. It started to pump. "When is the last time anyone made you feel this way?"

"Never," Gabriel gasped.

It was true.

Tears gathered behind his closed eyelids and slid down his cheeks in silence.

It wasn't supposed to feel good.

"No more saltines." Sir nipped at his ear. He growled low in his throat and tugged at Gabriel's lobe. "When you're to be rewarded, you will be rewarded properly. Do you like to come, Rabbit?"

"Y-yes."

It had to be a dream. There was no way it wasn't a dream. The way Sir touched him felt too good for real life. Nothing should have felt so wonderful.

"Then when you're good, you're allowed to come. This dick I'm stroking right now? The one that's so hard for me?" All of Sir's words were pretty, but Gabriel could barely string together their meaning. Pleasure swirled low in his gut and he knew it wouldn't be much longer before he couldn't hold it back. "It belongs to me. I don't want your hands on it. I don't want you to come unless I'm the one touching you. Do you understand?"

"Y-yes, Sir." Gabriel couldn't help it—he bucked forward into Sir's hand.

"I want you to know the full extent of the pleasure I can give you." The honey in Sir's voice was a new addiction Gabriel couldn't shake. "I want you to understand why it's important to be good."

Everything was tight. Gabriel squeezed his eyes shut and tried to loosen the clenching muscles in his gut, but it was no use. He was going to come. Sir was going to make him come, and he was going to make a mess of his pants.

"When we're together, I want you to know that your pleasure comes first," Sir uttered. His hand worked in rhythmic thrusts, tight enough that Gabriel wanted for nothing more. The pressure in his balls grew, and the urge to come welled up inside until it became irresistible. "I need you to show me that you understand, Rabbit. Your cum is your body's promise to me that it accepts. I need to feel it. I need to see you lose control."

Every breath was more strained than the last. Pinpricks danced behind Gabriel's eyes. No man had ever demanded he come before —at least, not without having come first.

A sharp cry pierced the silence of the kitchen.

Gabriel came into Sir's hand, spilling so much, he thought he'd never come again.

But Sir wasn't done yet. Gabriel's jeans sagged. Then, the elastic band of his briefs started to slip down over his ass.

Sir was going to breed him.

Gabriel's mouth opened again, and when he spoke, the words came naturally. He knew what men wanted to hear. It was what he'd been trained for. "That was so good, Sir. I want to make you feel good, too. Please, *please* use me. Let me show you the only thing I'm good at. Breed me, and make me do what I was born to do."

The elastic stopped moving, and Sir's hand on his shaft halted. Gabriel found the presence of mind to open his eyes. Sir must have needed more.

"Fuck me. I was born to take your cock. Let me take your come, Sir. Teach me what it means to be an omega."

Sir's hand parted from his cock, and Gabriel groaned at the loss of stimulation.

"Sir?" Gabriel looked over his shoulder, the pleasure of orgasm fleeting now that he'd lost the touch of another. He'd never come from another man's touch before, not even Garrison. It was strange and wonderful, and Gabriel didn't want it to stop. "Please, Sir. Please. I'm ready."

But there was a haunted look in Sir's eyes, and Sir wasted no time in raising the elastic of his briefs and lifting his jeans back into place. What had happened? Had he done wrong?

"Sir?"

"That's enough pleasure for tonight, Gabriel," Sir murmured. "I want you to do the dishes, then I want you to go to bed."

A lump rose in Gabriel's throat. Somehow, he'd done wrong.

But maybe, just maybe, he could fix things by being good. In that moment, all he wanted was Sir.

At Sir's hand, dreams of Garrison were eroding into nightmares.

13

CEDRIC

Breed me, and make me do what I was born to do.
Cedric braced his palms on the wall of the shower stall and squeezed his eyes shut. The memory of Gabriel's body still spoke to him—the heat of his torso against Cedric's chest, the silken sensation of his cock in Cedric's palm, and the smell of his omega as Cedric nuzzled against the back of his head and played with his ear. Gabriel's body language had indicated that he was ready, but the things he'd said revealed a story far more troubling.

Breed me.

Make me do what I was born to do.

No matter how Cedric tried, he couldn't escape what he'd heard.

If that was really how Gabriel felt, he couldn't have sex with him. Hell, he shouldn't have ever laid a hand on him. Disturbing thoughts like those ran deep, and until Cedric rooted them out, he couldn't reward his omega in the way he wanted to.

Above the noise of rushing water, Cedric heard Gabriel in the hall. The guest bedroom door closed, and Cedric's guilt built. He'd left his omega unsatisfied and wanting more when he should have been rewarded. It was *his* mistake. If he'd been strong enough not to shut down completely when Gabriel had demeaned himself in such a way, then he could have carried on and rewarded Gabriel in other ways—worked to stoke his confidence and knock down the walls of ignorance he'd locked himself behind. But that hadn't happened, and now Cedric had to live with the consequences.

Sterling's warning made more sense than ever.

Of course he was the Dom properly outfitted for the job—Cedric understood submission well, and that meant he understood that what Gabriel was doing was harmful to his mental health. Submission didn't mean defeat.

Cedric rinsed the rest of the soap from his body and worked the shampoo out of his hair. When the water ran clear, he turned it off and stepped out of the shower stall. His toes curled against the lush fibers of his bath mat, and for a moment, all he did was breathe.

He wanted Gabriel. The attraction had been instant, and the connection was there. Gabriel had been responsive to his touch, and his body had told Cedric that he was doing right. If he could only get his mind in alignment, then they could continue their sessions the way Cedric wanted them to progress.

But until then—until he knew that Gabriel understood his importance and his worth—Cedric couldn't touch him.

It was wrong.

He patted his face down with a towel, then wicked the water away from his hair and wrapped himself up. The en suite bathroom attached to the master bedroom was flush with the hall, and Cedric took a moment to be sure that Gabriel wasn't on his way back out of his bedroom. Right now, he needed some time to himself to think.

When he heard nothing, Cedric left the bathroom and started to change. He glanced toward the door to make sure it was locked. Living alone meant he wasn't used to closing doors behind him and locking them in his wake, but he was learning. Besides, having someone in the guest bedroom made the house feel more lively. He'd been on his own for so long now that he'd forgotten what it was like to have someone else around.

If only his heart could say the same.

Cedric toweled off by the end of his bed, then tossed the towel into his hamper and climbed across the mattress. He lay atop his blankets, chest down, and folded his arms beneath his head. What Gabriel needed was a gentle touch from someone who cared about him, but who could restrain himself enough not to take advantage of him when he was vulnerable. Cedric could fill that role for him. He was skillful enough to coax Gabriel from his noxious mindset and teach him that he had worth outside of sex and childbirth. It wouldn't be that hard.

Except the problem was, *Cedric* was hard.

Soft, golden-brown hair. Expressive blue eyes. A slender body...

Fuck.

It was going to be a balancing act between doing what was right for Gabriel and keeping himself in check, but Cedric was ready. Sterling had given him this job for a reason, and no matter how much of a temptation Gabriel was, he was damned well going to see it through to the end.

.

14

GABRIEL

The dreams were nothing like they'd been before.

Gabriel rose from bed, the sheets too soft against his skin to be real. It was the kind of soft that made him want to curl back up in bed and forget the rest of the world, but he couldn't do that. Something tugged at his soul and made him get up, like if he didn't, he might never feel comfortable again.

There was no weakness in his legs as he walked, and no sluggishness in his limbs as there usually was, but then again, the bedroom he was in didn't belong to Garrison—it belonged to Sir.

Padding barefoot upon the wooden floor, Gabriel found his way to the door that led out to the sun room. The curtain was pulled aside, and the door had been left ajar. Gabriel rested his hand on the brass knob and glanced into the room beyond the glass.

Sir stood there, one arm resting against the frame the screens were attached to, leaning casually as he observed the back yard. It occurred to Gabriel that he'd never been back there before, and that he had no idea what he might encounter. Still, the tug in his soul made him bold, and he pulled the door open and stepped into the room to join Sir.

Nothing was said as Gabriel crossed the floor, even though he was sure Sir heard his footsteps. Gabriel came to a stop at his side and gazed through the screen at what lay beyond. The sun room overlooked a forest. Trees with leaves in fall colors lined the distance, beautiful in ways Gabriel couldn't hope to explain.

Sometimes, from the upper windows of The White Lotus, he'd seen the trees in the distance turn with the passing of the season, but their browns and rusty reds were nothing compared to the splendor he saw here. Bright yellows, stunning oranges, and deep, gorgeous reds lit up the horizon. Every now and then, one of those colorful leaves would part from its branch and topple downward, spiraling as it celebrated its momentary liberation before it was brought to a stop by the ground. The sight filled Gabriel with gloom, and he tucked his elbows against his sides in the hopes that if he held himself tight, his weakness wouldn't be visible.

He was too late.

Sir wrapped an arm around his shoulders and drew him to his side. There were no words exchanged between them, but Gabriel got the feeling that his presence was welcome and appreciated. Wary, just in case that wasn't the truth, he leaned against Sir's side with the uncertainty of a dog seeking permission to do the forbidden. Sir did not correct him, and his body language didn't change, so Gabriel let himself relax. When he was settled, Sir's arm tightened around him, and Gabriel closed his eyes and let go of the anxious breath he'd been holding.

He wasn't going to get in trouble. Not now.

Sir was too kind to ruin an afternoon so beautiful.

Sunlight beamed onto them from outside, soaking into their clothes. It absorbed into Gabriel's hair, and he basked in it. He was vaguely aware that he was in his pajamas, and that he didn't look sexy at all while wearing oversized black, white, and blue plaid, but as long as Sir didn't mind, Gabriel didn't care. He rested his head against the crook of Sir's neck, right where it met his shoulder, and looked out at the fall forest.

"I want you to be mine."

The words came out of nowhere, and they turned Gabriel's cheeks as crimson as the leaves he watched outside. He remained motionless, still not convinced that Sir was talking to him.

For a while there was silence, but it wasn't uncomfortable. Gabriel remained pressed against Sir's chest, the scent of a crisp autumn day combining with the alluring scent of Sir's alpha. If there'd been a time Gabriel had smelled something so nice, he couldn't recall it. The scent teased out the tension from his shoulders and released him from his inhibitions. Even if it was just for a little while, Gabriel felt like one of the leaves on the horizon, spiraling on its way to the ground—free.

"I don't want you to think of him anymore, Gabriel." This time, there was no doubt that Sir was speaking to him. Gabriel opened his eyes to glance up at Sir. He was watching the forest, his gaze distant, but his energy present and modestly joyful. It was the quiet kind of happiness that made men glow—the kind that Gabriel wasn't really sure he understood. "You deserve better than him."

"I don't deserve anything," Gabriel whispered. He said the words peacefully, because they were the words he'd been taught. His familiarity with them allowed them to come like he'd been born saying them, and he said them without a second thought. "Garrison is good for me. He loves me, and I love him."

"You know that's a lie."

Gabriel frowned and nestled closer to Sir. He knew that he shouldn't be entertaining dangerous ideas like those, but when they came from someone like Sir, who'd been so nice to him, and whose strength was quiet and unassuming, it was tempting to forget.

"If he loved you, none of what happened would have happened. He wouldn't have made you give yourself away to others. He would have been too jealous to let anyone touch you at all."

"That's not true," Gabriel murmured. A cloud passed by overhead, and for a moment, the sunlight disappeared. A chill ran down Gabriel's spine in absence of the light, and he closed his eyes as he waited for the darkness to pass. "There's a difference between my job and my relationship. Garrison is my boss, but he's also my lover. We're going to get married, and he's going to give me a family. He promised."

"How many years ago did he promise that?"

The answer was five, all the way back when Gabriel was sixteen, but he didn't want to confess that to Sir. It was shameful. He'd been unofficially engaged to Garrison for five years, but they'd never once discussed anything to do with the wedding— even something as simple as the date they wanted to get married on.

"He's leading you on," Sir murmured. He kissed the top of Gabriel's head, and a shiver ran down Gabriel's spine. This time it wasn't from the cold—it was from excitement. "You're better than that. You're worth more than a crusty old man who promises one thing, then delivers another. He's never going to marry you, Gabriel. He's never going to give you the things in life that you want. But I can."

Tears formed behind Gabriel's eyes, but he willed them away. Crying in front of Sir would be disrespectful, especially if they were tears shed over another man.

The truth was, Gabriel had struggled with those thoughts before. On the hard days, alone in his room, he'd cried himself to sleep thinking that Garrison would never make good on his promise. In the morning, cried out and emotionally depleted, those thoughts receded into the dark corner they came from, but they never fully left. They lurked in the shadows, waiting for him to lapse in judgment again so they could claw their way through his subconscious and tear him to shreds.

Gabriel knew that until Garrison's devotion was his, and his alone, that he would never consent to marrying one of his boys, but how did Sir know that? It made Gabriel think that Sir was already inside his head, looking in on all of his secrets.

"I want you to be mine, Gabriel," Sir said again. "I can take care of you the way you need to be taken care of, and I can keep you safe. I would *never* give you to him."

"To him?" The sunlight returned, and Gabriel craned his neck to take advantage of it. His nose found the crook of Sir's neck. Every breath was full of him now.

"To the man without a name." Sir's hand traced along his arm, steady and predictable. "I would never give you to him, and I will never let him get you."

"How do you even know who he is?" Gabriel sighed. "You're not supposed to know who he is."

"Why?"

The question lingered between them. No matter how Gabriel turned it over, looking for an answer, he couldn't find it.

Why couldn't Sir know about the man without a name? If he knew, then he could keep Gabriel safe. They were both alphas, after all—strong, imposing, and dominant. Gabriel didn't stand a chance against a man like that, but Sir? Since Sir was an alpha, too, they were evenly matched—and if Gabriel had to guess, Sir was stronger.

He could be safe here, in this haven in the middle of the forest, with Sir by his side.

Sir, who was handsome like no one Gabriel had seen before. Sir, who was kind, even when Gabriel deserved punishment. Sir, who smelled so damned good...

"You want to keep me?" Gabriel asked. He parted from Sir's side only so that he could turn to face him. Sir looked away from the forest, his eyes the kind of green that would make the leaves jealous. "Why would you want to do that? I'm so..."

So boring. So plain. So broken.

Sir bridged the distance between them. His fingers tucked themselves beneath Gabriel's jaw, and his thumb traced over Gabriel's lips. On the outside, the touch was gentle, but inside, it was like Sir had struck flint against steel. Sparks, too brilliant and too hot for Gabriel to dare touch, cascaded inside of him.

He never wanted Sir's hand to go.

"So wonderful?" Sir asked. "So beautiful? So *good*?"

Sir's thumb crossed Gabriel's bottom lip, parting it from the top. Gabriel sucked in a tiny breath as arousal shot through him and flooded his gut. He was starting to get hard, even though he knew he shouldn't. He wasn't supposed to enjoy sexual contact with other men.

But Sir? Sir was ice water after a hike through a desert, and the first warm day after a harsh winter. His touch was insistent, but it wasn't demeaning. Gabriel didn't shy away from it—he wanted more.

"I *want* you, Gabriel," Sir whispered. The thumb crossed along his lip again, but this time, when it reached the plump middle, it ventured inward to trace along the tips of his teeth. "You don't have to feel unwanted anymore."

How did Sir know all the right things to say? How could he be so firm, and yet so kind? The tingling returned, but this time, it swept through Gabriel's body and left him highly aware of himself —the butterflies in his stomach longing to escape, the goosebumps down his arms, and the way his cock now nuzzled against the fly of his pajama pants.

He parted his lips and let Sir inside.

The pad of Sir's thumb traced over his tongue. Gabriel closed his eyes and set his lips around the digit, sucking gently as Sir explored his mouth. He could be good for Sir, if that was what Sir wanted. He could suck until his jaw was too sore to continue—until Sir became so aroused that taking Gabriel's mouth wasn't enough anymore.

"Good boy," Sir whispered, his lips so close to Gabriel's ear that Gabriel couldn't help but shiver in delight. "Good, beautiful boy."

All Gabriel wanted was to know he was pretty. His cheeks grew hot, and he lifted his tongue and ran it across the bottom of Sir's thumb, apprehensive of his reaction. Sometimes, when he was being too much of a slut, Garrison punished him—but Gabriel couldn't help himself. Not now. Not when Sir had whispered such exquisite things to him, and especially not after he'd called Gabriel pretty.

Gabriel wanted to give him everything.

"Do you know how good you feel?" Sir worked his thumb in deeper, and Gabriel hummed against it and let his tongue lave Sir with affection. "Do you know how beautiful you look, sucking me like that? You're gorgeous, Gabriel. You're the prettiest boy I've ever seen. He should have told you that. He should have told you that every damn day."

Tears swelled in the corners of Gabriel's eyes, pushing out from beneath his lids. They weren't born of sorrow—far from it.

For the first time in a long time, Gabriel was *happy*.

"He'll never give you the things you want from life." Sir's thumb caressed Gabriel's tongue as it worked back and forth, almost escaping the confines of Gabriel's mouth before pushing deep again. "He'll never protect you from the men who want to hurt you. You deserve better. You deserve me."

The tears fell fat and hot as they streamed down Gabriel's cheeks. Why was he happy? He wasn't with Garrison, and for so long, Garrison had been the only one he'd wanted. It was hard to imagine that he could be happy by the hand of someone else.

"If you want me as much as I want you, then you're going to let my thumb out of your mouth, and you're going to turn around." The words Sir spoke were stern, but they were not unkind. They offered Gabriel the chance to refuse if he wanted to, but Gabriel didn't want to. He wasn't sure he'd ever want to disobey Sir. "You're going to push your pajama bottoms down, and you're going to give your ass to me. You're going into heat, aren't you? I can smell your slick on the air. I want inside. I want to feel how wet your body is for me, and once I'm done feeling it, I'm going to be so slick with you that it'll be no problem to slide inside and breed you, will it?"

Gabriel's cheeks were on fire, and the loose sleep shirt he wore was too hot against his suddenly sweaty skin. Was he in heat? It seemed too soon, but who was he to argue? Slick already ran down his thighs, and his scent perfumed the air. Time didn't matter when his body told him in no uncertain terms that he was ready to conceive.

He was finally going to get what Garrison had never given him —he was going to give Sir healthy, beautiful babies.

The thumb parted from Gabriel's mouth. Roasting in the flames of his heat, Gabriel turned and braced his arms against the screen paneling. The wires bit into his skin, but he didn't care. For the first time ever, he was going to get what he truly wanted.

He was going to make a family.

But Sir's hands never gripped Gabriel by the hips, and Sir's cock didn't find its way between Gabriel's lubricated cheeks. Gabriel woke abruptly instead, short of breath and harder than he'd ever been before. With a keening, frustrated groan, Gabriel rocked his hips into the mattress of his new bed and tried to work out his arousal.

He couldn't feel this way. He *shouldn't* feel this way. He belonged to Garrison, not to anyone else—but there was Sir, with his dark hair and his green eyes, too beautiful for words and too kind to be real, watching from the back of Gabriel's mind.

What was he supposed to do?

The dreams were nothing like they'd been before, and they ended in unfamiliar ways, too—in orgasm, so crisp and sweet that Gabriel wilted onto the bed and had to take a moment to himself to recover. Guilt hit seconds later.

He was being bad—worse than he ever could have imagined. He couldn't stay here and face temptation, or he'd forget what he truly wanted, and who he truly belonged to. He had to get out now, before he did something he'd regret.

The dream was over, and he resolved to never have it again.

15

CEDRIC

"I t's going to take some work, but now that I understand my boundaries, I think it'll go well." Cedric held the phone to his ear as he pulled the overhead cabinet open and plucked the jar of coconut oil from the shelf. He picked up the spoon he'd left on the spoon rest and pressed it into the solidified oil, breaking off a small chunk to set in the heating frying pan. "There was an incident earlier in the day when he got spooked and bolted down the driveway for reasons I'm not entirely sure I understand, but other than that, there were no significant incidences. We spent the rest of the day getting to know each other so I could understand how best to approach the job. Sterling was pleased."

Oli hummed. "Like bringing home a rabbit, it sounds like. So, you called Sterling already?"

Rabbit.

Cedric grinned.

"First thing this morning." He pushed the glob of coconut oil around the pan and watched as it melted. "I wasn't even out of bed yet when I called him. He was awake and glad to hear from me. Apparently, Adrian was up all night worrying."

"I guess it's a good thing you called, then." The tone of Oli's voice led Cedric to believe that there was something he'd left unsaid. Oli didn't keep him waiting for long. "I think that it's good that you're being paid well for this job, but I'm not convinced that it's a good job to take, even if it means you're making a connection with Sterling."

"Why?" Cedric took four eggs from the fridge and rested them on the counter. He cracked the first one on the edge of the stove, then emptied its contents into the hot pan. "You don't think I can handle it?"

"It's not you I'm worried about. You're going to be fine. It's that little fidgety rabbit of yours I'm worried about."

"Mm." Cedric set the empty shell down and picked up the next egg. "What about Gabriel, in particular?"

"You said he spooked when you were outside. I'm no psychologist, but that seems to be a pretty big red flag, don't you think?"

"It was one time. He was with someone he barely knew in a place he'd never seen before. I came into this knowing that there was something strange going on. I think, if skittish is the extent of his damage, it's not the end of the world." The second egg struck the counter, the hairline fracture branching farther as Cedric pressed his thumb into it to split one half from the other. "I want him, Oli. I'm not giving up on him. I think he just needs to get settled."

"Well, you know better than I do." Oli yawned. "What are you doing up this early, anyway? It's not like you to be an early bird. Hell, if I could, *I'd* still be asleep."

"There's always excitement whenever a new client enters my life." It was partially a lie, but Cedric didn't want to get into the truth. Not yet. Telling Oli that he couldn't keep the damaged omega sleeping in his guest bedroom off his mind wouldn't have gone over very well. His friendship with Oli spanned years, all the way back to the time when they were both juniors in high school, and Oli was the new kid in class—the very first out of any of them to have manifested his omega characteristics. They'd tried dating for a while, but after one outrageously unsuccessful romp in the storage shed behind the high school, they'd decided it was better they stop being lovers so they could be best friends instead.

Oli still lamented the fact that he'd never had a chance to feel what the others from Cedric's short-lived high school relationships had so tactfully described as a huge knot, but by that time, there was no going back. The friend-zone had been firmly established, and they'd moved into almost-brothers territory. He supported Cedric, and he'd been there for him after he'd lost Brittany, but out of respect for Oli, Cedric did his best to keep sex-talk off the table.

"Well, I'd be careful if I were you," Oli said. "The Lowe family was weird during high school, and I get the feeling that they're even weirder now."

"Gabriel isn't weird."

"Mmhm. I thought so. I hear the defensiveness in your voice." Oli sighed. "You're up early because you were screwing him, weren't you?"

Gabriel, naked on his bed, the cute rounds of his ass almost heart-shaped as they tapered toward his waist. Pale skin and a smooth, hairless body. He'd perk that ass for Cedric, and then... Cedric blinked last night's dreams away. They were disrespectful when Gabriel's mental state was so fragile. What he needed wasn't sex, and Cedric had to remember that. "Of course not."

"That was a telling delay." Oli chuckled. "Listen, I'm just about to hit the road so I don't miss my interview. Do you want to touch base later when you're feeling a little less defensive, and we can have an actual conversation about how you want to screw the brains out of the omega you've been asked to dominate?"

"I don't—"

"Forget it. You can deny all day, but it's not going to do you any favors. The problem with having a best friend who knows you so well—*especially* an omega best friend—is that I can read you like a book. You might think you're being subtle about it, but you're not." Cedric practically heard Oli wink. "So I'll call you tonight, okay?

After this morning's interview, there's a career expo going on, and I'm going to dazzle them with my sunny brand of morning sarcasm."

"You're not going to need to go. You're going to land the job you're interviewing for."

"Details." Oli chuckled. "Listen, I'm letting you go. I'll call you back later. Let's say seven? That'll give me plenty of time to get home and change into pajamas, and it'll give you enough time to tie your new love slave up to the bed to make sure he doesn't bolt while we have a private conversation about him in the next room."

There was no reasoning with him. Cedric shook his head, but he was laughing on the inside. "Sure. Seven. I'll have my chains ready."

"Perfect. See ya."

The line went dead. Cedric set the phone on the counter, and he was about to pick up the third egg when he realized the two in the pan had turned to plastic. "Shit."

The overdone eggs were introduced to the garbage, two new eggs hit the hot oil, and a handful of minutes later, Cedric had breakfast ready. Eggs and toast. Simple, but satisfying. There were other ways to reward a submissive, and if that meant doting on him until they worked out Gabriel's issues, then Cedric would do so.

He wasn't sure if Gabriel drank coffee, so he fixed him a glass of orange juice and brought his meal from the kitchen to the bedroom. The door was closed, so Cedric balanced the plate on the crook of his arm and knocked. "Good morning, Gabriel."

One beat passed. Then another. There was movement in the room, and Cedric assumed Gabriel was getting out of bed to answer the door. He counted the seconds in his head.

Five. Four. Three. Two. One.

Nothing.

Cedric knocked again. "Good morning, Gabriel. This will be your last warning. When you are greeted, you are expected to respond."

Nothing.

Cedric frowned. He'd been of the opinion that Gabriel required a gentle touch, but it seemed like he was wrong. If he needed to be more forceful, he'd do it—but it upset him to think that he'd misread Gabriel like that.

Patience depleted, Cedric twisted the doorknob and pushed the guest bedroom door open. With Gabriel's fragile mental state, he hadn't wanted to enforce punishment, but Gabriel left him with no choice. He stepped into the room and opened his mouth to speak, but stopped short.

No one was there.

Gabriel was gone.

16

GABRIEL

R *un.*
Run, and don't stop. Never stop. Don't let him get you.
Gabriel skidded around the corner of the sun room and into the kitchen. Sir was at his bedroom door, looking to come in. If he didn't run now, if he didn't get out, then he'd be ensnared in this place. Sir would claim him, he'd be too weak to resist, and he would never see Garrison again.

He couldn't let that happen.

The side door leading to the carport was locked, but with a simple twist of his fingers, Gabriel worked it open and burst through the door. The cold morning air sent goosebumps up his arms, but he hadn't had time to grab a sweater. Sir had come in earlier than he'd anticipated, and he hadn't had time to pack like he wanted to.

It didn't matter. He had to get away.

He'd been *bad*.

Sir was nice, but Gabriel had met nice men before, and he'd never dreamed about defying Garrison for them. Sir was handsome, but appearances were shallow, and age would change his face and destroy his looks. Kind words and a willingness to understand wouldn't change Gabriel's life—action would. And while Garrison may not have whispered sweet words in his ear or given him much physical affection, he'd always provided for him.

Gabriel couldn't forget that.

This time, he didn't try to run for the woods. Gabriel dug in his heels when he arrived at the sidewalk and changed course, running in the direction Sir had driven to get back to the house.

Garrison was counting on him.

He hit the street corner, but there was still so far to go. Gabriel knew that if he kept following a straight path, Sir would find him right away. He'd been banging on the door right when Gabriel was getting ready to go, and that meant that he was running on borrowed time. Sir would be after him. He needed to get away, or he'd be taken back to the house and he would *never* get a chance to see Garrison again.

There was a mailbox on the corner, old, blue, and metallic. Gabriel rounded it, but before he could pass it, he came to a sudden stop. His hands and feet had gone numb, and pinpricks shot up his legs as his feet hit the sidewalk. A familiar, unsettling scent filled his nose, and his stomach balled up and squeezed until every pang of guilt Gabriel had ever felt was forced from the dark recesses of his stomach where they lived and up into his throat and lungs. Air deserted him. No matter how deeply he breathed in, he couldn't satisfy his body's needs.

Gabriel knew what was going on—he was having a panic attack.

There was no denying it. The numbness, the nausea, the shortness of breath... all that was missing was the dizziness, but that would come soon enough. It always did. The ground would fall out from beneath his feet, and the space just behind his eyes would start to spin, and from there, his whole world would shift out of focus. He'd stumble and fall if he tried to walk, like a sailor recently returned to land, while the harsh feelings built up inside until they overtook him completely. All he could do now was hide and hope that Sir wasn't interested in finding him.

Out here, his options were limited, so Gabriel hunkered down behind the mailbox and tried to talk himself through his panic before the dizziness had a chance to strike. Back in The White Lotus, when his panic attacks had started, he'd been told by the doctor on staff that counting was an effective way to manage his terror, and he'd been taught an exercise to help. He closed his eyes and drew in a deep breath, counting to five as his lungs filled.

One. Two. Three. Four. Five.

The scent didn't disappear, but it had to be in his head, didn't it? Wood and leather and rot. There was only one place Gabriel had smelled it before, but it couldn't be here, right now, could it? His brain was doing its best to sabotage him, and it was doing a wonderful job of it.

This was why he wasn't supposed to be on his own. Garrison had taught him that omegas were delicate creatures who needed guidance, and Gabriel had seen the truth of his words play out time and time again. Every panic attack, every jealous feeling of injustice, and every haywire emotional response proved that he wasn't suited to life without a leader. It wasn't wrong to have been born this way, but it was wrong to live life without an alpha for very long. The men and women who thought they could prove nature wrong were asking for trouble, and even if trouble didn't find them right away, it would track them down eventually. No one was immune. But Gabriel? Garrison had called Gabriel a perfect omega, and it meant that he was more susceptible to his submissive instincts than anyone else.

Gabriel curled his numb fingers against his palm and let the air out of his lungs slowly, counting down from five. All he had to remember was that his fear was trying to get the best of him. The scent on the air was a figment of his imagination. It wasn't real. Over the last few days he'd been pushed to his limits and forced to endure change after change—from Stonecrest, to Sterling's penthouse, to Sir's bungalow by the woods. It was natural that his body was shutting down. He wasn't made for high-pressure situations.

Fists balled, skin tingling, Gabriel flattened his fingers again and went back to counting. Five in, five out. He worked his toes, trying his best to drive sensation back into them. The dizziness was starting behind his eyes, as if his brain itself was spinning while the rest of the world stood still. More than anything, he wanted it to stop.

In five. The smell of wood and leather and rot wouldn't leave him alone.

Out five. There were footsteps down the block.

In five. Gabriel dared to open his eyes as the footsteps drew near, expecting to see Sir pass him by.

Out five. The face he saw was ripped straight from his nightmares.

Lungs empty and body weak, all Gabriel could do was watch as the man without a name strolled by the mailbox and kept on walking. His hands were in the pockets of his jeans, and he wore a black hoodie that zipped up the front. As he passed, he looked down at Gabriel with a brow arched and his lips pulled back in a grin that exposed the tips of his too-perfect teeth.

All Gabriel could do was stare.

Was it his mind? Was he hallucinating? Gabriel didn't want to reach out and touch him in order to find out. Terror coiled tightly in his chest, making sure his lungs stayed empty. His body screamed for air, but he couldn't breathe. It was like he'd been anchored to the bottom of the ocean and left to drown.

It's not real.

But the smell was, and so was the man's hawk-like nose and the piercing way his blue eyes tore Gabriel apart.

It's not real.

But the man's gait matched what Gabriel remembered, and the extra weight he carried fell exactly as Gabriel recalled it did.

It's not real.

But the cadence of the man's chuckle was impossible to mistake.

He passed the mailbox by, and as he stepped down from the curb to cross the street, he gave Gabriel one last, lingering look, then hitched the hood once slouched down his back over his head and kept walking. Gabriel watched him go, back pushed against the frigid metal siding of the mailbox, heart racing so fast he was sure it would explode.

How was this real? If it was real, the man without a name should have taken him. There was no one stopping him. Gabriel was on his own, and he was defenseless. Gabriel knew that there was no way he'd be let off the hook—he'd escaped, he hadn't been set free. So why wasn't the man without a name taking back what he thought was his?

Rust on the side of the mailbox caught the back of Gabriel's shirt, and he squeezed his eyes closed as a fresh wave of nausea consumed him. The world spun faster than it had before, and counting from five wasn't working. More than anything, he wished he could rip the useless part of himself out, if only so the spinning would stop.

"Gabriel!"

The sound of his name was distant, but it registered in Gabriel's ears, and it dragged him down from the spinning heights he'd climbed to.

"Gabriel!"

It was Sir, a foggy part of Gabriel's brain realized. Gabriel opened his eyes as the footsteps approached. Each beat of his sole against the sidewalk slapped the pavement at a frantic pace—panic. Gabriel wasn't the only one in the world who was alone and afraid.

"Gabriel!"

The voice was beside him now, and Gabriel looked up to find Sir standing next to him. His cheeks were red and his hair was messy, a combination of early morning and windswept. He wore a sweater, but the wind was whipping it, and his hair, in ways that made Gabriel feel cold just by looking at him.

Sir needed a jacket. Why hadn't he brought a jacket? Gabriel wasn't worth being cold over. Sir deserved so much better.

Gabriel only noticed that he was breathing again when Sir fell to his knees and swept him into a crushing hug. Gabriel froze, expecting punishment, but when none came, he carefully wrapped his arms around Sir and hugged him back.

"What the hell do you think you're doing?" Sir asked, but his voice was frightened instead of angry. "There were rules set in place. You weren't supposed to leave the house without my permission."

"I know," Gabriel whispered. He buried his nose against the crook of Sir's neck and tried not to remember his dream. Sir's touch felt too good, and it made him want to be bad, just like he knew it would. "I'm sorry."

One of Sir's hands tucked itself behind his head while the other barred across his back. The touch was intimate, but it was not demanding. It was the kind of touch that was grateful instead of possessive, and it made Gabriel want to know why.

Why was Sir treating him with kindness instead of disgust? Why was he being met with affection instead of pain? What was it going to be like when Sir got him back into the house?

Somehow, it didn't matter.

Gabriel breathed in Sir's scent and held it. Instead of anxiety, he was treated with release from his fears. Now that Sir had him, he was safe. He'd be kept secure inside the house, and even though he was going to be punished, Gabriel knew that whatever waited for him in the bungalow couldn't hold a candle to what the man without a name would do to him should he be reclaimed. Gabriel didn't like the thought that he was to go back home with the man he'd dreamed about—the one who'd encouraged him to forget about Garrison—but right now, he had no other choice.

He'd rushed his escape. Next time, he would give it thought, and he'd wait for the perfect opportunity. With the man without a name lurking nearby, and Sir intent on not letting him go, what other choice did he have? For now, he'd have to be strong.

Wilted against Sir's chest, Gabriel talked himself down from his panic. He was seconds away from announcing that he could walk when Sir's arms changed positions, tugging Gabriel to him that much tighter.

"Are you ready to go home?" Sir asked.

"Yes, Sir." Gabriel knew that he should stand, but he'd found safety in Sir's arms, and he was reluctant to part from them. Enjoying physical contact like this didn't mean that he was being bad. Right now, it was what he needed to get by. "Do you want me to stand?"

"No. You've lost the privilege to walk by yourself."

Gabriel blinked and pulled back from Sir's chest. He was about to ask what that meant when Sir lifted him from the sidewalk like he weighed nothing at all and tucked Gabriel against his chest. Gabriel gasped and locked his arms around Sir's neck, but all Sir did was chuckle. They rose together, Sir's body taut as he supported Gabriel's weight. He was slender for an alpha, but in that moment, he showed his true strength.

"Sir?" Gabriel asked, his tone pitched up a note from uncertainty.

"Your outside privileges have been revoked." Sir rounded the mailbox, carrying Gabriel bridal-style in the direction of the house. "I told you yesterday that you weren't allowed outside unless I gave you permission. That is no longer the case. You are to remain inside until you've proven that you can be trusted. If you test your limits again, your punishment will be *severe*. My patience is not unending. You know better."

"I know, Sir." Gabriel frowned, but he couldn't feel sorry for himself—not when Sir was holding him so close and sheltering him from the world.

"When we get inside, you'll have half an hour to eat the breakfast I prepared for you. After that, your time is mine."

"Yes, Sir." Gabriel's arms loosened around Sir's neck. He felt the sway of every step Sir took, but Sir's sturdy arms did not let him fall. "I won't do this again, Sir."

It was a lie. Gabriel knew it, and by the way silence descended upon them, he thought that Sir knew it, too. If Sir suspected he was lying, he didn't call him out on it. There was nothing he could do to keep Gabriel from going, and Gabriel was fairly sure he knew it. It was just a matter of when.

"Let's get you back to the house," Sir murmured, almost more to himself than to Gabriel.

Sir carried him the rest of the way home.

CEDRIC

Omegas who consented didn't run.

Cedric bent forward at the waist, resting his elbows on the kitchen counter as he held his head in his hands. He'd managed troublemakers before—men who liked pain and punishment more than they liked pleasure—but the way Gabriel acted didn't lead Cedric to believe he was looking for punishment. There was no sly twist of his lips or sparkle of mischief in his eyes. What Gabriel was looking for wasn't a spanking, or a lashing, or even a deprivation of his senses—he wanted to escape, and Cedric still hadn't come to terms with what that meant.

Did Gabriel want to be here? Probably not. Cedric had no clue what had happened with him, and Google wasn't telling him shit. All he knew was that one day, Gabriel had been a regular part of the Lowe family, and the next day, he'd been missing. He'd heard rumors about the aftermath as it related to the remaining individuals in the house—Adrian and his parents—but rumors weren't reliable, and they told him nothing about what he needed to know.

Timid Gabriel, who'd crumpled in on himself behind the mailbox, body shaking and eyes squeezed shut with terror.

What the hell had Cedric done to him?

Gabriel was locked in his room, the bolt secured on the sun room door. There was no exterior lock for the hallway door yet, but Cedric was already considering his options. He didn't want to lock Gabriel in a room like he was a prisoner, but at the same time, he was obligated to keep Gabriel safe. That left Cedric with two options—he could install a lock that would potentially piss off his landlords when it came time to move, or he could figure out what the root problem was and eliminate it.

One of those options was a much sounder solution than the other, if only Cedric knew how to go about doing it.

Breakfast.

Cedric's eyes traced up the kitchen wall to the clock hanging over the stove. Fifteen minutes had passed since he'd brought Gabriel inside and laid him in bed, but his nerves were still shot. Fifteen more remained before he would claim Gabriel's time as his own—fifteen more minutes to make a decision about what he was to do about his runaway omega. Two escape attempts in less than twenty-four hours. Was he a monster? Cedric had always thought he was the kind of Dom who operated with integrity and respect, and who was never afraid to give his submissive exactly what he or she needed. With Gabriel, he was beginning to doubt that was true.

Had he been too stern? Too tough? Too demanding?

Until he knew, he couldn't come up with a suitable punishment for what had just happened. Gabriel's state of mind was so frail that even a light spanking felt like it would be abusive. Until Cedric had a chance to pick his mind and get to know Gabriel for who he really was, his hands were tied.

Spinning his wheels wasn't getting him anywhere, so Cedric pushed off the counter and occupied himself with busywork. He scrubbed the few dishes in the sink he'd left from breakfast and swept away the crumbs left on the counter from making toast. He put water on to boil and prepared the French press. The unexpected cardio he'd been abruptly forced into hadn't given him a runner's high, and he needed *something* to make the morning a little better.

Boiling water poured, coffee left to brew, Cedric took a mug from the cabinet while he talked himself up. All he needed to do was go in there and treat Gabriel like he was any other client. Sterling wouldn't have given him a job that was beyond the scope of his capabilities—he knew Gabriel better than Cedric did, and if he thought it was a job Cedric could handle, then there had to be something he was missing.

Or maybe Sterling was setting him up to fail.

Cedric set the mug down. The ceramic clicked against the counter, joining the hum of the refrigerator to erase silence from the room. Was Sterling the kind of man who'd entrust a potential candidate with an impossible task in order to avoid rejecting him head-on? Cedric didn't want to think so, but the more he thought about it, the more his troubled mind tried to convince him it was true. The sudden change of plans, the alternate job offer, and the promise that *if* he did a good job taking care of Gabriel, the management position *might* be available to him when it opened up again.

It was all a ploy.

The realization was the kind of bitter Cedric couldn't chase away with sugar or cream. He strained the French press and poured his coffee, and by the time he'd sweetened it to his liking, the fifteen minutes he'd been so anxious for had passed—and so had his negativity. So what if Sterling had set him up to fail? He was young and green, and he would snap back even when put under pressure. So what if he didn't land the management position at The Shepherd? He'd built a perfectly good career for himself outside of Sterling's kink club—the position would only have helped broaden his horizons and connect him with the right people. The fact of the matter was, right now, he had a job to do. Gabriel was the one he should be concerned about—not himself—and conflating the situation with hypotheticals wasn't going to get him anywhere.

It didn't matter if Gabriel was damaged, or if the job was beyond the scope of his ability. The fact was, he'd taken it, he was being paid for it, and he was going to see it through to completion. Whether or not Gabriel wanted to be dominated was debatable, but there was no doubt in Cedric's mind that he needed help, guidance, and someone to catch him should he fall.

Cedric could do that.

Cedric *would* do that.

He picked up his coffee, approached Gabriel's bedroom door, and got to work.

18

GABRIEL

Three rhythmic knocks were all the warning Gabriel got before the door swung open. He looked up from his empty plate to find Sir coming through the doorway, a mug of steaming coffee gripped in one hand. He nudged the door closed with his heel after he entered, then came to sit on the bedside a polite distance away from Gabriel.

Polite wasn't something Gabriel was used to. When a man came to sit on his bedside, it meant that he wanted a certain thing, and Gabriel's body was quick to remember what it was. Partially, he knew, it was because his body remembered the way Sir had touched him the night before. Gabriel knew that it was wrong to get excited over a man he didn't belong to, but he couldn't help it. Besides, for as long as he was in Sir's custody, a reaction like that would be useful. When the time came that Sir did want to use him for sex, at least Gabriel would enjoy it.

Shamefully, he scooted across the bed to close some of the distance between them and sat so close to Sir that their thighs were touching. Usually that was all it took.

But Sir didn't turn and pin him to the bed, and he didn't try to kiss him, even though Gabriel had the feeling that kissing Sir might actually be nice. Instead, he turned his head and looked Gabriel in the eyes. Pinpricks, too light and too pleasurable to belong to a panic attack, spread through Gabriel's chest. They crept down his shoulders and along the length of his spine until he was sure he'd never get rid of them, and the pleasant buzz would stay forever. The depth of Sir's green eyes looked into him, like he was a painting to be appreciated rather than a blunder best ignored.

Affection, unexpected but welcome, bloomed alongside the pinpricks, and Gabriel fought the urge to smile. He knew that he shouldn't feel this way for another man, but he wasn't actively trying to. When Sir looked at him like that, Gabriel found it hard to remember he belonged to someone else.

For a long while, there was silence. Sir studied him, and Gabriel found himself too much in awe to look away. The sun was at an angle where its rays came through the glass door leading to the sun room and struck Sir's eyes in just the right way to intensify the color and amplify every undertone and highlight. But it wasn't the color of Sir's eyes that bound Gabriel—it was the emotion in them. Concern. Affection. Worry. Without a single word said, Gabriel knew he was cared for.

He never wanted to look away.

"What's going on with you?" Sir asked, his voice quiet. They sat so close that there was no need for him to speak any louder. He reached out and ran his fingers along the ridge of Gabriel's jaw, but didn't push for more. The pinpricks in Gabriel's chest turned frosty, like mint, and he shivered as he nuzzled against Sir's hand.

He didn't understand.

Sterling had given him to an alpha. They hadn't been together long, but the arrangement was unusual, and Gabriel wasn't sure what to make of it. If Sir didn't want his body, then what *did* he want? There was nothing about him that was particularly special. It wasn't like he was smart, like Adrian was. His genes meant that he wasn't good for much. Conception, child rearing, domestic tasks, sure... but Sir hadn't asked him to take care of any of those things, and the more he touched Gabriel with kindness instead of lust, the more confused Gabriel became.

When he'd left Sterling's penthouse to come live with Sir, he'd made peace with the fact that he'd have to be bad. Getting to Garrison meant struggle, and part of that struggle was the temporary rule of an alpha Gabriel didn't want. But this? Sir wasn't ruling him at all. Not really. Gabriel hadn't even seen him with his sweater off.

It made him feel like maybe he was doing a bad job at the only thing he was good at.

Sir said nothing, even when Gabriel held his tongue. The silence allowed Gabriel to think, and the more he thought, the worse he felt.

All his adult life, he'd worked to satisfy the men that Garrison brought to him. It was what made Garrison happy, and by doing it, Gabriel knew that he was being good. Even when he struggled with feelings of doubt or disgust, he knew that if he just pushed through, Garrison might recognize his hard work and devotion and finally deliver on his promise. No man he'd ever been introduced to had kept his hands off him for long, and Gabriel had grown accustomed to the fact that he was made to be touched.

Beautiful flowers attract bees to pollinate them, Gabriel. Beautiful omegas are no different.

Once, those words had comforted him when he hadn't wanted to go on. Knowing his life served a purpose meant that he was better able to rationalize the things he did, and the things Garrison wanted him to do. Now, those same words haunted him.

Wasn't he beautiful? Didn't Sir want him?

Why was he asking questions when they could be doing what they were biologically meant to do?

The world wasn't like Garrison had told him it would be, and it confused him. If he wasn't good for sex, then what was he good for? How would he ever impress Garrison enough to get him to stay if he couldn't even satisfy Sir?

117

Sorrow, insidious in nature, began to infect Gabriel's thoughts. Garrison was his future, but what good would the future be if he couldn't be the young man Garrison wanted him to be?

Words tumbled out of Gabriel's mouth, chased out by a creeping sense of worthlessness that lent the slow-moving sorrow inside of him a razor edge. "I-I miss my boyfriend."

There was a shift in Sir's eyes. The pretty green rings around his irises were darkened by regret, and the shape of his eyes softened, like he was looking upon something tragically broken. Gabriel didn't like to think of himself as broken, but as the poison inside him spread, he knew that he'd been fooling himself. He'd been broken for years now, held together by hope and willful ignorance. Now that he'd had the future stripped from him, he was doing his best to hold himself together by chasing the past. Sir had every right to be disgusted—Gabriel was in decay.

"You have a boyfriend?" Sir asked, his voice little more than a whisper. "I didn't know."

"I miss him." The dam had burst, and the truth spilled forth. Gabriel could spend the rest of his life pretending that he was fine, and that he could be good, but in that moment, he was too worn down to keep up the act. "I *love* him."

A cloud passed over Sir's face. For a moment, Gabriel thought he saw Sir break, too. Whether that look persisted, Gabriel didn't know. He ducked his head and looked away, ashamed of himself for being so weak, and humiliated that what he said had brought Sir pain, too.

"Where is he?" Sir asked. His hand parted from where it had once cradled Gabriel's jaw, and he returned it to his lap. "Why aren't you with him?"

"No one's helped me get to him." Gabriel curled his fingers, then let them go. "I want to go back to him. I want to go *home.*"

Sir bent over and set his coffee on the floor. When he sat up, he lifted his ass just enough to slide his phone out of his pocket. He laid it on his palm and held it out to Gabriel. "Do you know his phone number?"

Gabriel looked down at the phone, startled. No one had tried to help him before, let alone a man he was supposed to serve. What was going through Sir's head? Was it a trick? "N-No."

"Then why don't we Google him?" A half-smile perked one corner of Sir's lips, but there was sorrow behind it. It was a slow-building sadness, the kind that Gabriel thought he felt, too—like Sir had been robbed of purpose. "Everyone's online these days. Facebook, Twitter, Instagram... we'll find him."

The razor-edged worthlessness in Gabriel hit a wall so hard, the blade bent and became useless. He held his breath, sure that if he made one wrong move, the dream would end and the cruel realities of life would burden him again.

Was this for real? It wasn't just a trick made to fool him into misbehaving? It wouldn't be the first time someone had tried to deceive him. Only Sterling had ever asked him questions about Garrison, but in the end, he'd said that Garrison was a bad man, and he'd refused to help. Adrian was no better, and he was family. But Sir? Sir was a stranger. What was in it for him?

"Why are you doing this for me?" Gabriel asked uneasily. The phone remained on Sir's palm, untouched. Until he knew what Sir's motives were, he didn't want to push his luck. But the look in Sir's eyes wasn't malicious. No matter how hard Gabriel looked, he couldn't find cruel intention in them.

"Because I'm here to make you happy, Gabriel." The words were genuine in a way Gabriel wasn't prepared for. The pinpricks exploded, and Gabriel's heart fluttered. He bit down into his lower lip and dipped his chin, ashamed that he could ever think that Sir would want to deceive him. He'd been hurt before, but Sir had never wronged him. Why was he so distrustful of everything and everyone? "I know what it feels like to miss someone with all your heart, and if I can spare you that feeling, then I'm going to do everything I can to help."

The pain in Sir's voice was old, like it had long ago scarred over, but would never fully be gone. Gabriel wanted to ask about who he'd lost, but he knew it wasn't his place. So instead, he looked at the phone. It was sleek and flat, its screen smudged in the places that Sir's fingers touched most often. It had been half a decade since Gabriel had owned one—Garrison had taken his from him the same day he'd come to stay at The White Lotus. He didn't know the first thing about how it worked. "His name is Garrison Baylor," Gabriel said reluctantly. "Do you think you can find him, Sir?"

"I could." Sir shrugged. "But I think that I'll have you find him instead."

The phone passed hands. It was surprisingly light, and Gabriel looked down at it with equal parts apprehension and excitement. Was he really going to do this? Sir was putting the world in his hand.

"If... If I find him," Gabriel glanced up from the phone to look cautiously at Sir, "will you help me get back to him? Will you help me go home?"

"Of course."

Joy, golden and radiant, should have washed over him. It should have made the bliss of the pinpricks stronger, and the featherlight weight of his stomach that much more weightless.

It didn't.

The pinpricks disappeared. Gabriel's stomach sank. Dread, the same kind he'd felt when he was introduced to the men he was meant to service, made him pinch his shoulders tightly to his neck. He had unlimited resources at his disposal—everything he needed to track down the man he loved—but he couldn't bring himself to be excited about it. The joy had gone. Something had changed, but he didn't know what.

Sir's sad smile answered his question. Gabriel noticed the suffering behind his pleasant facade—and his heart did, too. It ached for the alpha he'd inadvertently damaged.

"I'm... I'm sorry, Sir." Gabriel fixed his gaze on the curve where

Sir's neck met his shoulder. He recalled the scent of his skin, and the way Sir's body had felt against his own. Whenever they touched, the pinpricks came back.

Whenever they touched, Gabriel was *happy*.

"What are you apologizing for?" Sir reached over and pressed a button on the side of the phone. It lit up, and Sir punched in a few numbers to undo the lock screen. "I'm glad that I know a little bit more about you. I would have never known you were in a relationship if you hadn't told me. What we need more than anything else is trust, and you can't build trust with a stranger."

You can't build trust with a stranger.

Gabriel looked down at the unlocked phone screen, searching the icons for a web browser as Sir's statement sunk in. When Sir had asked him to pretend to be someone else back in the driveway, how well had he known Garrison? He'd struggled to string together a single statement.

They'd been together for three years.

The screen dimmed. Before it could go out, Sir pushed the browser. It launched, and when it loaded, it presented Gabriel with a search engine.

"Type in his name." Sir tapped the search field and brought up the touch keyboard. "Let's see what we get."

Garrison Baylor, Gabriel typed.

He pressed enter, but his heart had already pressed escape.

19

CEDRIC

*G*arrison Baylor.

Gabriel's boyfriend. The name was familiar, but Cedric had a hard time placing it—likely someone from their school, he figured. A forgotten face from a lower grade that Cedric had never concerned himself with. Whoever this Garrison was, the news was hard to swallow, but Cedric was glad he'd found it out now before his heart got any more entangled than it was. Gabriel as a client wasn't enough to keep him from imagining what could be, but to know Gabriel was in a relationship? Cedric wasn't a home-wrecker. If Gabriel was with someone else, it gave him all the more incentive to stay away.

No matter how much it hurt, and no matter how much Cedric wished otherwise, Gabriel would never be his.

If only he could convince his heart of the same.

Gabriel's thumb hovered over the search button, as if he were having second thoughts. He glanced at Cedric, his lips tight and near the point of trembling, like he was on the verge of tears, but whatever was causing him pain didn't last long. He pressed the button and began the search.

Soon enough, Cedric would know the man who held the heart of the damaged omega at his side.

Over three hundred thousand results generated.

Cedric's jaw dropped.

Sex Offender Sentenced to Life in Jail

Leader of The White Lotus Sex Ring Found Guilty

Life in Prison for Baylor, Court Rules

Gabriel scrolled through the articles as if nothing was wrong. The tiny frown he wore didn't match the magnitude of the news on the screen. It was like he didn't care.

"Gabriel?" Cedric asked. He resisted the urge to take the phone directly from Gabriel's hand and turn off the screen. "Are you sure you have the right name?"

"Yes." Gabriel kept scrolling. All the articles were recently dated. "All I need to know is where to find him. He's waiting for his appeal to go through and for his lawyers to clear his name, and I want to be with him while he waits."

Either Gabriel wasn't reading the snippets beneath the articles, or he was willfully ignorant of them. Ignorant or not, the further he went, the more frantic his scrolling became.

Criminal Defense Attorney Marcus Hayes Takes on Role as Prosecutor in Jaw-Dropping Appeal

Sentence Maintained—No Freedom for Baylor

You'll Never Believe What This Lawyer Did to Keep a Sex Offender off the Streets...

What was Cedric supposed to say? Resorting to something tactful like, *I don't think it's a good idea I return you to a sex offender,* wasn't going to fly. The worry on Gabriel's face, and the growing concern in his eyes, proved that he didn't care about Garrison's crimes. Siding with something more blunt like, *Hell no, I'm not going to give you over to an imprisoned criminal,* felt just as weak and unsatisfactory. Cedric watched the feed scroll onward, loading story after story about Garrison's recently overturned appeal, until he could take no more. He pressed his finger against the screen, blocking

Gabriel's panicked scrolling, then spoke the only words he could think to say. "I'm sorry."

Three syllables were all it took. The phone dropped from Gabriel's hand, and he let loose with a choked sob so twisted that it almost sounded alien. Almost, because Cedric did recognize it—it was a sound that had once rattled free from his lungs and constricted his throat, too.

Grief.

The phone was unimportant. It toppled between Gabriel's thighs and met the bed, then slid off and landed on the floor. The impact was lessened by the silicone phone case cushioning the sides, but Cedric was unconcerned with the state of his device. In that moment, it didn't matter if his phone was broken or not—not when Gabriel was falling to pieces.

"I j-just want to go to him," Gabriel sobbed, his voice pitched so high that it was almost unintelligible. "I w-want to be with him. I don't c-care where he is."

"I'm sorry." Cedric hoped Gabriel knew his words were sincere. The situation bothered him more than he cared to admit, but that didn't mean Gabriel's pain went unacknowledged. Once, a handful of years ago, Cedric had been in the exact same place when he'd lost Brittany. The agony of losing a loved one was the same, whether that loved one was a criminal or not. "I know that it's not easy."

"N-no you d-don't." Gabriel squeezed his eyes shut, but tears streamed from their corners and traced glossy trails down his cheek. "I left him. I l-let myself be t-taken. If I'd been st-stronger, I would have been with him. We could have been *together*." Gabriel's sobbing reached a new, warbling peak, and he choked the last word out through clenched teeth. A few racking sobs shook his whole body before he pulled himself together enough to speak again. "W-we were going to get m-married. He was g-going to give me a family."

There was no ring on Gabriel's finger, and Cedric didn't think he was old enough to be thinking about marriage and babies. What was going on in Gabriel's head? What vile things had been done to him during his time with Garrison to shape his view of the world this way? Cedric thought he knew, but the truth was too ugly to reflect on for long. He let it go, and with it, he let go of every notion he had about the omega at his side to cling to fact, and fact alone.

Gabriel was kind, even if he was skittish. He was gentle, even when the world was against him. He was bold, because he had to be, and even when he was scared, he pushed past his fear to do what he felt had to be done. Cedric hadn't known Gabriel for long, but he already knew those things as truth, and he held them close to his heart. No negativity would affect his perception of the young man at his side. No dark history would shade Gabriel in his eyes. The past was the past—Cedric had reminded himself of that time and time again, and it was about time he started listening to himself.

He would not let past events influence his understanding of Gabriel as a person, just like he wouldn't let past events influence his understanding of himself. They were not tethered to history. History shaped them, but the present and the future were theirs to mold as they wished. Until he was proven wrong, Cedric would think of Gabriel the same as he always had—as the scared little rabbit who'd strayed too far from his burrow. What he'd learned changed nothing except his understanding of Gabriel's needs.

The reason why Sterling had wanted Gabriel cared for was obvious to him now—Gabriel didn't know how to take care of himself.

Always seeking guidance, even if that guidance was from strangers, timid to a fault, and so low in self-esteem that he was paralyzed when he took action into his own hands, Gabriel needed someone not just to dominate him, but someone who would be his advocate. He needed a partner whose stern touch would not only see him safely through the day, but whose interest in his wellbeing would ensure that he made steps toward being the best version of himself that he could be. A regular Dom wouldn't do. Gabriel's case required not just sensitivity, but the attention of a man who valued him as an equal, even as that man made Gabriel submit. What Sterling had proposed wasn't an attempt to sabotage Cedric's position at The Shepherd—Sterling saw in him a man able to chip away at the years of abuse done to an individual already so vulnerable within society. He believed that Cedric could do right by Gabriel.

A flood of emotion struck Cedric, and for a moment, as Gabriel sobbed inconsolably at his side, he allowed himself to let go of every fear that was holding him back.

There were no games being played. The task he'd been given was monumental, and it required unwavering trust on the part of Sterling and Adrian. There was no one conspiring to strip him of his opportunity to land the job at The Shepherd—in fact, it was the opposite. In Gabriel, he'd been given a chance at a future.

Now Cedric had to decide what direction he wanted that future to go in.

In Gabriel, Cedric saw himself as he'd once been—lost, confused, and hurt that life could be so cruel. No one had been there to help Cedric through those times, and the months he'd spent in mourning were cold and lonely things that he tried to push from his mind.

Not anymore.

The pain he'd suffered and the isolation he'd weathered gave him the experience he needed to help Gabriel through the worst time of his life. Sterling knew it, and he'd used it to make the best decision he could for his brother-in-law.

United in grief, they could rise together. Gabriel wouldn't have to feel so alone, and Cedric...

Cedric wouldn't have to feel so alone anymore, either.

There would be no more soft-spoken words, and no more walking on eggshells. Cedric understood what Gabriel needed, because for so long, his soul had needed exactly the same thing. He reached out and tangled his fingers through Gabriel's hair, directing his head upward until Gabriel opened his eyes and met Cedric's gaze. The distance between them was scant, and Cedric's heart jumped into his throat as Gabriel's blue eyes, puffy from crying, looked up at him.

He was beautiful.

Even in sorrow, even when he was uncertain of himself, there was underlying beauty in Gabriel that couldn't be denied. It was in the delicate angles of his face, and the way his slender form lent itself more to art than it did real life. It was in the soul behind his eyes, and the timid way he conducted himself. Like a piece of pottery broken and fitted back together with gold, the fragmented parts of who he was made him unique—they did not lessen him in any way. Cedric noticed because so often, he, too, felt like he'd been shattered. For so long, he hadn't been sure if he could piece himself back together. With Gabriel, he knew otherwise. He saw Gabriel's strength, even if Gabriel wasn't ready to embrace it yet. He noticed the pieces large and small, even the tiniest fragments that threatened to be lost. They were both works in process—finished pieces of art that had been subjected to undesirable conditions, but that could still be brought back to life. There was still growth to come. Gabriel would find himself, just like Cedric had once found himself. He'd pick up the pieces and he'd slot them back together, and he'd do it because there was no other way to move forward. No one else would do it for him—but Cedric could at least hold those pieces while Gabriel fought to give them order.

He would be there. He would be the pillar of strength Gabriel needed. And maybe together, as they worked toward restoring Gabriel's fragmented soul, the cracks in their foundations would be filled, and the pain they both harbored deep inside would be expressed.

Maybe together, they could heal.

"You will get through this, Gabriel." Cedric didn't try to offer condolence. Gabriel wasn't ready to hear it. In a state of shock, stripped of his future, his whole life was in free fall. Until he came close to hitting the ground, Cedric couldn't catch him, and he wouldn't try. The plunge was needed. Mourning was part of the process. Cedric would not take that from him. "You won't feel this way forever."

"Y-y-you don't know that." Gabriel's eyes were squeezed shut again, and he crossed his arms over his chest so tightly that Cedric was concerned he might pull a muscle. "You a-aren't me. You d-don't know."

"Then let me prove it to you." Cedric pulled Gabriel to his chest. In return, Gabriel uncrossed his arms to latch on to Cedric. His fingers curled so tightly in Cedric's shirt that the cotton collar bit into the back of his neck. "Be mine. You don't have to forget about where you came from, and you don't have to let go of your pain, but what I tell you, and the things I ask you to do? Listen to them. Obey them. Give yourself to me, and let me prove that it doesn't have to feel this way forever."

Gabriel's fingers tightened. Hot tears soaked into Cedric's shirt, wetting his skin. He paid them no attention. "Y-you promise?"

"I promise." Cedric let a hand wander along the back of Gabriel's head, hoping the touch might help soothe Gabriel's heartache. "You're not alone. You don't have to face this pain by yourself. I *want* to help you, and I will help you, if only you trust me enough to let me in."

The breath Gabriel drew was shuddering, but it didn't end in a sob like Cedric was expecting. Instead, he pushed himself closer against Cedric's chest and nodded in the smallest way. "Okay."

"Then it begins now, Rabbit." Cedric closed his eyes and rested his chin on top of Gabriel's head. The moment was still and silent, the sound of their breathing the only noise that marred it. "Every command, every reward, and every punishment will be shaped with you in mind. You might not always understand why I do the things I do, but I need you to believe that I know what's best, and that I would never do anything to hurt you."

"I do." Gabriel sniffled, but his fingers relaxed. The shirt bit less harshly against the back of Cedric's neck. "I believe."

It was all Cedric needed to hear. He directed Gabriel back from his chest so he could look into his eyes. Gabriel's were pink and puffy from crying, but beyond his misery, Cedric saw honesty. He'd meant what he said. "Then do as I say, Rabbit," Cedric murmured as his fingers worked slow, comforting circles on Gabriel's nape. "Take a hot shower, loosen your muscles, and then come back to bed and cry if you need to. It won't be long until I come to find you again."

"Yes, Sir," Gabriel whispered. His lips moved, but the sound of his voice was diminished, and Cedric barely heard it. It sent his pulse racing regardless. "I will, Sir."

The pieces had finally fallen into place—now all Cedric had to do was make sure they stayed that way.

20

GABRIEL

"Good morning, Rabbit."

Gabriel opened his eyes. Sunlight filled the bedroom. Sir was perched over him, the natural light glossing his hair. It made him look radiant, like he was a king of some faraway land. And this morning, Gabriel was his intended.

"Sir?" Gabriel croaked. Crying had turned his throat raw and cleared his sinuses, but at last, there were no more tears left to cry. Body warm after his shower, curled safe beneath Sir's blankets, he'd let all the pain and anguish out.

Garrison was gone, and there was no chance he was coming back. To read that his appeal had been denied and that he'd be serving a life sentence had crushed Gabriel's dreams of their happily ever after. If it had been ten years, or even fifteen, he might have been able to cope. In fifteen years Gabriel would be in his mid-thirties, and he'd still have time to conceive and bear children. But life in prison? There was no chance they would ever have the family Garrison had promised.

The loss of a dream was bitter, and Gabriel had mourned it until his tears were gone, even though he'd begun to suspect that Garrison wasn't the one he really wanted.

"We need to establish further rules this morning, Rabbit." Cedric ran his fingers along Gabriel's cheek, and for a moment, Gabriel wondered if he wasn't still in a dream. Sir's touch was electric, and the hurt in his soul lessened substantially from it. He tilted his head into Sir's hand and let Sir lavish him with affection.

Garrison was gone, but Gabriel's hope wasn't. There was still an alpha in his life—one who'd already sworn that he would protect him.

"Will you listen?"

"Yes, Sir." Gabriel closed his eyes. "I'm listening. I promise."

"Good." Sir came closer—so close that Gabriel could feel the heat of his body. His lips brushed Gabriel's forehead, the small metal balls of his snakebite piercings cool against Gabriel's skin. "The rules I gave you before are still to be respected. Up no later than nine, in bed no later than eleven. Your access to electronics will be limited if you misbehave, but otherwise, you are welcome to use whatever you find in the house as long as you are respectful of it, and replace it as soon as you are done."

"Yes, Sir." The rules were simple, but even slight structure provided Gabriel with framework. It was a comfort he sorely needed.

"When I ask something, you will listen, and you will do as I say." Sir's fingers brushed Gabriel's hair back from his forehead. "Failure to act will result in punishment. The severity of that punishment will vary depending on how you disobey, but I will never do anything that is detrimental to you. Everything I do, I do for you."

"Yes, Sir."

"Our arrangement is in effect from the moment you wake up in the morning, to the moment you go to bed." Sir's fingers played in Gabriel's hair, the kittenish touch keeping Gabriel relaxed beneath the sheets. "In essence, you will do your best to please me... and in exchange, I will do my best to please you. I will make sure that your needs are met and your comforts are considered. All I ask is that you be open for me—that you accept that your role in this is just as valuable as mine."

Gabriel opened his eyes, startled by the statement. "What?"

"If this arrangement between us is going to work, I need to know that I can trust you." Sir had drawn back, bent over Gabriel, but no longer so close that he could kiss Gabriel's forehead. "I want you to be able to speak your mind. If something is too much for you, you need to be honest about it. I won't push you any further than you're able to go, but you need to draw those lines for me if I misjudge them."

Equal partners? The concept was laughable, but the look on Sir's face wasn't playful. He was serious.

Nervously, Gabriel nodded. "Okay."

"It's okay to be afraid." Sir's voice dipped low and grew intimate enough that Gabriel's cheeks started to warm. "I was afraid once, too, but fear isn't something to want to avoid. Fear means opportunity. Fear means growth. Will you grow for me, Rabbit? Will you let me in and chase you from the safety so that you can start to live again?"

Everything Sir said made Gabriel's head swim, like his thoughts had to escape from thick syrup before they could make their way to his conscious mind.

"I'll grow for you, Sir," Gabriel promised.

Maybe, if he did, he could leave his pain behind.

21

CEDRIC

A week after Gabriel's attempted escape, Cedric watched from the couch as Gabriel reached for the upper shelf in the pantry in search of the popcorn. It hadn't yet occurred to him to pull a chair over from the kitchen table to stand on. Not that it mattered much to Cedric—he took selfish pleasure in watching Gabriel stretch himself out. The bottom of his t-shirt rode up his slender body, exposing the top of Gabriel's hip as he struggled to reach the box. No sexual contact didn't mean that Cedric couldn't enjoy what he saw—and so he did, even when it made him feel a little guilty.

"Sir?" Gabriel's cheeks were red, and when he turned to look through the kitchen doorway into the living room, he seemed both frustrated and embarrassed. "I... I can't reach it, Sir."

"You can."

Gabriel lowered his gaze to stare at his toes. "I'm sorry."

Since last week's talk, Gabriel had been obedient. The small, simple tasks Cedric had asked him to do had been executed flawlessly. Gabriel was eager to serve, and the job he did was always thorough and thoughtfully done. When Cedric asked him to wash the dishes, he did so without complaint and went so far as to dry them and put them away when he was done. When Cedric tasked him with sorting laundry, not only did it get sorted, but it got folded neatly, too. And at night, when they settled in together for the evening, Gabriel was always docile and pleasant. He'd curl up against Cedric's side and rest his head without pushing things too far, and Cedric rewarded him for his good deeds through innocent touch, even as his libido urged him to push things further.

Finding out about Gabriel's troubled past hadn't changed Cedric's perception, but it had changed his attitude. If Gabriel had been abused—if his disappearance at sixteen years old was linked to Baylor and his vile brothel—then sex was the last thing he needed. No matter what, Cedric would see his omega's needs met.

But tonight?

Tonight, Gabriel was falling short. The more he ducked his gaze and stood by his belief that he *couldn't,* the more Cedric wanted him to see that he *could.* If he pushed outside of his comfort zone and performed in the way that Cedric hoped he would, then maybe he could forgive this indiscretion. All he wanted was to see that Gabriel could think for himself.

But he wouldn't wait forever.

Five. Four.

Gabriel remained by the pantry, boring holes through his bare feet.

Three. Two.

He rubbed one ankle against the other, his hands folded behind his back.

One.

Gabriel stayed small in the doorway, nervously stroking his arm.

Zero.

Cedric stood and made his way to the kitchen. He was taller than Gabriel, and he wouldn't have had any problem reaching the box of popcorn on his own, but resolving the problem himself didn't satisfy him. Instead, he crossed the kitchen to stand behind one of the chairs pushed in at the kitchen table. "Come here, Rabbit."

"Yes, Sir." Gabriel crossed the kitchen to stand within arm's distance of Cedric. He looked so small and so timid that Cedric's heart broke for him, but he knew that if he wanted to help Gabriel piece himself back together, he needed to hold firm.

"I want you to take this chair over to the pantry," Cedric instructed. "When you set it down, I want you to stand on it. Do you think you can reach the popcorn then?"

From the way Gabriel's eyes widened, Cedric may as well have just told him the secrets of the universe. "... Sir?"

"Yes?"

"I'm... allowed to do that?" Gabriel glanced at the chair with frightened distrust. "I'm allowed to stand on it?"

"Of course you are. I want you to."

"Right." Gabriel ducked his gaze. "Okay."

As he picked up the chair and carried it carefully across the floor, Cedric considered what he was going to do about Gabriel's fear. Submission was beautiful, and it could be liberating, but in men like Gabriel, it was limiting. Cedric wanted him to listen, but he wanted him to be independent enough to solve problems on his own. Without a backbone, Gabriel wouldn't get far.

The felt sliders on the bottom of the chair dampened the sound of impact when Gabriel set it down. He tested its balance, then glanced back at Cedric questioningly. Cedric leaned against the kitchen table, arms loosely folded, and observed.

What could he do?

No matter what commands he gave Gabriel, his little rabbit would always be skittish. He would always blush, and bide his time, and lower his head to avoid Cedric's gaze...

Until he couldn't.

The solution dawned on him, and he stepped forward to help Gabriel onto the chair. He held out a hand, and Gabriel climbed up onto the seat, took the box from the shelf, then tucked it under his arm. The way his hand wrapped around Gabriel's felt right, and Cedric was reluctant to let him go when Gabriel was safely standing on the floor.

A boy like this is going to ruin you, Cedric...

Cedric blinked away the intrusive thought and let his hand part from Gabriel's. No matter how he felt for Gabriel, he was a client, nothing more.

"I want you to make the popcorn for me. When it's done, you'll pour it into a bowl from the cabinet—which you will reach yourself —and you will come to join me for the movie tonight."

Disbelief clouded Gabriel's eyes, and he shuffled his weight from foot to foot like he was nervous. "I'm not... I'm not going to have my privileges take away, Sir? I failed you..."

"I know, Rabbit." Cedric slid a hand around the base of Gabriel's head and massaged the soft hair there, like he was so fond of doing. Gabriel's eyes lidded, and he pushed into Cedric's hand. The distance between their lips was small, and Cedric found it hard to keep himself from making it even smaller. The air thickened with his desire, and the touch of Gabriel's hair against his palm left him wanting something he couldn't have. "I'm taking away another privilege of yours, but for now, don't worry yourself about it. I won't be ready to deprive you of it for another few days. Until then, you'll be good for me, won't you?"

"*Yes.*" The word was curled with pleasure, almost purred. Gabriel's head rested against Cedric's hand as his fingers worked slow, comforting circles against his scalp. It was for Gabriel's bene-fit, not his own. A simple touch wasn't pushing things too far. If Cedric had learned anything over the past few days, it was that Gabriel responded best to physical stimuli. Contact like this wasn't sexual.

Not really.

Not in the way that Cedric was starting to hope it would be.

His omega was gorgeous, and he deserved to be touched from time to time. Never below the belt, never on the lips, but elsewhere?

There wasn't anything sexual about that. Cedric wasn't breaking any rules, and he wasn't deluding himself into believing that a few tender moments between them meant anything more. Cedric was a professional, and Gabriel was his client—that was all. As a Dom, he needed to cultivate trust from his sub. There was no better way to do it than to play into what Gabriel naturally gravitated toward.

Constant physical contact.

Cedric couldn't help himself—he crowded the space between his lips and Gabriel's, and when he spoke again, he whispered what he had to say into the tiny space between them. "Then you'll make that popcorn, won't you? And you'll bring it to me?"

"I will, Sir."

"Don't keep me waiting, Rabbit." Cedric ran his fingers one last time through Gabriel's hair, then took his hand away. Gabriel's eyes opened, but the spell he held over Cedric, begging him to come closer, didn't break. "The movie is ready—all I need to do is push play. You will come back in a timely manner, and you will do as I've asked."

"Yes, Sir."

A shiver longed to work its way down Cedric's spine, but he resisted. He would not let Gabriel see that he wielded as much power over him as he wielded over Gabriel.

Not yet, at least.

That would be for another day. Tonight, Cedric had work to do. While Gabriel busied himself in the kitchen preparing popcorn, Cedric went back to the couch and opened up a search page on his phone. In three to five business days, Gabriel's training would begin.

22

GABRIEL

The bag of popcorn burned Gabriel's fingers, and he winced as he tossed it onto the counter and blew at his too-hot skin. It hit the metal bowl he'd taken from the cabinet, causing it to skitter across the counter and clatter into the sink. Gabriel winced and pinched his shoulders to his neck, expecting to be yelled at, but Sir didn't make a peep.

He wasn't like Garrison.

Gabriel didn't have to be so afraid.

The thought of it made Gabriel smile, and even though he was unsure what his punishment would be, he found that he didn't worry. Under Garrison's command, he'd lived in a state of constant fear and doubt, but with Sir, he had no worries. Every day they spent together reminded Gabriel that the life he knew and the life he now lived were separate entities, and it made him wonder if Adrian was right.

Maybe there was more to life than selflessly serving a man.

Sir demanded respect, and he asked Gabriel for things, but he allowed Gabriel to be selfish, too. Cuddles on the couch. Ghosted not-kisses on his forehead, or cheek, or shoulder. Tasty food and a soft bed to sleep in. What Gabriel gave, he got in return.

Everything except the knowledge of Sir's body.

Bowl rescued, popcorn poured, and as many whole kernels fished out as he could find, Gabriel returned to the living room. Sir had turned off the lights, but the dim bulb over the stove and the glow of the television helped Gabriel see the way. Careful not to disturb the couch, Gabriel settled at Sir's side and held the bowl of popcorn in his lap. The image on the screen was frozen, waiting for Sir to press play.

"I've brought the popcorn, Sir," Gabriel said. He kept his voice low, not sure if Sir wanted to hear him or not. "What do you want me to do with it?"

"Set it on the table," Sir instructed.

Gabriel leaned forward and set the bowl on the coffee table an arm's distance away from where they sat. When he settled, Sir turned at the hips and lifted a heavy blanket off the back of the couch. He draped it over Gabriel's lap and spent time making sure that Gabriel's lower half was covered before he pulled the remaining portion over himself. The gesture was subtle, but Gabriel didn't overlook it—the evening was cold, and Sir was doing his best to make sure that Gabriel's needs were taken into consideration.

Gabriel was glad for the blanket, because the heat radiating in his cheeks didn't stop there—it seeped into his groin and woke his cock. It was shameful to be aroused by nothing at all, but Sir had been so kind to him that Gabriel couldn't help it. Besides, Sir was handsome. More than once since he'd come to stay in Sir's house, Gabriel had dreamed about what it might be like to be his.

How Sir would feel on top of him, parting his thighs and pushing into his tight body.

How his knot would swell and leave Gabriel breathless.

How Gabriel would enjoy it like he never had before, and how if he was good, Sir might let him come, too.

There was nothing barring Sir from taking advantage of him. Every night for the past week, Gabriel had wondered if he'd wake

142

up in the middle of the night with Sir in his bed, stripping him of his clothes while his erection bobbed between them. Long. Hard. Ready to fill him...

Every night, Gabriel had closed his eyes, excited for the possibility that it might happen—that Sir might lay claim on him now that Garrison was no longer in the picture—but it had never happened. Maybe tonight, while they shared the same blanket, it would come to be.

For the last five years, Gabriel had clung to the notion that Garrison was the only man in the world who cared for him, and that he was the only man who Gabriel could ever be happy with. Rescued from a household that had never appreciated him, and that had only become more toxic once he'd succumbed to his first heat, he'd been convinced that there was no other path for him. Being unloved was part of being an omega. He'd seen it happen to his brother, Adrian, who'd once been their father's favorite before he'd manifested as his true self, and he'd seen it happen to himself, too. The withering looks his mother and father had given him when he'd come out from his room for the first time after his heat had ended, sweaty and exhausted, broke his heart, and their distance in the weeks afterward convinced him that there was no going back.

Garrison was the solution to a problem Gabriel couldn't fix on his own. Getting out of the Lowe house had been reasonable. Even Garrison had thought so.

But Gabriel had never thought that he could find love outside of the man who'd laid claim on him—that there might be someone else out there who'd want to take him in and save him from himself.

Love...

Love wasn't what Gabriel thought it would be. The future Gabriel had lost wasn't lost at all—it just needed to be reshaped.

The love he'd felt for Garrison hadn't been love at all, he realized. It had all the hallmarks of love, but on the inside, it was a hollow mockery. Garrison had never loved him. The realization was bitter, but Gabriel hadn't shied away from it. He'd been burying his head in the sand since the first day Garrison had brought him to the brothel. What Garrison loved was getting his way, and what he loved more than that was money. To him, Gabriel had been a physical release and a paycheck rolled into one.

He hadn't been the man Garrison wanted to marry. He would *never* be that man. Not unless Garrison changed his ways and opened his heart to Gabriel like he never had before, but that wouldn't happen now, not even with Seth gone.

Gabriel didn't want it to happen, anyway. Now that he'd met Sir, he knew better. What he needed wasn't a man who'd tolerate him as long as he continued to do whatever he asked—what he needed was a man who would treat him with kindness unconditionally, even when Gabriel was bad. He needed a man who wouldn't hit him, even when he was being petulant, and who thought of him first even when their needs were the same.

The future Gabriel wanted—a family he could take pride in, and somewhere quiet he could settle down—was still within his reach. All he had to do was re-envision the man who'd give it to him.

With Sir sitting beside him on the couch, re-envisioning wasn't hard.

Every now and then, painful feelings rose back up to the surface, but he knew that was a product of habit rather than sincerity. With every passing day, the ache in his chest lessened... and the force that took its place increased.

Sir would take care of him. Sir would chase away the demons and keep the man without a name away. And as long as Gabriel stayed good, Sir would keep him. He'd never have to go back to his parents, and he'd never have to burden Adrian and Sterling again.

"Rabbit?" Sir asked. He lifted his arm, and Gabriel took the invitation gladly. He leaned against Sir's side, and Sir draped his arm around Gabriel's shoulders. The scent of him, as appealing as it had been on the first day they'd met, flooded Gabriel's nostrils and sent pinpricks racing down his spine. He cuddled into Sir, unashamed that he was growing harder, and thought about the future.

If they started having babies with Gabriel's upcoming heat, Gabriel could give him a large family he could be proud of. Beautiful black-haired babies with green eyes, the spitting image of their father. With the fair genes Gabriel had inherited from his mother, they would grow up into elegant, sophisticated individuals. Proud like Sir, but made gentle by Gabriel, they would break hearts and change history—and if they were omegas, Gabriel would not cast them aside. He'd help them find their forever mates, and they would breed beautiful babies, just like he would.

There was no future sweeter than that.

When Gabriel was settled, Sir pushed a button on the remote and started the movie. Gabriel watched the screen without seeing what was on it. His mind was on the future, and what steps he might take to make it happen. Cuddling on the couch was step one, but if he wanted the family he'd dreamed of since he was sixteen, step one wasn't where his journey ended.

He needed to get Sir in bed, and then he needed Sir to take his heat. The days were ticking. It wouldn't be long before the first insatiable waves of arousal hit—a week, maybe, if he was unfortunate. Days, if he was lucky.

This time, Garrison wasn't there to force him to take contraceptives, and the staff at Stonecrest weren't on hand to suppress the symptoms of his heat.

He would breed with Sir, and Sir would give him the family he'd always wanted.

They'd be *happy*.

All Gabriel had to do was wait.

23

CEDRIC

I t arrived in a discreet white box on the third day after Cedric had placed his order. While Gabriel hid down the hall, frightened almost to tears by the doorbell for reasons Cedric couldn't understand, he picked the box up from the stoop and turned it around in his hands. It stood approximately half a foot tall, but it was light, and by the sound of the paper receipt rattling around inside of it, Cedric didn't think its contents took up much space.

He brought the box through the living room and into the kitchen, then laid it on the counter. The transparent circle of tape that secured the flap into its corresponding slot shone beneath the overhead lights, and Cedric worked it up and off with the nail on his thumb. Padded footsteps down the hall marked Gabriel's arrival, and Cedric heard the minuscule creak of the floorboards as he leaned around the doorway to glance into the kitchen.

"It's all right, Rabbit," Cedric said without turning to look. "It was a delivery. There's no reason to be afraid. In fact, I want you to come here. This is something for you."

There was a moment of hesitation, but before Cedric had to address Gabriel a second time, he came through the doorway and joined Cedric at the counter. Cedric spared him a quick look to take inventory of what he was wearing, then worked the flap out from its slot. Gabriel's jeans were a little tight, but his t-shirt was loose and comfortable. It would have to do. Once he'd adjusted to his new limitations, he would rework his wardrobe accordingly.

Cedric opened the box and took his purchase from inside.

The posture collar was worth every penny. Made of high-quality leather, its sleek, black exterior was complemented by downy padding on the inside. Cedric ran his thumb across it, testing it for comfort, but also for breathability. When he tightened the dual straps and fed them into their corresponding buckles, Gabriel's skin would need to breathe. It would do them no good if the collar was uncomfortable—Cedric wanted him in it for long periods of time. Training would not be effective if he had to remove it at regular intervals.

At his side, Gabriel tensed. The leather was intimidating, Cedric knew. There'd been a time when he'd worn a similar collar. Brittany had wanted everyone to see his face, and there'd been no better way to do it than to keep his head in place. But eventually, the thick D-ring on the front wouldn't look as imposing, and the heavy-duty build of the collar would become as natural to Gabriel's body as his own neck was. All it would take was time, and time was something they had plenty of.

"This," Cedric said, tracing his fingers along the D-ring on the front, "is yours from now until the end of time."

Gabriel said nothing, but there was buzzing energy in the air—nervous or excited, Cedric couldn't tell. He turned his head to look at Gabriel, hoping to source the change in the air, only to find Gabriel's eyes were partially lidded. His teeth had sunk into his bottom lip, small flashes of white that drew the eye to his tempting mouth. It wasn't nerves, and excitement didn't begin to cover it—Gabriel was aroused. Cedric detected the first stirrings of it in the air, and his cock throbbed at the thought that his perfect pet was turned on by the prospect of being so visibly claimed.

Doing his best to ignore the growing need behind his fly, Cedric continued, "This collar is your punishment for your misstep the other day, and you will wear it until I decide that it's time for you to take it off."

"Yes, Sir." Gabriel's voice quivered, but not from fear. The sound of it struck Cedric squarely in the gut, and he tightened his stomach as a fresh wave of arousal passed through him.

It wasn't right to think this way about Gabriel. Broken, abused, and twisted, Gabriel needed to know his worth before he knew another man's touch again. Right now, Gabriel needed to focus on getting better... but Cedric didn't know how much longer he could continue to deny himself.

Gabriel was special. It was in the way their bodies felt when they touched as much as it was in who Gabriel was at the core of his being. It was the same pull he'd felt to Brittany all those years ago, but intensified—made into something monumental by forces Cedric couldn't hope to understand.

And that force almost swept Cedric away as he fitted the collar to Gabriel's neck.

The unspoken tension between them swelled, and sparks the like of which Cedric had never felt before flew. Cedric gazed into Gabriel's partially lidded eyes and saw in them that what he felt, Gabriel felt, too. The tiny uptick of Gabriel's pulse and the scent of arousal on the air stirred Cedric more than it ever had before.

He wanted to touch. He wanted to pin Gabriel to the couch and knot him—to mark him as *his*.

Instead, he watched as Gabriel lifted his chin and accepted the collar. Cedric's hands were tied. There was nothing else he could do.

The collar molded to Gabriel's neck like it had been built for his body. Cedric tightened the straps and buckled them into place, then assessed how the collar hit Gabriel's clavicle. He ran a finger beneath to make sure the fit wasn't too tight or uncomfortable, then turned his attention to how it fitted against Gabriel's chin. Posture collars, rigid and tall, were made to restrict the movement of the head and neck. Gabriel would no longer be able to dip his head when he wanted to escape the reality of the situation, and he would look Cedric in the eyes when they spoke.

Pretty, ocean-blue eyes that left Cedric breathless.

Cedric bit the inside of his lip and pushed the thought away.

"How does it feel?" he asked. Unable to help himself, he ran his finger from the upper edge of the collar to Gabriel's neck, and then upward along his jawbone. Every time they touched, it stirred Cedric, and he couldn't get enough. It was selfish and irresponsible, but when Gabriel was so close, his body and his mind were at war, and there were some battles Cedric could not win. "Is it irritating your skin anywhere?"

"No, Sir."

Gabriel's skin was warm, and he smelled good. *God,* did he smell good. Cedric leaned a little closer, just to breathe him in. The war inside was being waged, and right now, his mind was losing to his body. "Is it comfortable?"

"Yes, Sir." What little was visible of Gabriel's eyes was glossy, and his pupils were blown out with lust. "It's comfortable."

"Then you'll wear it for me." It wasn't a question, but a statement whispered onto Gabriel's lips. They were too close and Cedric knew it, but he couldn't bring himself to pull away. "And when you want to sleep at night, you'll come find me, and ask nicely if I'll take it off for you."

Gabriel's eyes closed, and he tilted his chin upward as if he were expecting a kiss. "Yes, Sir. Of course."

Butterflies took flight in Cedric's stomach, and his cock strained against the front of his jeans. He knew that Gabriel had to be able to smell his arousal, but he didn't care. Gabriel had to know that he was desirable, and there was a chance that knowing Cedric wasn't immune to his charms would inflate his sense of self-worth.

Pink lips, ruddied by how Gabriel had worried them, were so close that all Cedric would have to do would be move a fraction of an inch forward to make them his. Gabriel wore his collar now, and he would until Cedric decided that he'd been taught his lesson. Wouldn't it be natural to make his lips Cedric's as well? To make sure that Gabriel knew that he was claimed?

Cedric leaned forward, ready to give in just this once, when a *thud* from the carport stole his attention away and jerked him back from the omega he was about to claim. He turned toward the side door as his heart raced, both glad for the interruption and gutted by it. A sound like that wasn't caused by the wind—whatever was out there was too solid, too heavy.

Too human.

Perhaps the courier wasn't gone, but then, what was he doing in the carport? It sounded like whoever was out there had hit Cedric's car with his thigh.

"Rabbit?" Cedric asked. "Go into your room. I need to go take care of business."

There was a response, but Cedric only heard the tone—his focus was on whatever was happening beyond the side door. There was no reason to believe that there was any kind of threat out there. He'd lived in this rental for the last three years, and he'd never had an issue with theft or vandalism. But as he approached, he couldn't help but feel like there was something out there that was wrong. Creeping instinct caused the hairs on Cedric's nape to stand on end, and a shiver swept down his spine. He kept an aluminum baseball bat by the door, just in case, but this was the first time he'd ever thought he'd need to use it. Cedric's hand curled around the handle, and he lifted it from where it had been leaning to keep by his side as he opened the door.

A man stood at the bottom of the driveway.

Cedric's hand tightened around the handle of the bat. He stepped down to stand in the carport, his eyes on the man in the distance. Technically, he was doing nothing wrong—he stood on the sidewalk, hands shoved into the pockets of his billowing black sweater, the hood drawn over his head. From where he stood, Cedric could only make out certain details.

A bulbous nose. A square chin. Broad shoulders... and his scent.

Wood, leather, and alpha.

Cedric knew that smell.

He set the end of the bat on the asphalt, the hollow *clunk* reverberating through the carport. Why was that smell familiar to him, and why did it put him on high alert? Cedric couldn't pin where he knew it from, but he knew that it wasn't the first time he'd come across it. There'd been a time when that scent had made enough of an impact on him that his body remembered it, so why couldn't he figure it out?

For a prolonged moment, they faced each other. The man stood where he was, posture wide and relaxed, while Cedric guarded the carport and prayed to god that he'd locked the front door after bringing in the collar. It wasn't that he thought he couldn't take care of the stranger, but with Gabriel in the house, he was nervous.

If anything were to happen to him...

Cedric couldn't risk it. He took a step forward, and as soon as he did, the man turned on his heel and continued on his way. Cedric walked as far as the front of the carport to keep an eye on him, but it didn't look like the man was interested in coming back. He crossed the street and continued on his way, leaving Cedric to question what the hell had just happened. Sometimes, in the fall, pedestrians stopped to watch the trees, but the forest was on the other side of the street. That man had been watching the house.

Had he been in the carport?

It didn't matter. All that mattered was that he was gone.

A light breeze stirred, disturbing Cedric's hair. He shook his head, pushed his fear aside, and returned to the house. He locked the door behind him, then checked the front door to verify it was secure. In all likelihood, he was overreacting. Strange things happened every day—there was nothing particularly wrong about a man standing on public property, looking wherever he pleased.

But that scent...

Cedric shook his head. He could spend the rest of his life trying to place where he'd smelled it, but it would do him no good. Right now, he needed to get back to the task at hand. There was an omega waiting for him in his bedroom who needed training, and no one else was going to step in for Cedric to get it done.

24

GABRIEL

The bathroom mirror was pristine—Gabriel knew because he'd cleaned it himself not even a day ago. Sir leaned against the meticulously scrubbed counter, his ass perched on the ledge while his hands were planted on either side of his thighs. Gabriel stood before him, his eyes never parting from his reflection. Sir was watching, and he refused to disappoint him, no matter how uncomfortable looking at himself was.

"What do you see?" Sir asked. The question was simple, but Gabriel didn't want to reply. What he had to say wouldn't be to Sir's liking.

So he was vague instead. "Myself."

"That's right, Rabbit. It's a good start, but it's not what I'm looking for. When you look at yourself, what do you *see?*"

The posture collar prevented Gabriel from looking down. Every time he tried to lower his head, the leather stopped him. It would not fold.

Gabriel looked himself over in the mirror and tried to find nice things to say. The posture collar was less than a week old now, and he'd never wanted it gone more than he did now. Talking to Sir while meeting his gaze wasn't half as terrifying as Gabriel thought it would be—but facing himself? Staring down his reflection while Sir demanded he report back?

It made Gabriel want to tear at his eyes until he couldn't see anymore. Why did he have to invent something nice to say? Sir already knew that there was nothing nice at all about him.

"I see a young man," Gabriel murmured.

"Expand on that."

It took all of Gabriel's will not to close his eyes. The longer he looked, the more intolerable his reflection became. "A young... omega."

"What about your reflection makes you an omega?" Sir asked.

Was it a trick question? Gabriel glanced at Sir's face to find his expression was affable, like he expected a genuine response.

"It's... young." Gabriel shifted his focus back to his reflection. "Younger than it should look, at least. Fine features. Round eyes. Full lips. Alpha and beta men don't look like I do."

"No, not all of them. But some of them do." Sir didn't show anger. His tone was conversational. "What else do you see?"

"Soft, blond hair." Gabriel frowned. "But it's too muddy to be beautiful. If it was blonder, like Seth's, or pale, like Lucian's, then... then maybe it would be beautiful, but it's not."

"Says who?"

"Says..." Gabriel wanted to say *me*, but that wasn't the truth. The truth was that Garrison had never found it beautiful, but Garrison was gone. The hold he had over Gabriel was no more. Even if he returned from jail, Gabriel wouldn't want him, so why was he letting Garrison's opinion poison his thoughts? "... says no one."

"What else?" Sir prompted, and Gabriel looked again. The posture collar gave him no choice.

"Blue eyes." Saliva pooled in Gabriel's mouth, and he swallowed it down. Blue eyes were common, and he'd always yearned to have Adrian's steely gray gaze. But the truth? The truth was that he'd wished that because Garrison had never noticed him in the way he wanted. The blue of Gabriel's eyes was deep and startling, dark and distinct. "Pretty dark-blue eyes."

"And your lips?" Sir's voice was firmer now, but it was no less friendly.

Gabriel fed from his prompt seamlessly. "They're full and pink. They're... they're pretty, too."

The posture collar forced him to look, and the longer he did, the more the man in the mirror changed. From too-skinny and plain to hauntingly beautiful, Sir tore down the lies Gabriel had worn as a mask for the past five years and exposed the stunning young man beneath.

Tears prickled in the corner of Gabriel's eyes.

"And my nose," he uttered. The words rattled, the tears not far off. "It's graceful and cute. It's *cute*. And my cheekbones are high and dignified, and my jaw is... is sharp, but not too drastic or masculine, and—and..."

Gabriel ran the back of his hand across his eyes.

"And it's good. All of it is good. The young man I see? He's *good*."

"Very good, Rabbit," Sir praised. He leaned over to press a kiss to Gabriel's temple. "Would you like to sit on the couch with me while I stroke your hair?"

The tears fell liberally now, and no matter how often Gabriel ran his hand beneath his eyes, he couldn't keep them away.

"Yes, please, Sir. I'd like that very much."

Fall days began to give way to winter nights. The sun had long ago set, and the darkness on the other side of the windows made Sir's house feel small and snug, like there was nothing outside their tiny slice of existence to worry about. With Sir there to protect him, Gabriel didn't worry about anything anymore.

The lights in the house were off when Gabriel headed down the hall to Sir's bedroom. A window at the very end of the hall allowed moonlight to enter, but it was a cloudy night, and visibility was spotty at best. Gabriel's fingers brushed the wall as he walked, guiding him forward. He felt each familiar doorway, and used them to mark the distance left before Sir's room.

Before he arrived, a light flicked on, shining from beneath the door. Gabriel stopped to listen, but all he heard was movement. It sounded like Sir was up to something—but as long as he was up, that was all that mattered.

Gabriel arrived in front of the door, touched the leather that kept his head upright, then took a breath in through his nose and lifted his fist to knock. The door swung open beneath the force of his knuckles, and he found himself looking across Sir's bedroom.

It wasn't the first time he'd seen it. Over the last few weeks, he'd stood at the door while Sir undid the straps to his collar one at a time, then slid the padded leather off his neck. He'd seen the luxurious hardwood and the cloudlike, king-sized bed on the other side, piled high with pillows that Gabriel would have sold his soul to be able to nestle into, and draped over with blankets both soft and warm. He was familiar with the heavy black curtains that Sir used to cover the windows, and sometimes, he saw something playing on the flat-screen television mounted on the wall.

What he wasn't used to seeing was Sir standing by the bed, nude.

His back was partially to Gabriel, and he held a towel in his hands that he'd been using to dry his face and hair. The bottom of it hung down to block Gabriel's view of his cock, but there was no hiding the magnificence that was the rest of Sir's body.

Sir was a work of art.

Gabriel stood frozen in time, soaking him in. The valley of Sir's spine was pronounced, the muscles of his back developed and taut against his skin. A broad chest tapered to a narrow waist, giving way to a bubble butt that even Gabriel envied. His thighs were solid and muscular, but still showed signs that Sir had once been delicately slender. He had all the markings of an omega, but he'd grown into an alpha's body—so beautiful and yet so strong that it wasn't fair.

But the beauty of Sir's body wasn't only attributed to genetics and time spent at the gym. As Sir turned to face him, the towel held loosely down his body, Gabriel got to see what Sir had been hiding from him beneath his sweaters and long-sleeve shirts—tattoos. Sir's right arm was consumed with color from his wrist all the way back to his shoulder blade. At a distance, Gabriel couldn't make out exactly what imagery the sleeve was comprised of, but the blend of colors was seamless, and it complemented Sir's skin tone as well as it did his personality. Sir's chest was inkless, but his left leg—from his hip to his ankle—continued the motif, as if his body housed a canvas that had been torn in two diagonally.

Gabriel sucked in a quick, shallow breath, but it did him no good. He remained frozen where he was, his eyes drinking in Sir as he'd never seen him before.

Are you interested in body modification, Gabriel?

Back then, Gabriel hadn't been sure, but now? Now he had his answer. He liked body modification just fine, as long as it was on Sir.

"Rabbit," Sir said softly. He made no move to hide his body. "Did you open the door without knocking?"

"No, Sir." Gabriel's voice was strained, but he did his best to speak as if the man he wanted wasn't standing naked no more than six feet from him. Nervous, he tried to duck his head, but the collar held him in place. He could not look away. "T-the door was open. When I went to knock, it swung, and... and I'm sorry."

"Hmm." Sir lifted the towel and patted at his face. The towel lifted away from his groin, and Gabriel did his best not to look. He swallowed hard, allowing the posture collar to keep his gaze level. "I guess I didn't close it. That was my fault. You don't need to apologize."

Sir wanted him to look at his face. His *face*. Not down. Not at... not at *that*. But he wasn't putting the towel back down. Why wasn't

159

he putting the towel back down? Gabriel's lips parted as his resolve wavered, arousal fighting his sense of duty to drive him crazy.

Was Sir doing this on purpose? There was no better test of obedience to see if Gabriel would dip his gaze than to tempt him like this. All he had to do was look down, and then...

"Are you here to ask to have your collar off, Rabbit?" Sir tucked the towel around his waist, ending Gabriel's torment. "It's about time, isn't it? I'm off-schedule today."

"Yes, Sir." The words were like sand in Gabriel's mouth. His cock strained against the fly of his pants, and for the first time, he regretted how tight they were. Sir had to be able to see everything. "Please, could you take it off?"

Sir's eyes looked into his. Gabriel had been trying to get used to the feeling of meeting another man's gaze, but despite his best attempts to acclimatize, it still sent a shiver down his spine whenever Sir looked his way. "Come here, Gabriel."

It was rare that Sir used his name these days, and so Gabriel heeded his word. He stepped forward, crossing the bedroom floor until he stood in front of Sir. Up close, he saw the details of Sir's tattoos—geometric patterns interlaced with feminine, floral imagery. The work was artful, photorealistic in its presentation. The colors were vibrant, and the line work was solid. Gabriel did his best not to look overly interested, but he wanted to take in every tiny detail and commit it to memory.

When he tore his gaze from Sir's colorful arm, he noticed what he'd missed before.

His nipples.

Both of them were pierced, run through with captive bead rings. Gabriel's cock twitched. All he could do was lift his chin and tilt his head up, hoping that Sir would take the invitation and undo the straps binding the collar to his throat. If he stayed next to Sir's naked body much longer, he wouldn't be able to help himself—he would be *bad*.

"You've been a good boy recently, Gabriel," Sir whispered. His words were articulated carefully, not muddied by the low volume at which he spoke. "Such a good boy. You've served your punishment without complaining once. I know that the collar isn't always comfortable. Being restricted takes getting used to."

"Yes, Sir." Gabriel closed his eyes. He'd hoped for an escape from Sir, but his attempt was unsuccessful—he saw Sir's image in his mind, body still wet from the shower, tattoos radiant on his skin, piercings glinting beneath the light...

The collar tightened—Sir always tightened it just a little bit when he was undoing the straps, and Gabriel was sure it was deliberate. It was a gesture made to remind him that if he was bad, his life could be made worse. Much worse.

But Sir was merciful, and Sir was kind. The tension lessened, and when it did, the collar came partially undone. Gabriel let out a breath and did his best not to look affected. He opened his eyes, focusing on Sir's face. Sir's eyes were downcast, paying attention to the buckle he was working to undo. "So I was thinking, since you've been so good, that you should be rewarded."

"Rewarded?" Gabriel squeaked.

"Mm. Rewarded." The collar tightened again. The last strap fell. Sir took the collar from Gabriel's neck, his touch delicate and thoughtful. "Here is your choice: you can either go shower and go to bed right now, then sleep as late as you want regardless of our schedule; or after your shower, you can come to watch a movie in bed with me. What is it that you want?"

Gabriel didn't need to think on it. "To make you happy, Sir."

A shudder ran down Sir's spine, visible even to Gabriel. He held his breath, knowing if he didn't, he'd have gasped. How was it that his words had power over a man like Sir? Could it really be that Sir was attracted to him, too?

"Then run the shower, Rabbit," Sir whispered. He leaned close, letting his lips brush the lobe of Gabriel's ear. "And make sure to dry your hair well. I don't like it when my pillows are wet."

25

CEDRIC

It was a mistake. The second Gabriel walked back into the bedroom from Cedric's en suite bathroom, his torso bare and his skin beaded with water, he knew he was in over his head. Gabriel was slender in a delicate, graceful way, like a glass ballerina at the peak of her arabesque. His face was young, and with his clothes cast aside, he looked younger than ever. Cedric had given him a clean pair of his boxers to wear, and they slouched down Gabriel's hips and flowed loosely around his thighs like he was a kid playing dress-up.

Twenty-one. Gabriel was twenty-one.

Was he really a kid? Cedric had always thought there was a world of difference between twenty-five and twenty-one, but he wasn't so certain anymore.

Gabriel approached the bed cautiously, meeting Cedric's gaze the whole time. When he arrived, he hesitated, then set one knee on the mattress. When Cedric didn't correct him, he climbed up and crossed the bed on his hands and knees. Cedric's cock couldn't have been harder. His body was reacting like Gabriel had crawled across the bed, straddled his lap, and begged him with those innocent eyes to put his collar back on so he could make him happy.

Fuck.

That didn't happen, thankfully, but what did come to pass was almost as bad. Gabriel settled next to Cedric on the bed and cuddled up to his side. He wiggled his hips so he could slip beneath the blankets, officially joining Cedric in bed. Bare thigh against bare thigh, Gabriel's chest against his side, a jolt ran the length of Cedric's body and buried itself in his balls. In an attempt to ignore it, he reached for the remote and hit play on the movie he'd pulled up on Netflix. It didn't matter what it was. What was on the screen mattered less than who was beside him.

The way Gabriel's omega smelled paired with Cedric's body wash and shampoo made him want to bury his nose in the crook of Gabriel's neck and breathe it in forever.

"Sir?" Gabriel whispered. He draped an arm lazily over Cedric's stomach as he got comfortable, his back toward the screen.

"Yes, Rabbit?"

"How long have you had your tattoos for?" Gabriel wasn't looking at the television at all—his eyes were on Cedric's body. Cedric wasn't sure if he meant to be obvious about it, or if Cedric was hyper-aware of every little thing Gabriel did, but he noticed.

"The first time ink pierced my skin, I was eighteen. I'm twenty-five now."

"Mm." Gabriel nuzzled against his side and cuddled a little closer. "What made you want to get them?"

Cedric was aware they were slipping toward informal conversation. The boundaries had been set when Gabriel had come to stay with him—respect was to be afforded to him at all times, and their relationship was supposed to be one of utility. Gabriel would obey Cedric and listen to his word, and in exchange, Cedric would guide him toward the best version of himself that he could be. Gabriel's chattiness could be a sign that he was growing too comfortable with their situation, and that Cedric would have to remind him of his place, but for now, Cedric permitted him liberty. He was to be rewarded, after all. If Gabriel continued to be so bold once tonight was over, Cedric would step in.

"I was a kid, and I thought they'd be cool." Cedric watched the screen, taking in the shapes and sounds, but none of the meaning behind them. "I was in high school, I had money, and I was going on to college. When I first started getting them, I was sure it was because I wanted the world to know I was tough... going from my senior year of high school where I was top of the food chain into the world at large felt like a big step. I knew I was going to be a small fish in a big sea, and I guess I was looking for validation."

"Oh." Was it his imagination, or were Gabriel's fingertips brushing his hip? If his arm nudged any lower, he'd feel the erection straining against Cedric's boxers, and then what? It wasn't like Cedric could explain that away. "Did you start with your arm, or...?"

"I started with this piece on my wrist." Cedric lifted his arm. His gaze parted from the television to focus on the honeycomb design that spanned six inches on his forearm, from his wrist upward. Framed behind the honeycombs, done in black and white ink, was a tree on a hill at sunset, where the horizon was light, but the sky above was darkened and speckled with stars. The honeycombs were in the foreground, done in bold lines, but the landscape was artfully expressed in pointillism. Since that piece had been made, the pieces around it had been blended in to match. Nothing on Cedric's arm looked disjointed or out of place—he was one smooth canvas worked upon by one skillful artist.

He carried her legacy wherever he went.

"I got this done in one eight-hour session. It was my very first tattoo, and my artist told me that I was crazy. She suggested that I stop being such a macho-bravado-tough-guy and take it in two sessions, so I fired back and asked her if she wasn't just afraid her hand would cramp up if she worked on me all day. I walked out of that session with her phone number and a fully finished tattoo, but she had the last laugh when I almost passed out three hours in."

"Eight hours for something so small?" Gabriel asked in awe.

Cedric held his arm in place to study, examining the honey-combs on his wrist. "Yeah. When you're passionate about some-thing, you want to do it right. She could have rushed, but she didn't. She took the time to invest herself in the piece, and you can still see her skill now, even all these years later. It's faded from light expo-sure, and it's going to need to be touched up in the future, but her spirit's there, if you look closely enough."

"You loved her," Gabriel murmured.

One corner of Cedric's lips twitched upward. "Do you think so, Rabbit? What led you to say that?"

"The tone of your voice." Gabriel settled down. His hair was soft from his shower—he'd taken Cedric's warning to heart and had dried it thoroughly before coming to bed. "And the look in your eyes when you talk about her. You said it was just one artist, right? So you must have been with her for a long, long time if that space on your wrist took eight hours."

"I'll have to keep in mind how perceptive you are. You're hiding all kinds of exciting secrets from me, aren't you?"

There was no reply.

"Her name was Brittany. She was twenty-five when I met her, and she was twenty-seven when she was taken away."

"Taken away?"

Cedric closed his eyes. "She was killed. No one knows what happened. Police investigation revealed the cause of her death, but not the motive, or who the perpetrator was. One day she was here, full of snark and laughter, and the next she never opened her eyes again. I dropped out of school and shut down for a year before I found my way again. It was the hardest time of my life, but it made me into who I am today. It shaped me into a man who appreciates life, and who understands that pleasures are only ever temporary, so they are to be enjoyed while they last. In the end, I like to think I'm a better person for it. She taught me to be the man I am today, and I'll always carry her with me because of it."

This time, it wasn't Cedric's imagination—Gabriel's fingers

traced across his hip soothingly. Cedric didn't open up about his past very often, but there was a promise in Gabriel's quiet ways that he wouldn't spread rumors or pass harsh judgment. The trust Cedric had in him extended beyond the professional—it bridged the way to his heart, and he was as cognizant of it as he was the rise and fall of his chest as he breathed. The part of his mind that desired Gabriel could not be shut off.

"Not everything has to be temporary, Sir." Gabriel's fingertips continued to paint patterns across Cedric's hip. "We can change that."

Gabriel's hand parted from Cedric's side and found its way amongst the sheets. He lifted his torso and repositioned himself slowly, so that one of his knees rested in the space between Cedric's legs. Cedric watched, slack-jawed, as the blankets fell away from them both, revealing the slender stretch of Gabriel's torso and abdomen, and the way Cedric's boxers pooled over his thighs. Gabriel settled down on his thigh and draped one arm over Cedric's shoulder, the distance between them almost negligible. The tip of Gabriel's nose brushed Cedric's. All Cedric would have to do was tilt his head and they'd be kissing.

He wanted it more than he cared to admit.

The television lit Gabriel from behind, playing with the blond in his hair. His skin glowed, and despite the dim light in the room, Cedric saw the color in his cheeks. He was gorgeous. Cedric couldn't resist him.

"I'm yours, aren't I?" Gabriel whispered. "Sterling and Adrian gave me to you. I'm your property now, and I will never leave you. Never. All I want is to be with you, Sir. All I want is to make you happy."

God, was this really happening? Cedric took in a staggered breath and tried to regain control of the situation, but Gabriel was a siren, and he was a sailor lost at sea. His arms found their way around Gabriel's waist, and he held him in place loosely.

Perfectly submissive. Perfectly behaved.

What was he doing not making Gabriel his? The invitation was there. They both wanted it.

They both wanted each other.

Cedric shuddered. His arms tightened, and he pulled Gabriel closer.

"So let's make something permanent together," Gabriel whispered. He tilted his head, and the tip of his nose traced the length of Cedric's as he brought their lips closer. "All you need to do is take me. All you need to do is use my body like you deserve to use it. I want to give you permanence, Sir. I want to take away your pain."

After all these years, there was still hurt in him, locked away in such a dark place that Cedric never visited it. Gabriel was his flashlight, illuminating the cracks and spaces he'd tried so hard to patch up over the last five years, and whose presence he preferred to deny. In this little, unassuming omega, Cedric had found someone who made him want to unlock the prison in his soul and set his hurt free. If Gabriel was his—truly his—then what did it matter if he gave in to what he wanted? If Cedric never left Gabriel, if he vowed to stay in order to make sure Gabriel recovered, then what did it matter if they had sex? Who was Cedric to stand in the way of love?

Was it love?

Gabriel's lips brushed his shyly, and Cedric found himself returning his affection. It may not have been love, but it was the beginning of something great—something Cedric wanted to encourage. His hands slid down from where they rested behind Gabriel's back to find the rounds of his ass, and he lifted Gabriel until he straddled his lap completely.

His submissive. His omega. His lover.

His.

26

GABRIEL

They were *kissing*. Gabriel's lips brushed against Sir's, and Sir's lips brushed against his, and that meant they were *kissing*.

Gabriel's soul sang.

Stripped down to their boxers, arms tangled around each other, lips brushing, it was the sweetest encounter Gabriel had ever known. He shifted his hips to rub himself against Sir's prominent erection, and the tiny gasp Sir rewarded him with was worth the risk, so Gabriel did it again. He wasn't in heat, so he wouldn't conceive, but if Sir would have sex with him tonight, it meant that he would have sex with him again. When Gabriel did go into heat, Sir would take care of it for him. He'd knot his ass over and over until the heat was gone and his body was his own again.

And then, Gabriel would give Sir permanence.

A relationship. A baby. A family.

They would have it all.

It was all Gabriel had ever wanted, and he hoped it was what Sir wanted, too.

Sir's lips parted, and they met Gabriel's with more intensity than before. The kiss became real, and Gabriel had to hold back from laughing with delight. Excitement exploded like fireworks in his chest, sporadic, but intense. Each burst made him want more, and he sweetened the kiss like he'd never been allowed to do in The White Lotus. No john he'd been with had ever wanted to kiss, and Garrison had told him his lips were too pretty not to see wrapped around his cock, but Sir? Sir wanted to taste him. He wanted to know how soft Gabriel's lips could be, and he wanted Gabriel to know what he felt like, too.

The way the smooth balls of Cedric's piercing rubbed against him, moving every time Cedric opened his mouth to revisit the kiss again, made it the sweetest kiss he'd ever had. Firm, but affectionate. Exploratory, but confident. Giving, and yet demonstrative of how they wanted to be treated.

Gabriel would never forget.

Sir's hands squeezed his ass, but they treated him with tenderness instead of greed. Gabriel knew the difference. To Sir, he wasn't a toy to be taken advantage of. He was an omega, and he always would be, but he was of value to Sir. For as long as Gabriel lived, he hoped that would never change.

Sir's hands guided him up, then pushed him back onto his lap. Gabriel followed his lead, grinding himself against Sir's cock through the boxers that separated them. His own cock was rock hard, pushing against the buttoned flap of the boxers he'd been given. How long would it be until Sir repositioned them and stripped Gabriel of his clothes? From there, all they needed was some lube, and they could truly be together. They could practice making a family until Gabriel's heat arrived.

Over, and over, and over.

The kiss continued, sweet and soft. Sir's lips were as delicious as his scent, and the certainty with which they moved awarded Gabriel with a new kind of stability. Sir wasn't only confident in himself as a person, but he was confident in sex, too. There was no shame in what he did. Gabriel knew what shame felt like, and how a man's stilted movements could affect intimacy, but Sir's kiss and the way he guided Gabriel even in silence was proud.

What they shared wasn't a transaction, and it wasn't being done out of desperation. Sir legitimately wanted Gabriel, and even though what Gabriel wanted was stability, deep down he wanted Sir, too.

Pretty babies, with their black hair and green eyes. A life beside a man who was strong, handsome, and merciful enough that he would not treat Gabriel like he belonged to the lowest echelon of society. A house by the woods, where they could raise their family quietly and embrace forever without the chaos of the city... Gabriel wanted it all. And tonight, when Sir took him for the first time and claimed him as his own, they would take their first step toward that future.

Together.

Sir's hands kept guiding Gabriel, grinding him down against his cock until Gabriel was so overwhelmed with lust, he trembled. There was a sensation between his body and Sir's that he couldn't explain, but that he didn't find bad—some kind of strange bunching in the fabric near Sir's shaft. Gabriel ignored it and moved in time with Sir's hands, and when he was pushed down against Sir's cock, he wiggled his hips to prove to Sir that he was ready for more. Sir listened. His hands remained on Gabriel's ass, but they no longer lifted him up and pushed him down. He left Gabriel on his own to do what Gabriel did best.

Gabriel would not disappoint him.

Arms looped loosely over Sir's neck, his head hung and his eyes closed, he rocked against Sir's cock. In his mind's eye, they were already nude, and Sir was inside of him. The excitement tightened Gabriel's throat, and the next breath he took hitched as he worked himself in controlled ways he knew would bring a man pleasure. Garrison might not have been his forever, but he'd taught him skills that would make keeping his forever-alpha easy. As soon as Sir stripped them and claimed him, he would never want to stray again. Gabriel would make him stay.

"Does this make you happy, Sir?" Gabriel asked in a whisper. His body moved while he spoke, never slowing or losing intensity. Every roll of his hips was calculated for best presentation and impact, and every time he lifted his ass and arched his back, he had Sir's pleasure in mind. Sight and touch were equally as important when it came to seducing a man, and Gabriel did not cut corners on either. He would be good for Sir. He would *always* be good for Sir.

So long as Sir was good to him, too.

"So happy," Sir whispered back. His voice was thin, stretched out by how he struggled to fight his arousal. "You're such a good boy, Gabriel."

The praise lit Gabriel up and manifested as a soft smile. He settled down on Sir's lap and lifted his head so that he could look at Sir's face. Sir's eyes were closed, but when Gabriel stopped moving, he opened them. They gazed at each other for a moment.

This was his forever. This was the face he'd look at every day for the rest of his life, and the body he'd bring pleasure to again and again.

Gabriel let his hands slide down Sir's shoulders, over his chest, and down his sculpted body until his fingers met the elastic band of Sir's boxers. "Then let me be a better boy, Sir. Let me show you how good I can really be."

Sir's eyes were glazed over with lust, partially lost to the alpha protector inside whose goal in life was to produce strong offspring worthy of his genes. When Gabriel went into heat, he would meet that protector in full, and they'd breed like the animals they were. Alpha and omega. It was how it was supposed to be. Gabriel had no hate in his heart for betas, but they would never understand what it was like to be so connected to another person that their bodies and souls screamed in unison that it was meant to be. Gabriel wasn't sure that he believed in the notion that somewhere out there was a soul made just for him, that when he met his alpha, the clouds would part, the light would shine, and his heart would never be lonely again. He'd thought he'd found that with Garrison, but it had been a lie.

But Sir?

If Sir wasn't that person, he was a sunny day after a month of rain. He was the sensation of waking up on a cold winter morning toasty and content beneath the sheets. He was sunrise, and he was sunset. But most importantly, he was genuine. Gabriel didn't believe that Sir would harm him any more than he believed that he could breathe underwater.

"Do you have lube, Sir?" Gabriel asked.

Life snapped back into Sir's eyes. He looked away from Gabriel and leaned over to access a drawer on his end table. From inside, he produced a bottle of lube and a box of condoms. Gabriel looked at the condoms, then looked back at Sir, wary. "Just lube, Sir. That's all I need."

They couldn't breed if Sir was shooting into latex. Gabriel needed to take him raw.

"And all I need is a condom, Rabbit." Sir took one from the box and went to tear it open, but Gabriel stopped his hand before he could. His fingers clamped over Sir's, holding them in place. He knew that if Sir wanted to, he could easily break free of Gabriel's grip, but Gabriel had to try. Condoms weren't supposed to come between them. When Sir took him, their bodies were supposed to understand each other in full. There could be no understanding if there was a barrier in the way.

"No," Gabriel insisted. He took the condom from Sir's hand and tossed it off the bed. There was a box of them sitting by Sir's thigh, but it didn't matter. Gabriel would throw every one of them away if he needed to. "I'm yours. You don't need to use condoms when we're together."

The arousal in Sir's eyes was gone. The alpha protector Gabriel had coaxed out of him vanished. "No."

One word. One crushing, disastrous word. Tears of frustration beaded in Gabriel's eyes, and he fought against the urge to slam his fists into Sir's chest.

"This was a bad idea, Rabbit. It wasn't your fault, it was mine." Sir lifted Gabriel off his lap and set him on the bed. Piece by piece, he dismantled Gabriel's future, and there was nothing he could do to stop it. "I shouldn't have kissed you. You deserve better than that. You're counting on me, and I let you down. I promise that I'll be stronger in the future."

"Stronger in the future?" Gabriel's voice trembled, his anger barely contained. "You want to be stronger in the future? For what? Why? I *belong* to you. I want you to take me. Why aren't you? Why are you holding back? What you're doing isn't strong—it's *stupid!*"

Sir looked like he'd been struck, but Gabriel couldn't bring himself to care. He pushed himself back from the bed and rose on trembling legs, knees threatening to buckle. Was this some kind of game Sir was playing? Was he trying to test his devotion? If that was it, he'd pushed too far. Gabriel wasn't going to take it.

"Rabbit." Sir's voice was flat, his dominance like steel. "You will calm down right now."

"No, I won't." Gabriel clenched his fists, only to find that his hands were trembling. He took a few hurried steps back from the bed and tried to do away with the energy swirling inside of him, but it was no use. "You took me in. I'm *yours.* So why won't you touch me? Am I really that ugly?"

"Rabbit." It was a warning.

Gabriel didn't take it.

There were hateful things he wanted to say. Scathing, hideous things that rattled loose from his soul like pebbles once stuck to the sole of a shoe—even when they were free of him, the impressions they left were lasting. They tumbled from Gabriel's lips, clunky and disjointed, their jagged edges meant to hurt. "If you don't want me, then give me to someone else. I won't take this anymore. I *can't* take this anymore. You're not an alpha. You're not... you're not anything!"

Sir didn't say a word, and his face gave nothing away.

"You don't know the first thing about being a man!" Gabriel took a stumbling step backward, too wired to stand still, but too terrified of what he was doing to keep himself steady. "You don't know anything at all! If you would just... if you would just fuck me, then it wouldn't be hard at all! But instead, you're keeping me between being yours, and being no one's, and I can't take it anymore!"

His clothes were in Sir's bathroom—he'd left them folded neatly on the closed toilet lid after stripping for his shower—but Gabriel couldn't go grab them now. He knew that he was pushing the limits and tempting fate, but he couldn't stop himself. Sir wasn't being fair.

"Just... just go away!" Gabriel wasn't sure if he was screaming at himself, or screaming at Sir. He took another few stumbling steps toward the door and hooked onto the knob. "If you won't f-fuck me, then someone will! Someone who deserves me!"

Gabriel didn't mean what he said, but the hurt twisted inside and made him react in ways he regretted. Sir was special to him, and sounding off on him like this was only going to come back to hurt him, but he couldn't bring himself to stop. There was anguish deep inside that needed to come out, and it all left him at once.

Garrison had promised him the world, then left him alone and hopeless, and now Sir was following in his footsteps with empty promises and half-truths. All Gabriel wanted was stability—a family to call his own. Was that too much to ask?

He twisted the doorknob, intending to return to his room to cry the rest of the pain away, but before he could step through the threshold, Sir rose from the bed. All he wore was his boxers, their front tented by his arousal, but even naked, he was intimidating. Taller than Gabriel remembered, body held rigid with anger, Sir swept forward like a cloud across the horizon to blot out the sun before a storm. Gabriel released the doorknob and staggered into the hall. His back hit the wall, and the air left his lungs all at once.

Sir towered over him, the only light coming from the television in the room they'd just abandoned. Its dim presence outlined Sir's body and encouraged shadows to play across his face in menacing ways.

Gabriel knew that look, and he braced himself for a beating. He'd been bad, *very* bad, and now Sir was going to punish him like he deserved to be punished. He'd overstepped the boundaries, and he deserved whatever rage Sir wanted to unleash upon him.

But no rage ever came.

Instead, Sir whispered words detached of emotion—and somehow, that hit Gabriel just as hard as his fists would have. "Go to your room, Gabriel. You've been bad, and you need to be punished."

27

GABRIEL

The room was dark, but Gabriel didn't need to see in order to feel the sharp impact, or hear the *slap* that rang through the room. The burning pain that spread across the tender skin of his ass brought him down from his fear and sobered his mind.

What had he been thinking?

Sir's hand came down again, the sound of his open palm striking Gabriel's ass crisp in the otherwise quiet room. Gabriel buried his face against the blankets and pushed out a breath through his teeth as the sharp pain of impact diluted into lingering, tingling discomfort that refused to leave him alone.

He'd been bad. He'd gotten frustrated and yelled at Sir when Sir was the one in control. What did it matter what Gabriel thought? What had given him the right to speak his mind freely? He was the omega, and that meant that he was the one who had to listen. Sir was right to punish him—he'd stepped out of line.

"In this household, Rabbit," Sir's hand traced over the skin he'd just struck, chasing some of the pain away with affection, "you won't yell. You won't scream. You won't blow up. It's okay to be angry, but you will express your anger like a normal, adjusted human being. That means that all the hurt you feel inside? You need to express that to me with words. You need to open up and let me know when you feel neglected or unfairly treated so we can fix the problem before it becomes an issue."

Sir had pulled the boxers Gabriel wore down from his ass so it was exposed. The elastic dug into the underside of Gabriel's cheeks, right where his butt met his thighs, but all he could do was squirm in an attempt to correct it. The lower half of his body rested over Sir's thighs, and the upper half was supported by his bed. Gabriel buried his face in his blanket and tried not to make a sound. He wanted to howl in disappointment and in pain, but he knew that now more than ever, he had to be good.

He'd been so close to officially becoming Sir's, but he'd ruined his chances by being too hasty and emotional. Sir wasn't like Garrison, and he would never be. One day, Sir would give him a family. All Gabriel had to do was hold on until that happened.

The hand that stroked pulled back, and Gabriel braced to be spanked again. When Sir treated him like this, he saw just how childish he had been. There was no reason for him to have gone off like he had. If he'd just talked to Sir like an adult, none of this would have happened.

Smack!

Gabriel sucked in a breath and tensed. He buried his head in the blankets and tried to stay still, but the sudden pain was hard to tolerate. He wiggled his hips and inadvertently rubbed his dick against Sir's thigh.

Sir's hand went back to caressing. When Gabriel was bad to Garrison, Garrison had never rubbed the places he'd hit, and his voice had always been full of hatred and spite. When Garrison had punished him, he'd wanted Gabriel to hurt, and sometimes he'd beaten him badly enough that Gabriel couldn't get up the next morning. Sir wasn't like that. Even though it hurt to be spanked,

Gabriel noticed that Sir didn't put the full force of his body behind it, and he never struck the same spot twice. The pain wasn't even that bad—if it wasn't for the sudden, unexpected nature of each smack, it wouldn't have hurt much at all.

In fact, every impact of Sir's palm pushed Gabriel forward, causing Gabriel's hardened cock to rub against Sir's thigh in secretive, sinful ways.

"Do I need to remind you that whatever happens to you is my decision?" Sir's fingers smoothed over Gabriel's sore cheeks. "Your body belongs to me. That's easy. Anyone could own you like that, you know. Anyone could exert force over you and demand that you succumb to their desires. The physical is just as easily taken as it is given. There is nothing special about that."

All the men he'd slept with as favors to Garrison. All the times Garrison had demanded he perform. All the long, lonely nights with no one but himself to keep him company...

"But why I'm punishing you right now, Rabbit?" Sir struck him again, his open palm bouncing off Gabriel's rounded cheek. Gabriel cried into the blankets, but even as he did, he pushed his hips forward to rub his cock against Sir's thigh. Pleasure and pain wove through him in tandem, twin sisters who sweetened each other by proximity. "It isn't because I want to dominate your body. Your body is already mine. What I want from you is something I can't take by force. What you need to give me isn't something you can hand over so thoughtlessly. What I want from you, Rabbit? It's your mind."

Gabriel gripped the blankets tightly and clenched his jaw. His mind? What was so special about his mind? Sir couldn't hold it. He couldn't brag about it. He couldn't fuck it...

"When you act in defiance of me, you prove that I own some of you, but not all of you. Your body is mine, and it has been since the day we met, hasn't it? I've seen how willing you've been to give it to me." Sir's hand ran from his exposed cheek to the small of Gabriel's back, and Gabriel couldn't help but grind against his thigh, seeking friction. He'd been hard in Sir's bedroom, and he was still hard now. After so long without physical contact, he needed release. "But your thoughts? Your emotions? Your devotion? Those don't belong to me. Not yet. And we need to fix that, don't we?"

Sir's hand ran back down over the curve of Gabriel's ass. His hand was exploratory, mapping out Gabriel's body like Gabriel was of value. Even with the lights off, he got the feeling that Sir was soaking him in, drinking in the feeling of him rather than the sight.

"Yes, Sir," Gabriel uttered. The harsh words he'd said and the emotion behind them was gone now. Beneath a firm hand, he was docile and obedient. He remembered his place. He belonged to Sir, and he had to treat Sir with respect. "Please, Sir, punish me so I'll remember. I never want to forget again."

"You say such beautiful things, Rabbit. Do you say them on purpose?" Sir's hand dipped low, following the curve of Gabriel's ass to the space between his thighs. Gabriel sucked in a needy breath, certain that Sir was going to start stroking him, but Sir's fingers met the elastic band of the boxers he wore, and he toyed with it instead.

"No, Sir."

"I almost don't believe you. Almost..." Sir drew the elastic back so it was taut. "... because you wouldn't lie to me, would you? You wouldn't tell me pretty lies to avoid a punishment you deserve."

Gabriel panted his reply, too starved of breath and addled by arousal to give Sir anything more than that. "No, Sir, I wouldn't."

The elastic snapped back into place. It hit the back of Gabriel's thighs, causing Gabriel to grunt into his blankets. The sting was temporary, but his body didn't know that. It pushed forward involuntarily with pain, his cock brushing Sir's thigh to bring him pleasure.

"Tonight was supposed to be your reward for good behavior. I wish it didn't have to end like this." Sir's fingers slid back and forth over the band, and every now and then, he tugged it as if to draw it back again. "Do you understand why it's gone this way?"

"Yes, Sir."

"Then you understand how to make it never happen again?"

Gabriel squeezed his eyes shut so tightly the darkness behind his eyelids speckled. He did understand. He'd taken Sir for granted, thinking Sir wasn't as powerful as Garrison, but he'd taken it too far. There was a difference between power laced with brutality, and power laced with kindness. Sir was not made weak because he had compassion—the fact that his control was so refined he exerted it over himself was a testament to his will. He did not lash out, even when Gabriel deserved it. He punished Gabriel in ways that would make him understand what he'd done wrong instead of ways that would allow Sir to get his frustration out in full.

"If you understand, then you'll want to be punished, won't you?" Sir's hand was on his ass again, caressing his skin. "I want you to count for me as I punish you, so you can see how much you're valued. Every spank is meant to honor you—to encourage you to be the best you can be, so that you can please me, body and mind."

"Yes, Sir."

Gabriel's body was on edge, left tingling in anticipation. He hung on Sir's every word, goosebumps running up and down his arms.

He would count. He would count and remember that he'd been bad, and that Sir truly knew what was best for him. It wasn't the way the evening was supposed to have gone, but he didn't regret it in the least. Sir was teaching him a lesson, and Gabriel would remember it forever.

The first spank startled Gabriel, and he cried out in surprise. When he caught his breath, he crowed out a broken, "One."

Sir's hand smoothed over his skin, then drew back and struck again. Pain seared Gabriel's backside, but it disappeared as quickly as it came. He jolted forward, and his cock rubbed against Sir's leg. "T-two."

"Good boy, Gabriel," Sir whispered. "Keep counting. I want you to know how much I value you. I want to hear you acknowledge it. You're better than this. Don't ever pretend that you're not."

The hand drew back, and a *smack* rang through the room. As his cheek jiggled from the impact, he rubbed his cock against Sir's thigh. Pleasure mixed with pain. Was Sir doing this on purpose? Gabriel never wanted him to stop. "Three."

Another *smack*. Gabriel's hips moved against Sir's thigh at a steady pace now, giving his cock the stimulation it craved. The spanking didn't hurt anymore—Gabriel's mind had gone haywire, and pleasure was the only thing that registered. "*Four.*"

How many more was Sir going to give him? Tears ran down Gabriel's cheeks, but he smiled. There was no other feeling like this. He'd never been punished and made to feel good at the same time.

Why had it never been like this before?

This wasn't a beating. This wasn't *anything* Gabriel had ever experienced. He'd been waiting for the day Sir lost his patience and struck him, but this was pleasure masquerading as punishment. Would he always be so spoiled?

Sir wanted this to happen to him. He wanted to guide Gabriel, but at the same time, he never wanted to hurt him.

Sometimes, pleasure had to be delivered in a package more purposeful than kittenish tenderness to get the point across.

On the next spank, Sir's hand found a part of Gabriel's ass that had been struck before. Pain spiked through Gabriel's pleasure receptors and made itself known. Gabriel cried into the blankets, but his hips rutted forward, and he worked his cock against Sir's thigh harder than ever to compensate. Pain morphed into pleasure and tightened in his balls. Did Sir notice? Gabriel wasn't sure. "Five!"

So close. He was so close. The small part inside of him that clenched whenever orgasm was on its way was clenching now, and with it, the rest of Gabriel's body. His toes curled and his fingers locked into the blankets. His eyes remained shut tight, and he bit down on his jaw as the sensation overwhelmed him.

One more spank. Just one more, and he'd come.

But the last spank never came. Sir repositioned him on the bed and rolled Gabriel over so that he was on his back. The change of position was jarring, and Gabriel opened his eyes to find that his vision had adjusted to the dark. He saw Sir looking down at him, on his hands and knees at Gabriel's side. "A first offense is five counted spanks, Rabbit."

Only five? Gabriel ached for more. Sir had to know it, and it was why he was limiting the punishment. He had to know that Gabriel was seconds away from coming.

Sir's hand on his ass wasn't his punishment—the denied orgasm he'd teased Gabriel with was.

"If you are bad again, it will be ten."

How quickly could Gabriel be bad? If he grabbed Sir's face and yanked him down to kiss him hard, would Sir punish him all over again? "What will happen if I'm good, Sir?"

"If you're good?" It was hard to tell through the dark, but Gabriel thought he saw Sir smile. His hand cupped Gabriel's jaw, and sparks shot through Gabriel, speeding his pulse. "If you're good, then you'll be rewarded."

"If I'm good, will you spank me again? Please?"

The only answer Gabriel got was the sound of Sir sucking in a breath through his teeth.

Sir leaned down, so close that their lips almost touched again. Gabriel already hungered for his kiss, and he'd only just gotten his first taste of it. Breathless in anticipation, Gabriel closed his eyes and let his head fall back just a little, so his lips were more easily accessible. He was ready.

"We'll talk about that later, Rabbit," Sir whispered. Gabriel felt his words, and he imagined the touch of Sir's lips. Passionate, eager, and all for him. "For now, you need to get to sleep. You will wake up at your regular time tomorrow. You've lost the privilege of sleeping in."

"I understand, Sir." What Gabriel got was better than sleep. The ache in his balls was torture in the most deliriously blissful way. "Thank you, Sir."

"Goodnight, Rabbit," Sir whispered against his lips.

"Goodnight, Sir," Gabriel whispered back.

The mattress shifted. Sir stood and left the room, closing the door behind him.

28

CEDRIC

"You've gone and fucked it all up now, Cedric."

"Not helping." A cup of coffee steamed in front of him, sweetened with Bailey's, but not even the alcohol was helping the panic steadily rising inside. After what he'd done last night, Cedric would need a whole bottle to get over the guilt. He pressed the phone closer to his ear until it smarted. The pain was well-deserved. "I need advice, Oli. What the hell am I going to do?"

"To be honest, I thought you were kidding when you said you hadn't already slept with him."

"How is that something to joke about?" Cedric asked, exasperated. "When is the last time I slept with anyone?"

He could almost hear the shrug. "I thought the whole BDSM thing was just a polite front for lots and lots of anonymous sex."

Cedric pinched the bridge of his nose and sighed loudly. "I am *not* a prostitute, and I will never be one. I sell a service that may or may not include sexual stimulation, not my body."

"Well, after last night, you might want to reconsider that claim. You got the condoms out and everything. Admit it—you were going to fuck him senseless."

"Remind me why I called you?" Cedric asked. He pushed away from the table and sank against the back of the kitchen chair. There was a cobweb in the corner of the ceiling. It drifted, caught by a breeze Cedric couldn't feel.

Oli snorted. "Because I'm your best friend, and who else are you going to call at, oh, half-past five in the morning? You're damn lucky that I'm at my wit's end trying to find a job right now, or I'd be pissed that you woke me up. Not everyone can take off their shirt, strap on a little leather, and ask a fifth of the world's population to pay their bills for them. Some of us have to kiss ass instead."

Oli's particular brand of sarcasm wasn't helping. Cedric, defeated, watched the cobweb drift in the breeze. "I don't want to be a jerk, but can we talk about my massive fuck-up, please? I need some help. You're the one from the outside looking in. What the hell am I going to do?"

"Not much you can do, is there? I mean, the way seems pretty straightforward to me." Oli clucked his tongue, like he was think-ing. "Step one: you've already made your mistake, so if you want to get your dick wet, go get it wet right now before you do anything else. Like, massively wet. Have lots of sloppy, satisfying sex. You might as well take advantage, right?"

Gabriel, looking over his shoulder with lust-lidded eyes as Cedric's length slid between his ass cheeks... Cedric's cock throbbed at the thought. "Not helping. I want him, but I can't have him. He's too damaged to be able to give consent, and I *won't* take advantage of him. I already feel like a monster over what I did last night. I should have had the willpower to tell him no. I shouldn't have so much as kissed him. What I did was wrong, and then I punished him for *my* mistake after he was justifiably pissed that I stopped play midway through. I'm losing my goddamn mind over him."

"Okay, okay, so if you're finished with step one, move on to step two: coming clean."

"You're not going to tell me to hop in the shower, are you?"

Cedric asked, words as dry as he could make them. When Oli teased, he went all the way.

Oli scoffed. "Okay, so sometimes I'm a dick, but I'm not that much of a dick. I mean coming clean as in, you need to get in touch with whatever idiot thought it would be a good idea to leave you alone with a little sexpot omega and admit that you did a nasty thing by kissing him last night. You don't want to sweep this under the rug."

"That *idiot* is Sterling Holt."

"And that name should mean something to me because...?" Oli sighed. "Listen. I know that you're freaked out, and I know that you've got a lot riding on this job, but we all make mistakes. So okay, this Sterling dude might be mad at you, but on the bright side, you didn't knock anyone up. You didn't even touch his dick."

That was a lie, but Cedric let it go. Oli didn't need to know about how he'd denied Gabriel an orgasm last night—or how he'd fisted Gabriel's cock on their first night together before he knew any better. "So I call him and tell him I did, and then what? How is this going to make things any better for Gabriel? He needed me to keep my hands to myself, and I fucked up and victimized him. What am I supposed to do to make things right with him? How the hell am I supposed to apologize after I almost raped him?"

There was a long pause—long enough that Cedric took his phone from his ear to check that the call was still going. It was. Seconds ticked by. He returned the phone to his ear in time to hear Oli speak, his voice hollow. "I thought you were asking me how to save your career."

"No." Cedric closed his eyes and let his shoulders slump. "I couldn't give less of a shit about my career. Right now, all I can think about is how I hurt Gabriel. How am I supposed to make this right?"

Another long silence passed between them. Cedric opened his eyes a sliver, staring at the ceiling through his lashes. Gabriel was broken—shattered into a million little pieces. He'd shown tremendous progress over the past few weeks, but was it enough? He'd pieced together the dirty truth about Gabriel's past, and he'd learned about his heartbreak. Until just a few weeks ago, he'd been in love with Garrison Baylor, whom Cedric had come to believe was one of the most deplorable men on the planet. He wasn't ready to sleep with anyone yet, let alone Cedric, who'd been acting as his pillar of strength after a highly traumatic event.

Gabriel couldn't give consent. Cedric had fooled himself into thinking that he could because his attraction to Gabriel burned like wildfire set loose on a field of dryer lint, and the only way to extinguish the flames was to give in to the heat. But now? Removed from temptation and left to process what had happened, he knew he'd done wrong. Gabriel trusted him, and he'd betrayed that trust by taking things between them too far. It didn't matter how much he liked Gabriel—the fact was, there was no way Cedric could give in to his desire without turning Gabriel into a victim.

If Brittany were there to see what he'd done, she never would have forgiven him. He *knew* better.

"I'm not ignoring you," Oli said, choosing his words carefully. "I'm just... I'm kind of in awe that your biggest concern right now is making things right with the omega who wants to jump on your dick instead of the alpha who could rocket your career to superstar levels. From what you told me, he came on to *you*. Why are you feeling so torn up about it?"

"Because he doesn't know any better." Cedric sat up straight, then thought better of it and slumped down onto the table. The Bailey's-infused coffee waited inches away from his head. "This Garrison Baylor guy he was going on and on about? He ran an omega sex ring, Oli. He took kids from their homes—kids who'd just gone through their first heats—and pretended that he was their boyfriend... that he could make things right for them, if they would only do him this one little favor..."

"The White Lotus bust?" Oli's tone changed. "*That* Baylor?"

"You know about it?"

"It was all over the news. Some hotshot attorney dating one of Baylor's boys just shot down that bastard's appeal and made sure he's serving life in jail for what he did. It's kind of big fucking news, Cedric."

"The name sounded familiar, but I guess it never clicked."

"Because you aren't an omega, I guess." There was distance in Oli's reply, not spiteful, but not exactly friendly, either. "If you were an omega, you would have known. It's been... it's been showing a lot of people's true colors, who stands up for what's right, and who casts a blind eye. There was trouble deciding on a jury, because good old prejudice runs that deep, even today. When he was able to appeal, there were almost riots. If your boy was trying to get back to that creep, then I can see where you're coming from. No sane person would want to go back to a situation like that. He beat those boys. He abused them. He raped them. I've been reading the court transcripts, and it's... it's ugly."

Cedric didn't want to hear more. Imagining the things done to Gabriel at the hands of a monster was too hard to swallow. "Then what am I supposed to do? He can't give consent, but I went ahead and tried to have sex with him, anyway."

Nothing that Oli said was sarcastic anymore. "But you didn't. You stopped yourself. It's okay to be tempted, especially if he was trying to seduce you, but the fact that you took control of the situation and shot it down before you went any further shows that you're aware that he's off-limits. I think now, the kindest thing you can do for him is call your boss and tell him what happened, then ask him to remove Gabriel from your care. He's not going to understand right now, but one day, when he's better, he's going to appreciate what you did for him."

It was the conclusion Cedric had been dreading, but the one he knew they'd come to. There was no other way. He'd taken things too far, and now he had to take drastic steps to make sure they never went that far again. Last night was proof that his body was weak, and his mind was even weaker. If Gabriel tempted him again, he'd give in.

The only thing to do was send Gabriel away before he made a mistake he couldn't take back. A kiss was one matter, but anything more? Cedric couldn't live with himself if that happened.

"I know it's not going to be easy for you, but it's the right thing to do." Oli's voice was sympathetic, but sympathy did nothing to unwind the struggle tying Cedric's soul into knots. "And I think... I think in the end, maybe it's a good thing. No matter what happens to you professionally, you've acted with integrity. And more than that, I think it's a good step forward. Since Brit passed, it's... you haven't been yourself, you know?"

Cedric said nothing. He already knew it was true.

"I don't know if you've been hooking up with people since she was laid to rest, but you haven't... you haven't been interested in people for a long time, and I think maybe this is a positive step forward. Even if you can't be with him, it's proof that you can still feel. One of these days, you're going to meet someone who knocks you off your feet again. Your heart isn't dead. There's still so much out there for you to celebrate, and so much love for you to give. He may not be the one for you, but he's the one who's given you what you need to find that person."

"Right." It was hard not to sound bitter when Cedric's heart told him one thing, but his mind told him another. Injured or not, Gabriel was someone special. Cedric had met enough people in his life to know that he wasn't right for everyone—but Gabriel? Without trying, Gabriel had lifted his spirits and made him feel again, and that was more precious than Oli could ever know.

Oli hesitated. "So you're going to call that Silver dude, right?"

"Sterling. And yes."

"And you're going to ask him to take Gabriel back home?"

"... Yes." Even the thought tasted bitter. Cedric didn't want Gabriel to go, but he couldn't see a way around it. He'd failed, and this was his punishment. "I'll give him a call once the sun's up."

"Sounds like a good plan." Oli paused. "And Cedric? I'm proud of you. It really takes balls to do what you're doing."

"Thanks."

The call ended after half-hearted goodbyes. Cedric curled his arms on the table and buried his face in them, facing the reality of what he had to do, even as his heart begged him to do otherwise.

29

GABRIEL

Heat.

Sweltering, blistering heat.

It manifested as sweat on Gabriel's brow and radiated from a place so far inside of him, it might as well have come from his bones. The ache inside lit to a dull roar, like wind blowing over the tops of tall trees, or the sound of a train barreling down the tracks.

Gabriel opened his eyes and he knew it.

Heat.

It had come for him at last.

Arousal pulsed low in his gut, a creature rising from the depths that could not be pushed back down. Dark and full-bodied, it addled his mind with thoughts of sex, but only one man he wanted it from.

Sir.

Everything was disjointed. The heat came on like a fever dream, and it robbed Gabriel of his senses. He rolled onto his side to gaze at the digital clock on the nightstand. It was just before six in the morning. The heat must have come on in the early morning hours, after he'd come again and again remembering Sir's firm hand and the beautiful things he'd said.

Gabriel was glad his heat was here. After last night, Sir would breathe him in and fall to his knees in want. He'd bury his tongue in Gabriel's slick and lap him up, and then, when he was high off Gabriel's pheromones, they'd breed like they were supposed to, and Gabriel would enjoy every second of it. In the sparse moments of lucidity his heat-addled mind afforded him, he would take full advantage of Sir's body and ride him like he'd wanted to all along—because if he was being truthful to himself, he'd wanted Sir since the very first time he'd seen him, even before his conscious knew what his subconscious had known all along... that Garrison was no good for him, and that he deserved an alpha who would live up to his promises.

Sir would keep his word. Sir was kind and merciful.

They'd make wonderful babies together.

Gabriel's body urged him to stay in bed, but his mind wanted him to seek out companionship. He peeled the sheets back and crossed the room on wobbling footsteps, uncertain of himself. In his sleep, he'd kicked off Sir's loose boxers. They'd been drenched in his cum, anyway. He couldn't wear them out of the room. Instead, Gabriel freed his favorite pair of panties from his duffel bag and shook them out.

Navy blue. White polka-dots. Cheeky.

Sir wouldn't even have to take them off to get to his slick—all he'd have to do would be to push them aside.

Gabriel stepped into them carefully, but he still came close to losing his balance. The world was a lot less stable than he remembered it, but the risk of falling was worth it—he was going to have sex with Sir, and then they would be a family.

Trembling with excitement, Gabriel slid his hands over his ass to make sure his panties were sitting just right before he crossed the room and opened the door quietly. Sir's bedroom door was open, and that meant he was already awake. Gabriel would have preferred to surprise him in bed, but it didn't matter. If they bred in the living room or if they bred in the bedroom, the results would be the same. It was the action, not the location that was important.

One hand braced on the wall to keep him stable, the other toying with the hem of his panties, Gabriel headed down the hall. He heard noise in the kitchen—a mug being placed in the sink.

Sir.

The double-wide doorway was within reach, its white trim a beacon. Gabriel bit down on his lip in anticipation, knowing that as soon as he crossed the threshold, he would belong to his alpha at last. A few more steps, just a few more steps...

Gabriel's bare foot met polished wood. A shiver ran down his spine. Sir stood at the sink, hands braced on either side like he might be sick. He was still in his pajamas—a loose t-shirt that only partially hid his full tattoo sleeve, and a baggy pair of sweatpants that concealed the body Gabriel remembered so well.

Another step forward.

Sir looked over his shoulder, tired and wistful. That look didn't stay for long—as soon as he saw what Gabriel was wearing, his eyes widened. On the inside, Gabriel beamed. He was desired. He was loved.

He would have what he wanted most of all.

Sir turned. He took in a breath to speak, but before he could, realization dawned on his face, and his eyes clouded over. The alpha protector from last night was back, and Gabriel wanted him more than he wanted anything else.

"You're in heat," Sir murmured. He took a small step toward Gabriel, even as Gabriel advanced through the kitchen to reach him.

"Need you," Gabriel replied. He arrived in front of Sir, his mind already starting to lose itself to the swirling steam starting to fog his thoughts. "Please, Sir, I need you. You need to help me. It *burns*."

Sir set a hand on Gabriel's wrist. Gabriel curled his hands in the t-shirt Sir wore—an old band shirt Gabriel didn't care to investigate. He pulled himself forward and tilted his chin upward, and Sir did the rest. Their lips crushed together, and Sir's hands slipped down to squeeze his ass.

Slick flowed. Gabriel's body was ready to be penetrated—ready for however often Sir wanted to use him over the next several days while they worked tirelessly to conceive. When they were done and Gabriel's heat had been extinguished, Sir could punish him then. He could spank Gabriel until his palm smarted and he couldn't keep going anymore—Gabriel wouldn't mind. He wanted it. And when they conceived their next baby, Sir could spank him all over again.

Naughty omega, not taking precautions like I warned you to. Bad boy, Rabbit. You know better. Now we're going to have another baby...

Gabriel lifted a thigh and hooked it over Sir's hip. He wrapped his arms around Sir's neck, and Sir hooked an arm beneath his ass. He lifted him up like he weighed nothing at all. The kiss broke. The rock-hard erection beneath Sir's soft pajama pants pushed into the space between Gabriel's legs, and he knew that soon, that cock was going to be his. It would use him so much over the next few days that he'd feel empty without it. And the knot that would stretch him? Gabriel didn't know it yet, but he already couldn't live without it.

"Fuck me, Sir," Gabriel whispered into Sir's ear. "I went into heat for you. I *want* you."

"You need to go back to your bedroom, Gabriel," Sir whispered back, voice so deep, it rolled like tires over gravel. "You're in heat and you don't know what you're saying. You need to go back to bed, and we'll handle things from there."

"Only if you come to bed with me." It was all Gabriel wanted. He tucked his head against Sir's shoulder and kissed his neck, ready to be taken. This wasn't like any of the times he'd gone into heat at The White Lotus—in Sir's arms, he was happy. If Sir wanted his body and mind, Gabriel would give them to him—and he'd give him his future, as well.

They stumbled through the kitchen. Gabriel knew they were moving, but he struggled to cling to his conscious, rational mind. Soon enough, the heat would overtake him and he'd know nothing more, but he wanted to make sure that Sir was with him in bed before that happened. He wanted to remember the best moment of his life.

The bedroom door swung open. It took a second to realize it was his own.

"Sir?" Gabriel lifted his head to look Sir in the eyes, but Sir was already setting him down. Gabriel's feet met the floor, and he took a few staggering steps backward as he tried to find balance.

Sir's expression was painted with struggle, his lust-softened eyes plagued with indecision.

Then the dream turned into a nightmare, and it happened too fast for Gabriel to stop it—Sir left the room and closed the door, leaving Gabriel alone.

"N-no!" Gabriel whimpered. He couldn't find the strength to scream. "Sir! Please! No!"

The heat set in. He swayed on the spot and caught himself on the foot of the bed before he fell. Slick soaked his panties. There would be no more relief.

Gabriel couldn't walk. Getting to the door would be an impossibility. He crawled onto the bed and fell onto his side, then let loose with a shuddering sob that snagged in his throat and rattled his bones.

Why wasn't he ever good enough? Why couldn't he have any of the things in life he wanted? A family wasn't so much to ask for, was it? All he wanted was someone to love, and who would love him back.

Another ugly sob escaped Gabriel's lips, and he curled up on the bed as his body betrayed him. Slick flowing liberally, cock throbbing, he let go of his mind and let himself go into heat.

30

CEDRIC

All he needed to do was push the button. One touch of his finger to the screen would solve all his problems. The call would go through, Sterling would answer, and they'd figure out a way to get Gabriel out of the house together. Cedric wouldn't give in to Gabriel's advances, they'd part ways forever, and he'd never see the little omega who meant so much to him again.

But Cedric couldn't bring himself to call.

He stared at the contact information on his phone, tracing the numbers with his eyes until the screen dimmed, then went out. There was no way that Gabriel could stay, but Cedric didn't want him to go, either. His heart hurt too much at the thought.

Business was business—at least, it had been, until he'd met his match in Gabriel. In Brittany, he'd found someone whose lust for life exceeded his own—in weeks, she'd brought him to his knees and collared him as her submissive. He'd been paraded around The Shepherd like the trophy he was, and they'd been the envy of every soul in the building. A beta Domme with free rein over an alpha male? Cedric had lived for the looks he got—the greed of men who wanted him, but who would never get to touch him. And now here he was with his own perfect, exceedingly desirable submissive, unable to touch him even though Cedric wanted him most of all.

It wasn't just the power trip. It wasn't.

Gabriel meant more to him than that.

Gabriel, with his gentle eyes and his sugar-sweet innocence, reignited the part of his soul that Brittany's death had extinguished. He'd stitched him back together and reminded Cedric that it was okay to be vulnerable—being broken didn't mean that he was weak. The strength it took to look down at all the broken pieces of his psyche and pick them back up one by one was a testament to his perseverance and his endurance. Gabriel wasn't weak because he'd been tricked down the wrong path in life, just like Cedric wasn't worthless because his grief was long-lived. In Gabriel, he saw that there was more than one way to heal.

And one day, in retrospect, he hoped Gabriel saw the same from him.

Cedric woke the screen. Sterling's contact information was still there, the call one tap of his finger away from connecting.

He closed his eyes, said his goodbyes, and called.

"Hello, Cedric." Sterling was already awake, by the sounds of it. It didn't make what Cedric had to say any easier.

"Good morning." Neither man spoke, but this time, Cedric didn't have the stamina to hold out. He crumbled. "There's been an incident, and Adrian needs to come for Gabriel."

"Is everything okay?"

"He's fine. We're fine. I..." It was his last chance to lie and explain away the truth, but Cedric couldn't do that. The only way he could hope to apologize was to make sure that Gabriel was removed from his care and given a fair chance at normalcy. "I kissed him last night, and he went into heat this morning. I managed to get out of the house before anything could happen, but I can't go back inside. Right now, he needs Adrian. He can stay in my house for the duration of his heat, but once it's over, I think we should end the contract. After what I did, I don't think it's right to see it through to completion."

There it was, all of the unembellished details laid out for Sterling to see. Cedric would not hide the truth, and he would not pretend he was innocent—but more than that, he refused to muddy Gabriel's name. The trauma he'd been through meant Gabriel didn't understand what he was doing by coming onto Cedric, or how wrong it was. If Sterling was going to be disappointed in anyone, it would be Cedric. The blame was his, and his alone.

"A kiss?" It was hard to get a read on Sterling's voice.

"In the last few weeks, Gabriel has taught me what he really needs." Cedric tried to keep his voice from shaking, but it proved impossible. "What he says he wants and what he actually wants are different. I know it, and I think you do, too."

There was no comment from Sterling.

"I want him. I want to care for him body and soul, but I can't. I thought that I could coax him out of his mindset and convince him that his imagined path in life isn't the right path for him, but... but I want him too badly. I can't get him out of my head, and I know that even if I wait this heat out and take him on again, that's not going to change. If you don't take him away, I *will* fail in my role as Dom, and I *will* put him into a position that doesn't benefit him. I'll take him to bed, Sterling, and I can't do that to him. Not with how he is now."

All along, Cedric had been convinced that he could hold the pieces together for Gabriel while he put himself back together. He'd thought they'd become whole together. Instead, Gabriel had started to take him back apart. He'd opened up Cedric's soul and left Cedric to bleed for him.

And Cedric suffered it gladly.

He took another breath and spoke slowly and calmly. He couldn't show weakness now. "If you would be kind enough to notify me when my house has been vacated, I'll move back in and we can both go on with our lives. I'll refund you the money you paid, and you can invest it toward better care for Gabriel."

"The call is breaking up," Sterling said. "I've heard enough to know to send Adrian over. After he arrives, I want you to come see me at The Shepherd, and we'll have a chat face-to-face."

There hadn't been so much as a grain of feedback on the call. What was Sterling going on about? "I'll be there, but—"

"See you soon." Sterling's voice was the same kind of unreadable that it had been after learning about the kiss. "Don't keep me waiting."

The call ended. Cedric set down the phone and allowed himself a single, shuddering, tearless sob. It was over.

Goodbye, Rabbit.

Adrian's silver Lexus screeched to a halt by the curb. The engine cut so quickly that Cedric winced. He climbed to his feet from where he sat and prepared to greet Adrian, but when the door flew open and Adrian stormed up the lawn, Cedric didn't think a simple, "Hello, I'm sorry I victimized your brother, please let me get out of your life," was going to cut it.

"Adrian, I—"

Adrian shoved his shoulders, and Cedric had to take a step back to brace himself. Adrian was dressed in full business professional, but he didn't let a fitted suit stop him from showing Cedric exactly what he thought of him. "What the *hell* do you think you're doing?"

"Waiting for you to get here so I can make sure he gets the care he needs."

"You fucked him, didn't you?" Adrian clenched his fists.

"No."

"I swear to god, if he ends up pregnant because of this—"

Cedric caught Adrian's wrist in his hand. The move was instinctual, and so was the way he leaned closer to eliminate the space between them. By the time he spoke, Cedric was barely aware of what he was doing—all he knew was that he had to make sure that no one allowed Gabriel to feel guilty over this.

No one would make his omega suffer.

"I told you *no*."

There was a silence uncharacteristic of the Adrian Cedric knew from high school. His face was older now, but Cedric still saw the same refined features and the same distrustful eyes. Adrian hadn't always looked that way, but the older he became, the more jaded his expression was. Once, Cedric hadn't understood, but now he felt that he did. Someone, or something, had hurt Adrian back in high school, even before Gabriel's disappearance. He bore the scars of that time plainly.

It may have been the same thing that had brought Gabriel to run into Baylor's arms.

Cedric released Adrian's hand and took a step back. He nodded toward the door. "Gabriel is inside, down the hall, in the bedroom on the left."

"If I smell you in his bed, so help me..." But Adrian's voice had lost its edge, and there was uncertainty in his eyes. Cedric knew suffering, and he saw the storm inside. "Sterling gave me your number. I'll be calling you when Gabriel is safely removed from the house so you can come back. I'm sorry for the inconvenience."

Despite the guilt and disappointment dragging down his soul, Cedric managed a tiny grin. "Adrian Lowe, apologizing?"

"Don't get used to it." Adrian stepped around him. "You might be telling the truth about my brother, but that doesn't mean that I trust you."

"You don't have to. I'm not going to see either of you again."

"Just... go see Sterling." Adrian shook his head. "Is there anything I need to know over the next week? Leftovers that will go bad in the fridge? A pesky cat you need to feed? Any doors I shouldn't open?"

"There's nothing I have to hide." Cedric heard Adrian twist the doorknob. He didn't turn to watch him enter. "No matter what he tells you, everything was my fault. Don't let him convince you otherwise."

"I doubt that," Adrian murmured. "I know my brother."

"And now I know him, too." Cedric headed down the path leading to the carport. "He's a beautiful soul. All he needs is someone who can help him remember that. I'm glad that you found him, Adrian. I'm sorry this has happened to you... and to him."

The door didn't swing open—Cedric didn't hear the creak of the hinges. But Adrian didn't speak, either. The hairs on the back of Cedric's neck stood on end, and when he arrived at the driveway, he turned to look at the front door. Adrian stood there, one hand on the doorknob, his face consumed with worry.

Worry.

Not anger. Not rage. Not hate.

"You're telling the truth," Adrian murmured. The sound of it carried through the crisp fall morning. There was no traffic on the street to drown out his words—their only witness was the trees. "You didn't touch him, did you?"

"I would never do that to him." Cedric slid his hands into his pockets. A breeze nipped at his exposed skin and chilled him, but he didn't let it rush what he had to say. "The truth is, I'm not strong enough to take care of him the way he needs to be taken care of." The wind stirred fallen leaves. They crinkled as they abandoned the lawn and met the sidewalk. "No matter what happens, and no matter what you think of me, it doesn't matter. All that matters is that you get him someone who can help him—someone who can make him understand how precious and valued he is. I love him, Adrian. I love him, and I need to know that he's going to get better and lead a happy life. The only way I can make sure that happens is by making sure that responsibility is no longer my own."

Cedric's throat constricted. If he said anything more, he knew he'd start to cry.

"Cedric," Adrian said, startled. "Wait."

But waiting wasn't an option. Cedric had done enough of that already. He entered the carport, sank into the driver's seat, and got the hell out before he could change his mind. As he drove past, he spotted Adrian by the front door, his typically stern face softened by surprise—or regret.

Cedric set his eyes on the road and didn't look back. He couldn't.

Another future shattered. Another love stolen from him.

Cedric left his heart behind him, and as he did, all his carefully assembled pieces fell back apart.

31

CEDRIC

There was a buzzer beside the back door of Sterling's penthouse—a simple rubber button that glowed from the inside. Cedric pressed it in, then leaned against the metal railing out of the way of the door. No matter how bad he felt, he knew that coming here was the best thing he could have done. He would look Sterling in the eyes and admit that he wasn't man enough for the job, and he would shoulder whatever punishment followed. It was his burden to bear, and he wouldn't shy away from it.

The door opened. Heated air gushed out and warmed Cedric's cheeks. He looked up to find Sterling in the doorway wearing a simple button-down shirt, the top two buttons undone, and a pair of slacks. His blond hair was a little messier than Cedric was used to, almost like he'd been sleeping. "Cedric," Sterling said with a knowing nod. "Come in."

Coming in felt like a bad idea. When Sterling found out the truth, there was going to be bloodshed. "I think it's best we talk out here."

Before Cedric could so much as begin the conversation, Sterling stepped back from the doorway and gestured down the hall. "No, I insist you come inside. The longer we keep the door open, the more the cold will come in, and I don't want Lilian to catch a chill."

Lilian, the baby. Right. Cedric swallowed his nerves and stepped through the door, making sure it was latched behind him. Like ivy creeping across a foundation, anchoring its roots against all odds, Cedric's emotions had become entangled in what was, at its core, a business transaction. The only way forward was to pluck the roots out and leave behind barren subject matter. The simpler he kept this conversation, the better.

He stood by the doorway, unwilling to enter the penthouse any farther. He wasn't a guest here—this was business, nothing more. "I'm here to prematurely end the contract, and I want to return the money you gave me in compensation for Gabriel's care."

"It seems like a drastic step to take so suddenly." Sterling's face was as impossible to read as his tone. There wasn't joy in his eyes, but there wasn't anger, either. He kept his mouth neutral, no twist of his lips there to reveal what was going on inside his head. "You kissed him?"

"I..." A kiss was technically accurate, but it didn't encompass what had gone on that night, and what had happened earlier that morning. Cedric would be truthful—Gabriel deserved his honesty. "It's more than that. It's not the physical that bothers me, but the intention behind it. Over the last few weeks, I've learned what Gabriel needs, and sex isn't it. Gabriel needs someone who won't be tempted to drag him back into the same darkness he escaped from. I'm not a good fit for him."

Sterling looked him over, the track lights overhead hitting his shoulders and casting dynamic shadows that amplified the features of his face. Next to Sterling's greatness, Cedric remembered just how small he was—nothing more than a young man looking to find himself through kink, but doing a miserable job at it. Gabriel needed someone sure of himself, whose every move was made with purpose, and who spoke with confidence no matter what he said. At twenty-five, and after having suffered a tragic loss, Cedric wasn't ready to be that man. It was foolish to think he could take on a job so big when he, himself, was a work in progress.

Two broken souls couldn't heal each other. Gabriel needed stability. It was better to end things now, because Cedric knew if they continued, their pieces would start to slot together as they healed, and it would make their eventual separation that much more difficult.

"Cedric?" Sterling's voice was crisp, and it lacked the anger Cedric anticipated. Cedric lifted his gaze to look into Sterling's eyes. "Do you know why I chose you?"

"To assess my worthiness when it came to the management position," Cedric replied. The answer was obvious—Sterling had told him as much during their conversation at the interview. "You wanted to see my work ethic."

"Not quite." Sterling's blue eyes were soft, like he was looking upon his favorite son. "There are other ways to test a man's mettle than to entrust him with your vulnerable brother-in-law. The reason why I entrusted you with Gabriel was because I knew you understood."

Saliva pooled in Cedric's mouth. No matter how many times he swallowed, it never seemed to make a difference. What was Sterling going on about? He'd waded into the job blindly, and he'd only learned about Gabriel's past when Gabriel had opened up and subsequently broken down on him over Garrison Baylor. Cedric understood nothing.

"Five years ago, the young man who let himself be paraded around on a leash with stars in his eyes, beautifully submissive to a woman he loved, disappeared. In the blink of an eye, the man you were was stripped from you, but here you stand before me, risen from the ashes of your past, and stronger than you were before."

On the surface, Cedric kept his reaction impartial. He didn't allow his bottom lip to tremble or his eyes to widen with surprise. On the day of the interview, he'd walked in thinking that Sterling never would have looked into his past—but of course he had. When he'd looked across the desk at Cedric, searching the depths of his soul for the truth, he'd already known what secrets Cedric housed. All he was looking for was honesty.

"You're young, and many would say that you lack the experience necessary to take on my position at The Shepherd, but they don't understand what it's like to lose someone, do they? Or how it feels to grow up overnight? From starstruck and in love with the world to jaded and guarded out of necessity. I know your pain, Cedric, because it's a pain I share with you. I ended up growing up well before my time, and The Shepherd is my monument to that struggle."

There had to be a catch. Cedric held firm before Sterling, keeping his silence. Once, Sterling had used that tactic to encourage him to speak, and now Cedric returned fire.

"You've had your whole world reduced to nothing, and yet you still managed to rise back up and make something of yourself. You changed your life to fit your new goals and aspirations, and you did so on your own. Nothing could stop you—not tragedy, not hardship, and not yourself. That's why I chose you to take on what seems like an insurmountable task."

"Because I bested tragedy?" There were tears lurking behind Cedric's eyes that he refused to shed. Remembering what he'd lost when Brittany died was hard at the best of times, but as shaken as he was from abusing Gabriel, it hit him harder than it had in years.

"Because you were shaped by it." Sterling made no move to come closer, but Cedric felt so close to him in that moment, they might as well have been standing side by side. No one had ever put into words the way his life had changed after Brittany's death because no one had ever understood what it was like, but Sterling knew—Cedric heard it in his tone of voice as plainly as he heard it in his words. "And I had hopes that you might be able to see into the truth of a young man who's going through that same pain right now, and that you might grow together."

"Then why didn't you tell me that from the start?" Cedric uttered. His voice was hoarse, betraying the profound sorrow and hurt he kept buried inside. That hurt was clawing its way through the earth now, disrupting ground laid to hide it years ago. Its efforts eroded at Cedric's façade, like he was a house of cards built on a mechanical bull. "You kept information from me about Garrison. You smoothed over Gabriel's past. You made it seem like it was no big deal, and I wandered into a goddamn mine field without so much as a metal detector. That boy tore into my heart and left me bleeding. I tried to take advantage of him when he wasn't well enough to know better. I deserve to be arrested, not given a pat on the back and a motivational speech. I almost raped him, Sterling. I wasn't prepared for what I would encounter, and I almost raped him. You can't sweet-talk what I did—or what you did— away."

"We kept it from you because you, of all people, should know that Gabriel is a person, not a problem." Sterling's face was unreadable, but compassion lurked in his tone. "The struggles he's gone through and the experiences that have shaped him are part of who he is, the same way your struggles and experiences are a part of who you are. You know that. If you didn't, you wouldn't have cared enough to come here. So let me ask you this: why are you standing here, Cedric?"

The question demanded a response, but Cedric couldn't find words.

"You're standing here because you're a man of character. If you didn't care, a kiss wouldn't weigh on your conscience."

"It wasn't just a kiss," Cedric stressed. Maybe Sterling didn't understand. "We... I was seconds away from taking him. I didn't get him out of his boxers, but—"

"You're standing here," Sterling said as if Cedric hadn't spoken at all, "because you're looking to make things right. You want what's best for Gabriel, not for yourself. You're putting the needs of others

211

before the needs of yourself, and you're coming to me to let me know where you fell short, and what is needed to correct the situation."

No matter how much Sterling analyzed the situation, it didn't change what had occurred. Cedric shook his head. "What does it matter?"

"In some ways, everything, both good and bad." Sterling's expression tightened, and the affection in his eyes dulled. "I will be removing Gabriel from your care. I've already started to investigate alternative treatment options, since he did so poorly at Stonecrest."

At last, something that made sense. Cedric accepted the news, and he let himself mourn his loss. Losing Gabriel stung, but there was no other way.

"But the qualities you've demonstrated this past week?" Sterling continued. "The rigid moral and professional standards you hold yourself to? I would be a fool to look for someone else to manage The Shepherd in my place. If you're still interested in the position, it's yours. I couldn't picture a man better suited for the job."

The job offer didn't fill the void unearthed in Cedric, and it did nothing to push his sorrow back down into the bog it had clawed its way up from. "Gabriel is worth more to me than a job offer. I can't, in good conscience, accept when it means that our paths might cross again. Until he's healed, I don't want to get in his way. I wouldn't want to hinder his recovery."

"I'm not ready to step down just yet," Sterling said. He kept his voice level, and Cedric couldn't pinpoint exactly what his underlying motives were. "You'll have a month to think about it before I reopen the position and entertain other candidates."

"You're wasting your time. I've given you my answer."

"Time is never wasted if it's spent in hope." Sterling met his gaze. "I'd offer you a place to stay while Gabriel sees his heat through to completion, but I get the feeling you'd refuse."

"You're right."

"Then I want you to know that I don't hold you accountable for

212

what you did." Sterling's eyes bore through him with the same contemplative look he'd given Cedric during his interview. "There are two sides to every story, and although Gabriel's view of the world is skewed, I know that there are details that have been omitted or overlooked. You aren't the villain you make yourself out to be. Bad deeds aren't what make a villain a villain—inaction in correcting those deeds is."

"I should go." The longer he stayed here, the worse he was going to feel. What Sterling said was reassuring, but it did nothing to assuage Cedric of his suffering. The fact was, he'd let his heart get in the way of a job, and that job had morphed into something he wasn't ready to handle. If he'd been strong enough, could he have seen Gabriel through to the end? Could he have made him realize that suffering made men as much as it broke them?

That after he was done pulling himself back together, Cedric would be waiting for him?

It didn't matter anymore.

Cedric pushed the door open and stepped out onto the metal-grate landing. Sterling stood in the doorway, watching.

"You have my number, Cedric," Sterling told him. "I'm not upset. You've made a mistake, but you can still recover from it."

"Thanks. I'll wire you back the money tonight, once I find a place to stay."

"Don't."

Cedric squared his shoulders and returned Sterling's gaze. "I will."

Nothing more was said between them. Sometimes, silence didn't need to end. Cedric turned and headed down the steps to the alley a little more quickly than he would have liked, a chilly autumn wind biting at his cheeks. He hadn't had the presence of mind to grab a hoodie before he'd left the house. Everything was in disarray, and it would remain that way until he pulled himself back together.

Another atmospheric high met with a meteoric fall. He should

213

have listened to his common sense when he'd met Gabriel for the first time and felt the sparks between them—if he'd refused the job outright, he never would have had to feel this way. Now, a part of his heart was missing all over again. Cedric didn't know how many more pieces it could break into before it crumbled into dust.

32

GABRIEL

A damp cloth dabbed the sweat from Gabriel's forehead, and for the first time in what felt like ten years, Gabriel opened his eyes. It wasn't Sir who sat at his bedside, like he thought it might be, but Adrian. In some ways, the sight of him took a load off Gabriel's mind—he hadn't realized how much he'd missed his brother until he saw him in person. But mostly, it made Gabriel feel miserable. He closed his eyes and tried to hide the fact that he'd woken up.

"You can't fool me, you know." Adrian took the cloth away, and Gabriel heard saturated fabric splat as it landed on water. "It's been two days. Are you finally coming down?"

"No." Gabriel wasn't lying. He knew that he was far from finished with his heat—snapping back to lucidity partway through estrus wasn't uncommon for an omega. "My body's just letting me get something to drink, and maybe something to eat, if I'm lucky."

"You've been eating and drinking just fine. I've been making sure of it." Adrian's voice was stiff, like he was angry. He had every right to be. Gabriel had pushed Sir away, and now once again, he was going to be his brother's problem. "What the hell were you thinking, not telling anyone you were going into heat? You're not even on birth control, for Christ's sake."

"I'm sorry."

"You'd better be. You were living with an *alpha*. Do you know what that means?"

Silence. Gabriel didn't open his eyes. His mouth was dry, and every inhaled breath he took tracked that dryness farther down his throat. It felt like if he breathed in anymore, he'd start to strip his vocal cords.

The bed creaked. Sopping fabric twisted, and beads of water trickled downward. The cloth met his head again, cold, like frost seizing a desert at midday. Gabriel exhaled and held his lungs empty for as long as he could. Maybe if he didn't breathe, his body would be so worried about air that it would forget about making a baby with an alpha who didn't think he was good enough.

"You do know what that means. Of course you do." Adrian spoke so quietly, Gabriel wasn't sure he was meant to hear. "Why would you do something like that, Gabriel? Cedric was taking care of you, wasn't he? Wasn't he treating you nicely?"

Why did Adrian always have to make him feel bad? Gabriel rolled onto his side and curled into a ball. The cold cloth on his forehead plopped onto the sweat-damp pillow he was resting on. "Sir was treating me very nicely."

"Then why would you hurt him like that?" Gabriel heard the cloth move, and soon after, it met his forehead again, held there by Adrian's will. "What you did was really low."

"You gave me to him," Gabriel whispered, almost too ashamed of himself to speak. "Omegas are designed to be bred, Adrian. Why else do we go into heat? Why are we so soft and slender when alphas are so hard and broad? If I can't give Sir a baby, then what use am I to him?"

"Jesus Christ. Nine months in Stonecrest and you still think that way?" The cloth blotted his forehead, then hit the water again.

"That bastard really got to you, didn't he? What you just said isn't right. It's not right at all."

Garrison had always warned him to be careful of the nonbelievers. Brainwashed omegas who argued that there was more to life than to serve the purpose they were born for were dangerous, and their way of thinking was toxic to happiness. At least, so Gabriel had thought. But he was starting to question what he believed. When had Garrison ever told him the truth?

"What you did to Cedric? That wasn't okay. You need consent from someone before you do something like that, Gabriel. Heat isn't something you drop on someone out of the blue."

It hurt to hear, but Gabriel knew it was true. In pursuit of his own selfish desires, he'd tried to harm Sir by making him do something he didn't want to do. If he'd truly respected Sir, he never would have done something like that. "I'm sorry."

"I'm not the one you need to be saying sorry to."

Gabriel opened his eyes. The room was bright, light streaming in through the sun room to dance across the polished floors and bring out the color of the paint on the walls. It had to be early in the afternoon—the days were getting shorter, and bright light like this didn't last for long. "Where is Sir? In his bedroom?"

Adrian snorted. He picked up the basin of water on the floor by the bed and moved it aside. There were empty bottles of water left haphazardly on the floor, and he nudged one out of the way with his foot as he walked by. "No. Cedric called Sterling to tell him what had happened between you, then disappeared. It's not a good idea for him to come back until your heat is finished. Your scent is everywhere. He's going to have to deep clean to get it out. We should probably pick up his cleaning bill."

Cleaning bills didn't matter to Gabriel. He propped himself up on his elbow as Adrian set the basin of water on the table by the door and looked across the room. The door to his bedroom was closed, and as far as he could tell, there wasn't anyone waiting outside of it to surprise him. He didn't hear footsteps down the hall or noises in the kitchen. The house was dead.

"Adrian?" Paranoia was starting to set in. It was an unwelcome but natural part of heat. "How much longer until my heat is gone and Sir can come back?"

"How long are your heats in general?"

It bothered Gabriel that he didn't know. Most of the time, Garrison put him on contraceptives and sold his heat, and Gabriel had never thought to ask. All he knew was that when he woke up after it was done, he was always exhausted, filthy, and badly dehydrated. "Normal length, I guess."

"Then we're looking at another five days until you're one hundred percent okay to take out of the house. I'm not going to bring you back to the penthouse until your heat is completely gone. I need Sterling to look after Lilian while I look after you, so we can't chase him out."

The world came to a stop. Gabriel sat up, head spinning. "The penthouse?"

"We don't have another treatment option lined up for you yet." Adrian returned to the bedside, but didn't sit. He hovered, nervous energy keeping him on his feet. It fed into Gabriel's paranoia, and he pulled the covers up to his nose but couldn't find it in him to hide his eyes. "Until we figure out what your next move is, you'll be staying with us again. We have the same space set up we did last time, with the screens. You'll have blankets, and pillows, and all the privacy you could want."

Privacy wasn't the issue, and Gabriel couldn't care less about the screens. He didn't understand why he'd be heading to the penthouse when his heat would only last another five days. "You said Sir is coming back. Is it because my heat is all over the house? Y-you want to get it cleaned up first before I come back, so Sir doesn't take advantage of me... right?"

Adrian gave him a sorry kind of look, like someone who'd just witnessed a small child try their best, but still fail. "You're not coming back here, and you're not seeing Cedric again. It didn't work out. He knew what was best for you, but he still touched you inappropriately."

Inappropriate? There was nothing inappropriate about what he'd done with Sir. For years, Gabriel had been involved with the inappropriate. He'd fallen into bed with men who made him feel bad about himself, and he'd touched strangers in ways he wished he hadn't needed to. Inappropriate was having sex with a man he had no interest in. But Sir? There was nothing inappropriate about him.

"I want him." So often, Gabriel was afraid to speak for himself. Why make a scene when silence was just as effective? Speaking for himself always led to argument, and argument led to punishment, or worse. He'd long ago relinquished control of his free will and embraced the inevitable—but for Sir, he would fight. If he didn't, what choice did he have? "I'm in love with him, Adrian. I was the one who was touching him. He never touched me first. *Never.*"

"We are not having this conversation. You're not well enough to be in love with anybody." Adrian set a hand on his shoulder. "All you need to do right now is lie down and get some rest. You've still got a long way to go."

The touch of Adrian's hand on his skin was like a live current coming into contact with water. Gabriel tore away from him and scrambled across the bed, heart in overdrive. More than ever, he wanted to run, but he knew his body would fail him. What would he do if he managed to get out of the house, anyway? Lose himself in the woods? Without a water source, he'd die. Addled by heat, he wouldn't be able to care for himself. And for what? For an escape from the harsh reality of his life? As a physical rebellion against what was being decided for him? He could run all he wanted, but he would never solve any of his problems if all he did was avoid them. During the bust, he'd buried his head in the sand and let himself be guided, and it had ended in ruin—but now he'd found someone he actually cared for, and someone he thought might care for him.

Gabriel couldn't listen to Adrian. He wouldn't. "Don't tell me I can't love. You have no idea what I can do. You need to take me to see Sir."

"You're not going anywhere." Adrian's voice was shielded and used the same flat, emotionless register he often adopted when talking to their mother. "You're in heat, Gabriel. Your thoughts are jumbled, your body is weak, and if you leave this house, someone out there is going to knock you up. You're under my care again, and you're going to do what I say."

Why was Adrian so stubborn? Gabriel balled his fists, squeezing the blankets. "I'm not going to do what you say!"

A flicker of emotion returned to Adrian's face—surprise. It parted his lips and widened his eyes almost imperceptibly, but Gabriel saw it. If he could get a reaction like that out of Adrian, then all he had to do was keep pushing, and eventually, he would cave.

"You can tell me until you're blue in the face that I can't love anyone, or that I'm b-broken, but you're wrong! I can fall in love just like anyone else. I can know happiness, Adrian! Maybe I'm not normal, but that doesn't mean I'm incapable of emotion. I hurt like you. I laugh like you. I cry like you. And you know what? I love like you, too, and I *love* Sir."

"You loved Garrison what, a month ago?" Adrian wasn't angry—he was crestfallen. Surprise had bled into regret, like he was standing vigil over a tragic event. "How can I believe you? You're in heat. The last week, your hormones have been influencing your thoughts and urging you to settle down with an alpha who can fulfill your biological drive. I know it feels like love, but—"

"Go." Gabriel's hands trembled. What Adrian was suggesting made him feel dirty. It was *wrong*. "Get out!"

"Where am I going to go, Gabriel?" Adrian frowned. "If you don't have me here, you're not going to make it through your heat.

220

You didn't prepare for it. If it wasn't for Sterling dropping off supplies—"

"GO!" Frustration brought tears to Gabriel's eyes and pumped through his veins like fire. Paired with his heat, the sensation was unbearable. Adrian didn't want to understand, and he would keep saying hurtful things until he broke Gabriel all over again and forced him to let go of the one good thing in his life. "I don't want you here!"

The mask came back on. Adrian's surprise and concern disappeared. "You're not doing yourself any favors by acting out like this. I know that you're not operating on all cylinders right now, but if you keep fooling yourself into thinking you're the only one in the world who can fix your problems, you're only going to cause more trouble for yourself. Ask me how I know."

Nothing Adrian said could fix the hurt that had been done. Discouraged, Gabriel dropped onto the bed and flipped onto his side, his back to his brother. He didn't want to think about what was about to happen to him—about how he was about to be taken away from the one man who'd ever meant anything to him.

"You probably won't even remember this conversation," Adrian admitted with a small sigh. He made his way toward the door. "I know that you're going through a lot right now, but I need you to stay strong. I promise, no matter how much you hate me, I'm not going anywhere. I'm not going to let anyone else hurt you, Gabriel. I won't."

Maybe it was the truth, but Adrian was doing a fine job of hurting Gabriel all on his own. Gabriel squeezed his eyes shut, curled up on himself, and let his heat take over his mind once more.

In the scorching fires of nothingness, he knew no more pain.

33

GABRIEL

Lucidity came in fragments. The air was too hot, and the
sheets too warm. There were times when Gabriel came
back to reality to find himself at the door to the sun room,
the muscles in his arm strained as he tried to twist the handle the
wrong way. The cold air from the cracks beneath the door felt good,
and his heat-addled brain wanted relief. Usually, it wasn't long
before Adrian swooped back into the room, a bottle of water or
some easy-to-eat food in hand, and put him back to bed. Gabriel
only had the time to step into the sun room once, and when he did,
the chilly autumn air took away his pain.

At least, some of it.

The heat had robbed Gabriel of his mind, but it hadn't robbed
him of his emotions. An emptiness swelled in his chest, a void
between his lungs that was as dark as it was bottomless. As he
gazed through the screen separating him from the world at large, it
hit him in full.

He was alone.

Darkness came, and when Gabriel stirred again, he was back in
bed where the sheets were too hot and the clothes he wore clung to
his body. Adrian laid across the foot of the bed on his back,

holding his phone up over his head as he browsed the internet. He didn't turn to look at Gabriel before he spoke, and his thumb kept flicking across the screen. "Are you awake now? Do you need some water?"

"Adrian?" Gabriel asked, heartbroken. "I don't feel well. It *hurts*."

Adrian set his phone down and sat up. He squinted at Gabriel, but whatever thoughts passed through his head were hidden. "Are you aware now? Did you shake it?"

"I don't know." Gabriel closed his eyes and pulled his knees to his chest. He wanted to strip off his t-shirt and fling it across the room. The way it clung to his skin frustrated him. "There's something inside of me that *hurts*."

Adrian got up and settled by Gabriel's side. "Where?"

"In the middle of me." Gabriel hugged his knees closer to his chest. If he curled up on himself tightly enough, maybe he'd be able to fill the empty space inside. "It's empty."

"Gabriel..." Adrian sighed. He reached down and plucked a water bottle off the floor, then twisted the cap right off. The serrated plastic snapped, the sound so loud in the room that Gabriel jumped. "You're okay. I promise. I know that a lot is going on, but you're fine. All you need to do is rest."

The last thing Gabriel wanted to do was rest, but with Adrian keeping watch over him, he didn't have much of a choice. Miserable, he laid back down in his too-hot bed and did his best to dodge the spots where his body heat had made the fitted sheet almost unbearable.

"Things will get better, I promise." Weight shifted on the bed, and Adrian peered down at him. Gabriel blinked a few times to clear his vision, then closed his eyes and tried to forget. "We're going to get you home as soon as we're able, and from there, we'll figure out our next steps. You're not going to feel this way forever, I promise. I'm going to make things right."

"You can't," Gabriel croaked. Tears formed behind his eyelids and escaped down the sides of his face to soak into the pillows. "You can't fix this."

"Then who can?"

Gabriel pinched his lips together. The answer simmered inside until it grew red-hot, but he couldn't let it out. How was he supposed to take care of fixing his problems when he wasn't even good enough to get Sir to stay?

"You're going to be okay." Adrian's voice was soft and solemn, like he understood what Gabriel was going through. "I know how heartbreak feels. It's hollow, isn't it? Like this solid construct you thought would be the pillar of the world for the rest of your life turned out to be made of cardboard, and there's a storm on the horizon." Something solid, flat, and circular pressed against Gabriel's lips—the neck of the water bottle. "Drink. You need water. You'll feel a hundred times better after your heat is over if you drink enough now."

The water was warm. Gabriel drank, but with every swallow, the ripple of muscle down his throat increased in severity until he couldn't handle it anymore. He tore away from the bottle and rolled over so his back was to his brother.

"You're stronger than you think." Plastic slid against plastic. Gabriel listened to the cap find its home on the bottle. "You're going to get through this. It's okay to hurt. Life is pain in the same way that life is pleasure. We're creatures of experience, so—"

"Don't tell me that." Gabriel curled up tighter. Deep down he knew Adrian was trying to help, but his mind was fogged with the urge to find an alpha—*his* alpha—and start a family. It was hard to think of anything else. "Right now I need to hurt. I don't want to know what it'll feel like in the future. I don't."

"Okay." Adrian didn't sound angry, but he didn't exactly sound pleased, either. He ran a hand through Gabriel's hair, then stepped away. The sound of his footsteps let Gabriel track him from the bedside to the hall door. "But know that when you're tired of feeling like this, I'm here for you. I know it's not the same as having someone to love, but we're family, and I will always have your back."

There was a lump in Gabriel's throat that he couldn't swallow. The doorknob turned, its metal latch scraping on the strike.

"There are good people in the world, whether you want to believe it or not," Adrian murmured from the doorway. "There are people who want to help you—who'll love you, if you give them the chance. But behaving like this? Pushing away everyone so you can cling to the one person you think will turn your life around? It's not doing you any favors."

Gabriel squeezed his eyes shut.

"I love you, Gabriel." Adrian spoke firmly, but not unkindly. "Sterling loves you. We're here for you. But you have to be here for us, too."

The lump stayed put no matter how Gabriel tried to swallow it down. He clawed at his face and choked back a sob. The heat came back to swallow him whole.

On the seventh day, the vestigial symptoms of Gabriel's heat vanished, and with it went his excuse to stay in Sir's home any longer. The last few days he'd been alert, but traces of his fertility clung to the air, and Adrian refused to move him back to Sterling's penthouse until they subsided completely. Conversation had been stilted and awkward, and Gabriel took responsibility for it. Adrian had gone out of his way to make sure Gabriel knew that he was loved and looked after, but the pain inside remained.

No matter what he did, or what thoughts he clung to, Gabriel couldn't make it go away.

"Gabriel?" Adrian called from the kitchen. He'd started to amass their belongings and bring their bags to the door. "Before we go, I want you to take one last shower, just to make sure none of your heat is sticking to you."

"Okay." Gabriel stood in the living room, turning the collar Sir had given him over in his hands. The tall, firm leather had held his head up when Gabriel wanted to do nothing more than look away. It was supposed to have been his forever, but now, Gabriel wasn't sure if he wanted it anymore. If he couldn't be with Sir, what was the point?

"And Gabriel?" Adrian poked his head out of the kitchen, saw the collar, and made a face. "Can you please find a box or something to put that in? Just for my sanity?"

"Yeah." Gabriel nodded. "Okay."

The box the collar had arrived in was in the living room closet near the front door. Gabriel tucked the collar beneath his arm and went to get it, only to find it was on the top shelf far at the back, beyond his reach. Memories of the time in Sir's kitchen rushed back to him, and the collar met the floor as it tumbled from his grip. Gabriel blinked back tears and took a step back. If he could run, he could escape this. He could start over and try again.

But what good had running done him? And where would he run to, now that he knew that Garrison had never loved him?

The obstacle was small, but the emotional turmoil it brought was great. For years, Gabriel had been told that his only purpose in life was to be tied to a superior member of society—that even the simplest tasks were outside of his capability. Sir thought differently. Sir would have wanted him to get a chair from the kitchen so he could reach the box.

Gabriel looked over his shoulder toward the kitchen. Adrian was grumbling to himself as he wrestled to jam the last of Gabriel's heat-soaked clothes into his duffel bag. Ever cautious, Gabriel made his way to the kitchen table and took one of the wooden chairs. The hair on the back of his neck stood on end, and his instincts screamed at him to stop what he was doing and leave the task to someone better suited for it, but he didn't let old habits stop him from doing what he needed to do. Gabriel brought the chair into the living room while Adrian continued to grumble and squish clothes down as far as he could into the duffel bag, then set the chair by the closet door and took a deep breath.

He could do this. He didn't need anyone else to tell him what to do.

Gabriel stood on the chair and brought down the box, then put the collar inside.

"After your shower, we'll get going." Adrian tugged the zipper the rest of the way, then sat so his back rested against the wall. He looked from the kitchen at Gabriel. "I left fresh clothes on top of the toilet tank. We'll toss your old ones in the trunk of my car and leave them there so we don't bother Sterling. I don't have any more space in the duffel bag. Maybe tomorrow, while I'm at work, you could do some laundry. Sterling's composed enough about heat-laced scents that it's not going to be much of an issue, but I'd rather have it done and out of the way than looming over our heads."

"Okay." Gabriel bit the inside of his lip. "Will Sir be at the penthouse?"

"No." Adrian glanced downward. "Cedric's not going to be around anymore, Gabriel. We went over this. It's not healthy for you to be with him. You need to heal—not fall in love."

Fall in love.

Gabriel's heart fluttered, but at the same time, his stomach churned. The axis his world balanced on shifted, and the urgency of his situation made itself known. In a handful of minutes, he'd leave Sir's home and never return. He'd never see Sir again. A part of him had known it all along, but that part had been hushed by willful disbelief. Now, there was no time left to play dumb. If he didn't do something, he would never see Sir again.

"I'll go shower," Gabriel murmured. He dodged the subject, bowing his head as he took a few steps toward the living room door. When times had gotten tough in the past, and when he hadn't known what to do, he'd bolted. But now, even as his hamstrings readied themselves to sprint and his heart picked up the pace, his brain worked to piece together a new way forward.

He *could* do this. If he let himself breathe and told himself that there was a way forward, he could find it. Years under Garrison's command didn't mean that he was useless. Sir had taught him better. All he had to do was believe.

When Adrian didn't object, Gabriel continued on his way. As he went, he grabbed the notepad and pen Sir kept on the table by the couch, then closed himself in the bathroom and locked the door. A twist of the knobs sent water gushing from the showerhead, creating the white noise he needed not only to think, but to mask his activities. Secure in the knowledge that Adrian wouldn't suspect a thing, Gabriel sat on the toilet seat, clicked the pen open, and began to write.

34

CEDRIC

Oli slammed his beer bottle down on the table a little too hard and ran his arm across his mouth. The television was off, but the stereo system was on, and Oli's phone streamed music directly to the speakers. It was at a low enough volume that it didn't interrupt their conversation, but the background noise was appreciated—the quiet wrecked Cedric more than he cared to admit.

"And you know what I told him?" Oli asked with a snort. He shook his head. "I told him that if he wanted to knot my throat, he was better off swiping left, because oh hell, no. There's no way I'm letting someone clog my trachea. Some people may be into that whole breath control thing, but I prefer not to die by choking on alpha dick, thanks."

Oli stretched out his legs, arched his back, and lifted his arms skyward as he yawned. Cedric watched him from where he sat, unable to carry the conversation.

"Not even a chuckle?" Oli frowned. "I expected maybe a face, at least. Or a snort. Or some kind of quirky Cedric comment to tell me to broaden my sexual horizons and get with the times. But nothing?

I thought we worked through the worst of it last night. You know it's not your fault, right? Please tell me you're not sliding back down that slippery slope of guilt, because I spent all my energy pushing you back up it this past week."

Cedric breathed out steadily through his nostrils until his lungs were empty. He looked Oli over, from the undone dress shirt he wore to the black socks with a single hole on the bottom of his right toe. For the last week, Oli had been alternating between trying to find a job and helping Cedric feel better, and Cedric knew he owed it to his best friend to smile, but he felt like there was very little to be happy about.

Once more, what he wanted had been taken from him. He'd failed to keep another lover safe. There was no worse feeling than that.

"Shit," Oli mumbled. He repositioned himself on the couch, curling his legs beneath him while leaning heavily against the arm. "Alright. Well, I guess this is what resistance training is all about, right? If I've got to do more heavy pushing, then I'll work through the pain. Where are you at right now? Lay it on me. If we've got to work you back up from the very bottom, we'll do it."

"Do you ever feel like life is pointless?" Cedric looked away from Oli to stare at the wall. The rental Oli occupied had strict rules about driving nails through any surfaces, so Oli had decorated with photos cut out from art books and stuck the prints to the wall with mounting putty.

Oli snickered. "I think the better question is, when haven't I?"

Cedric shot him a withering look, and Oli raised his hands defensively.

"All right, all right, so I'll cut back on the gloom." Oli settled back onto the couch and looked Cedric over. "Yeah, I feel down from time to time. I guess that's how you're feeling now?"

"I feel like..." The tangled mess of emotion in Cedric's chest was hard to put into words. For a second, he struggled to pinpoint exactly what it was he wanted to say, fearful that if he dwelled on it too long, he might become ensnared. "I feel like maybe I'm cursed, and that I'm not meant to be in a relationship. I know that's a bleak outlook, and that it's not healthy, but this is the first time I've opened up to anyone since Brittany passed, and..."

"Oh, Cedric." Oli got up from the couch and sat on the arm of Cedric's armchair. "You ridiculously sad creature. You're going to put puppies out of business, you know that? If your whole BDSM career thing doesn't work out, you should take up making memes of yourself. #SadCedric might be the next big thing."

Cedric rolled his eyes. "Not helping."

"Well, what do you want me to do? Be sad with you?" Oli offered a sympathetic smile. "The way I see it, one of us needs to stay upbeat, right? If we were two sad sacks wilting across the couch bemoaning the obstacles in our lives, our negative energy would accumulate until it reached critical mass and we'd both probably explode from terminal sadness."

No matter how much Oli joked, there was always a hint of truth in what he said. Cedric knew it, and as much as he despised it, he couldn't let the kernel of truth from Oli's statement go. "I'm being dramatic about this."

"Of course you are." Oli punched his shoulder. "But you have every right to be, you know? You've been through shit. You deserve to mourn... but I don't know if I understand why you're mourning now. That omega must have really done a job on you if you're this hung up on him."

Being hung up didn't begin to describe how Cedric felt. It wasn't so simple. The matter was far from clear-cut, and the more Cedric thought about it, the more complex it became. Oli could boil it down all he wanted, but he'd never catch the essence of what Cedric had been through.

"It's... different." Cedric floundered for meaning. Explanation didn't come easily. "It's not the same as when Brittany died, but it's… it's hurtful in the same way. I lost him. Through my actions, I lost him, and I know I'm never getting him back."

"With an attitude like that, you're not." Oli leaned over to snag his beer from the table. He set it to his lips and drank, then took in a loud, satisfied gulp of air. "The difference between Brittany and Gabriel is that with Brittany, you have closure. There's no coming back from beyond the grave, unless we're talking seriously-messed-up-horror-movie shit."

Cedric shot Oli a glance, and Oli hid his grin behind his beer. When he was done, he set the bottle on the table and rolled his shoulders.

"Not helping," Cedric said.

"Details. Details." Oli waved a hand dismissively. "But you know what? I mean, apart from my little tangent, you can see what I'm getting at. There is nothing you can do about Brittany, and you know it. You have closure. It might not be the closure you want, but you can't deny it's there."

Cedric bit his tongue. What Oli said wasn't meant to hurt, but that didn't mean his words didn't claw at Cedric's soul.

Oli leaned forward, his eyes narrowed conspiratorially. "But you know, with Gabriel, you can still make things right. You might have sent him off in a selfless act of love, but you know what? You know where Sterling lives. That's his brother-in-law, right? You can track him down, and when you do, you can talk to him about what you're feeling. You can work things out. You may have made a mistake, but that doesn't mean you have to keep reliving that mistake forever. You can make things right."

"I'm making them right by staying the hell away."

"No." Oli's eyes flashed. "You're making them wrong by staying the hell away, and you can't convince me otherwise."

Silence fell. Cedric stewed in those words. Oli didn't understand because he didn't know Gabriel in the way Cedric did. Until he knew how delicate and broken Gabriel was, he'd never really get it.

But Cedric also knew that there was truth in what Oli said. As long as they were both still alive, there was always a chance to make things right. He'd spent the last week licking his wounds and feeling miserable about himself, but the truth of the matter was, he'd acted with integrity. He'd done what was necessary for Gabriel, and he'd acted with his best interest at heart. There was a chance that, given time, he could recover from this—that *they* could recover from this. In a few years, when Gabriel was in a better mental state and adjusted to the world, then maybe...

Cedric's phone rang. He jumped, and Oli hopped off the armrest he'd been perching on and went to sit on the couch again.

Sterling was on the line.

"Shit," Cedric muttered. The timing was too coincidental—Sterling's call was a sign from the universe, either that he was never meant to ever patch things up with Gabriel, or that he was. Cedric couldn't tell which. Heart in his throat, Cedric answered the call. "Hello?"

"Good evening, Cedric." Sterling was cordial as always. "Gabriel has just come home, so the house is vacated and safe for you to re-enter. Are you sure you don't want me to send a cleaning crew in to make sure the house is tidy when you get back?"

"No. No, that's not necessary." Cedric rubbed his eyes and tried to let go of the tension in his chest. "Thank you for letting me know. I really appreciate it."

"You're welcome." Sterling paused. It sounded like there was something more he wanted to say, but if there was, it went unsaid. "Have a good night."

"You too."

Cedric took the phone from his ear. The call time froze—Sterling had hung up.

"I'm guessing that wasn't your dentist." Oli laid back on the couch and turned his head to look at Cedric. "You're going home?"

"Yeah." Back to a house that would be too quiet, and whose

rooms held memories Cedric didn't want to recall. "Thanks for hosting me this past week. I really appreciate it."

Oli chuckled. "Hey, having a built-in dishwasher slave isn't so bad. You know, I could get used to this whole cohabitation thing. If you ever need a roommate, just let me know."

"You'll find a boyfriend before that happens," Cedric told him. He got up from the armchair and put his phone back in his pocket. "Then you're not going to want anything to do with a roommate. Why have someone living in your house who cooks and cleans for you when you could have all that plus a sex life?"

Oli raised a brow. "Right, because I've had so many men fighting each other for the chance."

The humor in Oli's words gave Cedric hope, and he shook off some of his melancholy. He'd move onward, and as he did, what was meant to happen would happen. All he had to do was get his head on straight and decide which future was the best one for him —and for Gabriel. "Seems like you've had plenty of interest, if this last week's ramblings about your dating site adventures say anything."

"Uh, no." Oli snorted. "When the highlight of my week is that a guy waited three days before telling me he wanted to ram his knot down my throat, then yeah, my prospects aren't all that great. Which means you have to try your hardest to make things right for you, okay? You've mourned Brittany for years, and you've honored her memory, but she'd want you to be happy. Isn't that what you always told me?"

Late nights at The Shepherd. Punishment by Brittany's hand. The thrill that came from proving his submission. The tug around his neck as she pulled at his leash...

All I want is to make you happy. Let it all go, and I promise, you'll find the way.

So many eyes on him, wanting, craving, who'd never been able to touch...

Cedric let out a breath steadily and slowly and nodded. "She'd want me to be happy."

"Then it's obvious what you have to do." Oli gestured at the door. "And it's up to you to make sure it happens. Like it or not, you're in charge of your own happiness now. If you're miserable, there's only one thing you can do: go out there and *do* something about it."

35

CEDRIC

The house was the same as when he'd left it, but the energy had changed. Cedric stepped in through the side door and overlooked the kitchen, letting it sink in. The light above the stove was on, and every small detail was as he'd remembered it, but the hum of the refrigerator and the airflow through the vents fell flat on his ears. The house he'd called home had lost its vibrancy. Cedric's heart had separated itself from this place.

There was a note on the kitchen table. Cedric spotted it through the dark and flipped on the overhead light before heading over to check it out. It had been written on the magnetized notepad he usually kept on the fridge in small, meticulous handwriting.

I stripped the sheets and pillowcases from the guest bedroom bed and tossed them in the washer. The blanket wouldn't fit. I left it in the basket by the washer, so all you need to do is stuff it inside. Figured it was the least I could do.

We ate some of your food, and I took out the trash before we left. Otherwise, everything is where it should be. If there's a problem, you can call.

Sorry for the inconvenience.

-Adrian

By the sounds of it, the washer wasn't running. Cedric stuck the notepad to the fridge on his way past, then headed to the basement to swap out the laundry. The blanket was where Adrian claimed it would be, folded neatly, like Cedric gave a shit about what it looked like. The gesture was small, but it impacted him in a large way, and Cedric sank to his knees and sat on the unfinished floor as the reality of his situation hit him hard.

Gabriel was gone.

In Oli's apartment, denying the truth had been easy. Separated from his home, his subconscious had tricked itself into thinking everything would be alright. Cedric plucked the blanket from the laundry basket and held it to his chest. The scent of Gabriel's heat clung to it, muted by time, but still present. It wouldn't be long before it disappeared completely. Before that happened, Cedric rested his head against the blanket and breathed.

Gabriel.

The steel of the washing machine was cold against his back, and a damp chill met his thighs, seeping up from the floor. Cedric closed his eyes and let it go, just like Brittany would have wanted. He detached from what he knew and what he believed to side with what he felt.

Arousal, of course, but that was natural. The scent of an omega's heat was made to stir an alpha, and Cedric understood that no matter how respectful he was, it was bound to happen. Longing, another given, but not because of biological drive—Cedric longed for what his heart had claimed, but what his head had pushed away. Then, beneath that, was something Cedric wasn't expecting. Determination strengthened his resolve and told him that he had to wait a little longer—that throwing himself back into Gabriel's life would do more harm than good. If he wanted Gabriel to heal, he couldn't keep picking at his scabs. The issues Gabriel struggled with were complex, and they would only worsen if Cedric aggravated them with his presence. Instinct told him to stay away, and he'd trust it. There were other ways to win Gabriel back than to spring headfirst into action.

He would be patient. He would bide his time and wait, no matter how much it hurt.

Pain is the precursor to pleasure, Cedric. Don't fear it—welcome it. Let it take you. Let it heighten your experiences. I promise, it won't be long now until you understand how good suffering can be...

Cedric shivered. He stood, knees wobbling, and dropped the blanket back in the laundry basket. The damp linens in the washer were free of Gabriel's scent, and he transferred them quickly to the dryer before they could be recontaminated. A twist of the knob on the dryer's control panel started the tumble cycle, and Cedric picked up the blanket once more. He carried it up the stairs and followed his heart not to the living room, but to the sun room. In the winter, Cedric kept the doors shut and sometimes went so far as to cover the windows if the temperature plummeted low enough, and on chilly fall nights, he avoided the room entirely, but a gut feeling told him it was what he needed to do. More than once, he'd seen the appreciation in Gabriel's eyes as he looked toward the room, like it bore a secret only he'd been trusted with. When Cedric's sock-clad feet met the chilled wood floor and his gaze focused on the dark forest beyond the screen covering the closed windows, he thought he knew what that secret might be.

Freedom.

For the duration of Gabriel's stay in his house, he'd been kept like a bird in a cage. It was the world he was used to—the only world he knew—but out here, divorced from the city and its claustrophobia, he'd glimpsed what it meant to be free for the first time. Cedric buried his nose in the blanket again and looked through the dark. Beyond the damage that Baylor had caused, and beyond the trauma Gabriel still suffered from, was there a young man inside of him who longed to be free? From his situation, from his keepers, and from himself? Every furtive glance, and every small act of rebellion... what was going on in Gabriel's head?

There was a lot to think about. Cedric lowered the blanket and went to head inside, but he stopped before he went any farther. There was a scent on the air that struck him as familiar. Wood and leather, and...

Just beyond the screen, a shadow moved. Cedric shook his head and turned. The night was starting to play tricks on his eyes, and his heart wasn't helping. What he needed was a good night's sleep. Tomorrow would be brighter, and the day after that brighter still, until his heart was healed enough that the way forward was obvious.

When that time came, he wouldn't hesitate. He would do what he had to do.

For Gabriel. For himself.

There was still a way out of this. All he had to figure out was which routes would lead to happiness, and which would lead to ruin.

36

GABRIEL

Gabriel packed leftovers into portion-sized storage containers, his body present, but his mind elsewhere. The granite countertops in Sterling's kitchen were beautiful, and the appliances in the penthouse were cutting edge, but Gabriel took little joy in them. Even a week after leaving Sir's home, his mind was elsewhere, lost in the reds and oranges and yellows of a place he'd left behind.

The kitchen lights were off, and only the tiny bar of LEDs supported beneath the kitchen cabinets lit the counter. The darkness was better. Sometimes, when it got dark enough, Gabriel could trick his mind into thinking he'd never left.

It was a different kind of pain from when he'd been dragged from The White Lotus by the man without a name. The hollow, empty feeling between his lungs remained, but the distress that absence caused wasn't anything Gabriel had felt before. In the past, he'd been afraid to be alone, but now, loneliness didn't frighten him. He'd been afraid when he'd been taken from Garrison because he'd believed he couldn't survive on his own, but Sir had taught him that wasn't true. The pain he felt now was linked to something different.

Regret.

Gabriel sealed the top of the container and started on filling the next. He'd prepared a stew earlier that morning that had simmered all day, and there was plenty of it left over. Slices of potatoes tumbled over tenderized meat, and Gabriel had to put the ladle down. The first night, in Sir's kitchen, where Sir had played with him like Gabriel deserved pleasure, too...

How different those times had been. Over the course of a few weeks, under Sir's tutelage, Gabriel had bloomed.

It wasn't like at Stonecrest, where the counselors were nice, but whose therapy sessions never spoke to Gabriel where he needed to be reached. For nine months he'd resisted what all of them had to say because he hadn't wanted to listen. There was no connection between them—no reason for him to want to change. Back then, no matter how they tried to convince him otherwise, he'd stubbornly clung to the notion that he was in love with Garrison, and that they were the ones in the wrong because Garrison had said so.

It took actually falling in love to realize that he was the one who'd been mistaken.

Gabriel brushed tears away from his eyes and picked up the ladle again. For so long he'd been passive, thinking it was what would make him worthwhile. Whenever a problem got to be too big, or he became too scared of its outcome, he ran. He allowed the worst to happen because he was afraid that playing an active role in the solution would make Garrison turn up his nose in disgust.

Omegas aren't made to do anything but be bred, Gabriel. Don't make me remind you again.

Who the hell was he worried would hate him now?

Sir?

Gabriel finished with the leftovers and sealed the last container. He stacked them one atop another, then picked them all up and brought them to the fridge. With the toe of his foot, he pried open the fridge door.

Sir would want him to take action. All along, that's what Sir had wanted from him. There was a reason why Sir hadn't done what Gabriel had asked him to do in his note—he wanted Gabriel to be the one to take responsibility. He wanted to know that Gabriel wasn't afraid.

The popcorn. The collar. The mirror.

Gabriel placed the leftovers on the shelf and closed the door. He needed to take action. If he didn't, he'd always regret the choices he didn't make.

The penthouse was quiet. Sterling was downstairs in the club, doing whatever it was that he did night after night, and Adrian was asleep in bed. Lilian's crib had been moved into his room since Gabriel had come to stay, and he knew that the sooner he got out, the sooner life for his brother would return to normal. Lilian would move back to her own room and there would be no hard feelings.

All he needed now was a plan.

Gabriel left the kitchen and returned to his small, screened-off section of the living room. Next to his duffel bag, now stuffed with laundered clothes free of heat, was the box he'd put his collar in —the same one that had shipped to Sir's home. On the top flap was a sticker with Sir's address. Trembling, Gabriel tore the section of the flap with Sir's address off and held it loosely in his hand.

No one was chaining him to a bed. No one was locking him in a room to force him to stay put. The shackles were gone. All he had to do now was find the courage to open the cage door and fly away.

Adrian's belongings were by the back door of the penthouse, assembled so he could grab them quickly before heading to work. Keys, wallet, briefcase. Gabriel stood in front of them, heart heavy, but knowing what he had to do.

There was a time in his life when he was willing to be bad so he could be good for Garrison. It was time to extend the same courtesy to Sir.

Gabriel opened his brother's wallet and took the money from inside. One day soon, he promised the universe, he would pay

Adrian back—but if he didn't do this now, he would never forgive himself. He needed to try.

The back door opened. When it closed, the penthouse was short a soul.

There would be no more inaction. Gabriel *wanted* this.

Garrison's lies wouldn't keep him from happiness anymore.

37

CEDRIC

A paper tumbled from the medicine cabinet a week after Gabriel's departure. It slid across the floor until it bumped against the bathtub and came to a stop. Cedric abandoned his quest for a Q-tip and picked it up—it matched the paper he kept in the living room. There was a message written on it shaky, chicken-scratch handwriting. In parts, the ink had run, and the paper showed signs of water damage in scattered, circular spots. Tears.

Cedric's breath caught in his throat and his heart lurched forward like he'd just hit a drop on a roller coaster. Without reading what the note said, he already knew who it was from. Reading it confirmed his suspicions.

I'm sorry I did that to you, Sir. It was wrong of me to do, and I'm not just saying that. I wish I got to treat you better. I know that you're disappointed in me. In the future, I'll do my best to remember not to mess up. Adrian says we're not going to see each other anymore. I don't want that. I don't want to be taken away, but Adrian says I have to go. I want to see you again. Can you come see me at Sterling's penthouse? I don't want to have to miss you anymore.

Cedric stopped reading before the note was finished. He

blinked away tears and tried to talk himself down from his sudden emotional high. Getting riled up over a note Gabriel had left him a week ago wouldn't do him any good. He'd already talked himself down from acting out of desperation. Right now, Gabriel's recovery mattered more than his feelings—but knowing that didn't make the note hurt any less.

In the future, I'm going to do my best to be good. I know that I'm not—

A few words were crossed out, struck through and scribbled over so intensely that Cedric couldn't make out what Gabriel had written. The text resumed.

—well, but I also know that you mean the world to me. I told you that I have a boyfriend and that I was in love with him and that I was supposed to make a family with him, but when I told you that, I was lying to you. I didn't know I was lying when I said it, but I was. I know that now. You showed me that. Garrison was a bad man, and he did bad things to me. I know that I'm—

A few more words were struck from the page, and the paper had torn where Gabriel had pressed the pen too hard. Cedric blinked away tears and ran his thumb over the wrinkled paper.

—not okay, but I'm doing my best to get better even if you can't see it. I want to please you. I want to make you proud and wear your collar and share your bed. I want to make you feel as good as you make me feel. I didn't know that it was possible to feel good like that, but you showed me it is. All you did was be kind to me and I hurt you and I'm so sorry.

A whole paragraph was blotted out. Cedric wiped the tears from his eyes with the back of his hand.

Adrian says that I can't love you because a few weeks ago I said I loved Garrison, but I don't think that's true. He's smart about a lot of things, but he's not always smart about me. He doesn't know that I never loved Garrison. I don't think anyone does. I only found it out for myself after I met you because I figured out that I love you, Sir. I love you, and I went about showing it to you the wrong way, and I'm sorry. I wish I hadn't messed up so bad.

Cedric's hand trembled. He sat on the toilet and set his hands on his lap, but it did little to keep the paper from rustling.

Please come see me. Please. I hurt inside because you're not here, and I promise I won't try to get you to take my heat next time. I promise I'll be good. We can work together to make sure that I'm better and then we can be happy and I can give you a family when you want it and then we can be happy together. I won't ever be mean to you or disobey you or make you angry. You won't ever have to send me away again.

The last of Cedric's willpower ran out. Tears streamed down his cheeks, and he let out a single, shuddering sob that he couldn't swallow no matter how hard he tried.

I love you, Sir. I'm sorry I didn't know how to show it. When we get back together, can you please teach me how to love properly so I don't hurt you again? Because all I know how to do is wrong, and I want to do right. All I want is to be good.

There was no signature. There didn't have to be.

Cedric set the note on the counter and covered his face with his hands. Grief had never felt like this before. The profound ache in his chest crushed his lungs and shrank his stomach. It stole his will to keep going, and urged him to abandon logic and act on impulse. Cedric couldn't let that happen. Gabriel needed kindness. For now, all he could do was hold on and hope.

A noise jolted Cedric from a dead sleep. Light from the television bathed the living room in its glow, but the volume was muted—the sound hadn't come from it. Cedric rubbed his eyes and pushed Gabriel's blanket away. There was a chance that it was the furnace clunking back on after a period of inactivity, but it had sounded too loud and too close, like someone had bashed in the front door.

Cedric rubbed the sleep from his eyes. The front door was a few feet from the couch, and it was still in one piece. The lock was engaged, and the small, frosted window at eye level was undisturbed. It must have been a dream.

Groggy, Cedric searched for the remote and turned off the television. Memories from the night before returned, and with them came the same despair he'd harbored all evening. The note in the bathroom had torn him to pieces, and he still wasn't over it. To know that Gabriel was hurting and that there was nothing he could do about it shook Cedric's faith in himself. If he was this easily ruined by another, then what good was he as a Dom? The career he'd built for himself was founded on lies. At heart, he was still the meek submissive eager to listen and obey. Who was he, playing at something he wasn't?

Before Cedric found the remote, another clattering *crash* broke the silence of the night. This time, Cedric knew he hadn't imagined it. He bolted up from the couch, head spinning from the sudden change in position. It wasn't the front door that was under attack—it was the side door in the carport.

It happened again, and this time, Cedric heard the knob crash against the wall-guard. Booted feet struck the kitchen floor.

Someone was in the house.

Cedric grabbed the closest thing he could find—the lamp off the table. The plug separated from the wall and hit the ground. The noise was much louder than he would have liked, and the footsteps stopped.

A man chuckled in the kitchen. Cedric's blood ran cold.

He grabbed the lamp's cord and wrapped it around his free hand so the plug stayed off the ground, then slowly, he crept forward. If he could get to the kitchen doorway and hide to the side, he could surprise the intruder and clock him over the head with the lamp.

Cedric didn't get the chance.

The footsteps in the kitchen started again, and when they did, they came quicker than before. All Cedric had time to do was widen his stance and prepare for attack. The intruder barreled through the kitchen and came to a stop in the doorway. He didn't need to come any closer. The light from the television bathed his face in haunting shadows, and Cedric's eyes widened.

"Hello, Cedric," the man said. His teeth gleamed in the dim light, and his eyes shone with unmasked cruelty. The air smelled of wood, leather, and... "It's so nice to see you again."

GABRIEL

"I t'll be $21.85, kid."

Gabriel unfolded a twenty-dollar bill from his pocket, then counted his singles. One. Two. Three. Four. He handed the money to the driver, then opened the car door and stepped outside. In his hand was the jagged piece of cardboard he'd torn from the box his collar had arrived in.

Cedric Langston
514 Goldfinch Rd.

The rest of the address had been left behind, but Gabriel didn't need it. Sir lived in Aurora, and the taxi driver had plugged the address into his GPS and found it without issue. There was no mistaking the bungalow. Soon, Gabriel would be home.

"Thank you," Gabriel said before he shut the door. He stepped around the taxi and onto the sidewalk, taking in the house he'd thought he'd never see again. As the taxi left, Gabriel gathered his wits and approached the front door. It was early in the morning, and he knew Sir would be sleeping, but if he needed to, he could figure out which of the house's front-facing windows belonged to his bedroom. If he tapped at the window for long enough, Sir would wake up and open the door for him. They'd have a frank conversation about expectations and how Gabriel could be good, and then all would be well with the world.

He approached the front door.

The doorbell was a slender rectangular button set to the right of the frame. Gabriel lifted his hand to push it, then stopped.

There was conversation happening on the other side of the door.

It was early in the morning, and Gabriel was certain that Sir lived alone. Nervous, he pressed his ear closer to the door and tried to hear what was going on. Sir wasn't the type of man who'd bring an omega home so soon after his last one had left, was he? If that was the case, Gabriel was out of luck. He'd only borrowed enough money from Adrian to get him to Sir's house—he had no way to get home.

"Get the hell out of my house." Sir's voice was darker than Gabriel had heard it before, but it was stronger, too—unyielding. "You're not welcome here. Get the *hell* out."

Gabriel laid his palms flat on the door and closed his eyes, trying to hear the response. The other person stood too far away from the door, and all he heard was a distant, masculine rumble. Jumbled noises like those offered no answers.

"You need to leave." Sir's voice was steel. He didn't sound like himself at all. "I swear, if you don't…"

The voices behind the door drew closer. This time, Gabriel heard the reply. "You don't have any say in this, Cedric. It's not your place to make demands anymore."

The bottom dropped out of Gabriel's stomach, and he pushed back from the door in horror.

He knew that voice.

He *hated* that voice.

It was the man without a name.

Reeling from what he'd heard, Gabriel took a few, hasty steps backward and almost tripped down the stairs. He caught himself on the railing and gasped for breath as his throat convulsed. Sickened, he leaned over the railing and dry heaved into the shrubbery by Sir's front door. It had to be a nightmare. The man without a name couldn't be inside. He *couldn't*. Now that Gabriel didn't live with Sir anymore, the man without a name had no reason to be there. He should have given up and left Sir alone.

The nightmare would end if Gabriel walked away. The man without a name didn't know he was standing outside the door. All Gabriel had to do was leave—to take the sidewalk and turn the corner, then lose himself in the city until he found a pay phone so he could call Adrian to pick him up. But if he did that, there was no telling what the man without a name would do to Sir.

One year.

For one hellish year, Gabriel had been at the mercy of the man without a name. He'd suffered at his hand and done things he regretted. He hadn't had a choice. If he left now, there was a chance that the man without a name would take Sir, and he'd do the same terrible things to him that he'd done to Gabriel.

Or maybe he'd do worse.

Gabriel couldn't let that happen.

Sick to his stomach with nerves, Gabriel hobbled down the stairs and sucked in a breath. A small voice inside told him that he was foolish—that all he was good for was serving an alpha, and that there was nothing he could do to help Sir. But Sir had taught him better than that.

It was okay to be scared. It was okay to feel weak. What wasn't okay was giving up without trying.

Sir deserved his best.

Gabriel rounded the side of the house and entered the carport. The lights were off, but the door was open. The man without a name spoke from deeper within the house, gloating. The individual words were lost, but their malice wasn't.

One at a time, Gabriel took off his shoes and left them in the carport. The gritty asphalt of the driveway stuck to the bottoms of his socks, and he said a silent prayer that no small stones would catch on the cotton. What he was about to do, he needed to do in silence. Stones tapping against the kitchen floor with each footfall would give him away.

Gabriel let go of one last, shuddering breath, then filled his lungs and held the air inside. As his panic built and his world started to spin, he set foot inside Sir's house and started to creep across the kitchen floor.

CEDRIC

The back of Cedric's thighs hit the arm of the couch, and he winced. The hand he'd wrapped around the lamp cord shot down to brace himself, but the cord went taut before he could reach, and he stumbled. The force pulled the lamp from his hand, and it swung down and clattered against the table. Cedric grabbed at the couch to steady himself, but by the time he'd regained his balance, it was too late. The familiar stranger was right in front of him, and the gun he carried nuzzled the underside of Cedric's jaw to force his gaze upward.

Leather and wood and something... off. Cedric gazed into the man's eyes and remembered that smell.

Five years ago, wearing nothing but a sheer black thong and Brittany's collar, he'd seen those eyes leering at him from across The Shepherd. He'd tasted that scent on the air as Brittany brought him to his knees in one of the private rooms and ran the leather tails of her flogger across his back.

Pain is the precursor to pleasure, Cedric...

Those eyes, boring through him as the tips expertly bit into his back. That gaze, piercing him as Brittany struck again, never high enough to wrap around his shoulders, and never low enough to do damage to his kidney area. The surge of endorphins, and the way the world melted away.

Let it take you. Let it heighten your experiences.

There'd been so many who gathered to watch the fall of a young, virile alpha male at the hands of a beta Domme, but only one set of eyes stayed with him, their hunger unparalleled. And now, so many years after his last appearance at The Shepherd, Cedric looked into them again. The hunger had grown more wolfish over time.

Eyes like those would eat him up.

"Look at you," the man murmured. The pistol pushed Cedric's head up farther, and Cedric had no choice but to bare his neck for the man. "Five years older, but no less handsome. I wish I wouldn't have waited so long. I can only imagine what it would have been like to have you by my side as you grew into the young man you've become."

Cedric's lips twitched, but there was nothing he could say. With the muzzle flush against the underside of his jaw, he was afraid to speak.

"But you're lucky—I'm done waiting now. It's time to pluck you while you're in your prime. I won't have you stray from me. Not again. Never again."

"Please, put the gun down," Cedric said through gritted teeth. He closed his eyes as if doing so would erase the danger he was facing.

"And what? Have you swing that lamp at me?" The man laughed. He reached out and glided the wrapped cord from around Cedric's hand. The lamp clattered to the floor. "No. That won't do. I'm not going to give you the chance. Until I have you where I want you—where I know you'll be good—I'm going to use this to keep you docile. You've grown wild over the years without someone to look after you, haven't you? Playing at Dom, pretending that you're strong when deep down, all you want to do is submit..."

The man brushed his fingertips along Cedric's cheek. His skin was cold to the touch, and Cedric had to fight the impulse to yank his head away.

"I'm glad I found you when I did," the man admitted. His fingers found their way to the back of Cedric's head to caress his hair. He'd drawn so close that Cedric could almost taste his vile breath. Alcohol, Cedric noted, and nicotine. "I knew if I was patient, you'd come back. The Shepherd is there to guide lost souls like your own—souls who need the stern, commanding hand of someone far more experienced. And what a coincidence it is that the second you came back into my life, you brought with you my beloved toy."

Toy? Cedric opened his eyes to search for meaning on the man's face, but there was none to be found. The crazed look in his eyes overshadowed reason.

"When I've got you where I want you," the man explained, weaving his fingers through Cedric's hair until his hand cupped the back of Cedric's head, "then I'll turn my attention on bringing him back, too. A full toy box. I know that you like him, Cedric. I've seen how you've looked at him—how he makes you forget who you really are."

Cedric's pulse rushed in his ears. *Gabriel.* "You leave him out of this. He didn't do anything."

"He did more than enough." The man tutted. "I got bored trying to find you, you know. I thought after I killed Brittany that you'd come back to The Shepherd and look for comfort, but that never happened, did it?"

No.

For a second, the world stopped. Cedric looked into the bestial eyes staring him down as the dam burst, and every emotion he'd repressed over the last five years gushed back to the surface. "What did you say?"

"You were supposed to find me," the man murmured. His fingers tightened in Cedric's hair. "What's a sub without his Dom? Nothing. Alone, frightened, unable to cope... you should have come

259

back to the club, and I would have taken care of you. I would have taken all your pain away."

"What did you say?" Cedric demanded, his voice warbling as it raised in pitch.

"But you never came back for me, and then you moved, and I lost you. Can you imagine that? I *lost* you. The only one I wanted, and you vanished. Do you know what pain you put me through?"

The gun didn't matter anymore. Hot lead embedded in his skull didn't frighten him. Cedric lurched forward with a strangled cry, but the man's grip on his hair held him in place, and all he succeeded in doing was sending searing pain through his scalp. "You *killed* her?"

No suspect. No known motive. No trail. The mystery of Brittany's death had haunted him for years. All the nights he'd spent awake in bed, unable to sleep as his mind tripped over every "what if" and "if I'd only...", were for nothing. It was his fault. Brittany had been killed because the psychopath crouching over him wanted to keep Cedric for himself.

"Shh. Keep your voice down, Cedric. It's not polite to yell. You don't want me to punish you when we get home, do you? Not when you're still so new, and my love is still bottomless. Let me spoil you. Let me make you feel good. Don't give me a reason to make you suffer."

"Who the fuck are you?" Cedric snarled. Each breath he took was labored, and his chest heaved from the exertion of keeping still. "Tell me who the *fuck* you are right now."

"I'm your new Master."

The man twisted the hand in Cedric's hair to redirect his head, then pushed the gun tighter against his jaw to make sure he followed through. Cedric had no choice but to tilt his head to the side and accept as the man leaned in close so their lips could brush. Sickness and anger rose as one inside of him, and Cedric sucked his lips into his mouth and bit down on them to keep the man from touching him any further.

"That's no way to treat me, you know," the man murmured. He pulled back and looked Cedric in the eyes, and Cedric committed to memory every repulsive feature of his face.

A bulbous nose, its large pores blackened with clogged sebum. A pronounced, square chin—deceptively handsome. Broad shoulders, powerful and muscular instead of hunched. A thick neck with pronounced tendons. Narrow, hungry eyes that devoured instead of appreciated. He was the same man Cedric had seen at the bottom of his driveway the day he'd heard the noise in the carport, and the same scent he'd smelled when he'd walked into the sun room with Gabriel's blanket and had seen the shadows shift.

All this time he'd been watching, and Cedric hadn't clued in. He bit back on his frustration and remained silent. Until the gun wasn't nudged against his jaw, there was nothing else he could do.

"I want to treat you nicely, Cedric. I want to reward you. I saw you playing with my old toy, and if you're good, I'll bring him back so we can play with him together. You'd like that, wouldn't you? To have a toy of your own to play with?"

"No," Cedric hissed through his teeth. He kept his mouth shut, afraid of the consequences if he moved too suddenly or put pressure on the gun. "You leave him out of this. He's innocent."

The man cackled. "Innocent? You don't honestly believe that, do you? When I found him, he was wasting away in Baylor's filthy brothel, throwing himself at whatever men Baylor wanted. When I took him home, he didn't fight me. He was mine for a whole year, you know, before he ran away and found his way into your arms. There's nothing innocent about him. A boy like that was made to be bred."

Nothing mattered anymore. Not the fact that the man was holding him by the hair, not the gun pressing against his jaw, and not the fact that he was confronting a confessed killer. With a roar summoned from the depth of his being, Cedric launched forward and swung at his aggressor. Blind rage dictated his movements, and he barely felt as his fist slammed into the man's face. They toppled together onto the ground. Cedric had no idea where the gun was, and he couldn't bring himself to care.

The monster that killed Brittany wouldn't take Gabriel, too. He'd lost one lover to this scumbag—he wouldn't lose another.

Cedric's fist connected with the man's face once more. Spittle flew from the man's lips as his head jerked to the side, but it wasn't enough. It would never be enough. This disgusting excuse for a human wanted to harm Gabriel, and Cedric wouldn't stop until he wasn't a threat anymore.

He drew his arm back to strike again, but before the punch connected, the man lashed out and grabbed him. They rolled over so the man was on top, pinning him to the floor.

"Don't make me hurt you, Cedric," the man rasped. The gun was a fraction of an inch away—the man had dropped it to pin Cedric's wrists to the floor. "All I want is to take you home and make you mine. Can you imagine the life you'd lead? Free of responsibility, worry, and thought, you could indulge in submission all you wanted. No one else could tame an alpha like I could. You'd never be satisfied with another partner."

"I'll kill you if you touch him," Cedric snarled. He fought against the man's hold, but failed to break free. "If you lay a hand on him, I'll end you."

"He's just a toy, Cedric," the man said, saccharine regret tinging his words. "There's nothing special about him. He's a sad, broken, useless waste of skin that we'd be stupid not to play with."

"No, I'm not," a voice said from just behind the man a second before a metallic *clang* echoed through the room. The man slumped onto Cedric's chest, dead weight. Behind him stood Gabriel, a frying pan in his hand, his chest heaving with every breath. "And I'm never going to let you forget it again."

40

GABRIEL

The frying pan was too heavy in his hand, and Gabriel cast it aside. It clattered on the living room floor, louder than it should have been. The world spun and his fingers were numb, but Gabriel didn't let the terror win. As long as Sir was in danger, Gabriel would not give in.

Sir shouted at him, but words had lost their meaning. The whole universe rang, like a gong had gone off in the distance, and its vibrations were everlasting. All Gabriel could do was trust his instinct, and his instinct told him to get the man without a name off his lover.

Gabriel grabbed the man without a name and dragged him to the side, his task made easier by Sir's eagerness to get up from the floor. When Sir was freed, Gabriel picked up the gun and lifted his gaze until he met Sir's eyes.

"Here," Gabriel said. Even he heard his voice wilting.. He pressed the gun into Sir's hand. "It's not safe for me to touch it anymore."

The world grew small and frightening once more. Gabriel didn't fight it. His knees gave out and he fell forward, but he never hit the ground—Sir caught him and held him close, and in his arms, Gabriel let his panic rob him of his senses.

There were lights when Gabriel opened his eyes, red and blue against the cold night. He blinked several times. The last time he'd seen police lights, he'd been at his parents' house, freshly returned from a failed expedition to find Garrison after escaping from the man without a name. Had everything else been a hallucination?

Sir's hand slid protectively over his thigh and shattered that possibility. They were perched on the sidewalk, Gabriel cuddled up against Sir's side, as officers stormed the house behind them.

"Sir?" Gabriel asked. His voice broke, and he cleared his throat.

"Everything's okay, Rabbit," Sir promised. The hand once on Gabriel's thigh wrapped around his shoulders instead. It brought with it a blanket—the same heavy kind that Gabriel remembered from the day he'd returned to the Lowe household. "You're safe. I've got you. No one is going to take you away from me. No one."

Safe.

Gabriel closed his eyes and let go of his fear. The man without a name was being apprehended by the police, and Gabriel was back at Sir's side. No one had been taken and kept against their will, and as far as Gabriel could tell, Sir wasn't hurt. Really, that was all that mattered. Against all odds, they'd come out victorious—*he'd* come out victorious. For the first time in his life, he'd gone up against an alpha, and he'd *won.*

The screech of nearby brakes brought Gabriel to open his eyes. Adrian's silver Lexus almost ran up on the curb. The second the car was in park, the driver side door flew open, and Adrian bolted from the car. Gabriel blinked, and as if by magic, Adrian had arrived at his side and dropped to his knees by the time he opened his eyes.

"Gabriel?" Adrian took his arm, as if the only way to tell if Gabriel was real was to touch him.

Gabriel managed a smile, but did not budge from Cedric's side. "I'm okay."

"What the hell are you doing out here?" Adrian was breathless, his voice shaking with fear instead of darkened with anger. "You know you're not supposed to see Cedric anymore. We talked about this."

"I needed to prove to myself that I could do it," Gabriel murmured. "... So I did. I'm sorry. I took money from you that I shouldn't have, too. I'll pay you back."

Adrian opened his mouth to speak, but he was cut off. Sir spoke, his words gentle but firm. "Gabriel saved my life."

There was a moment where the only sounds were police chatter and the heavy thud of boots on the sidewalk. Gabriel let that moment sweep away the rest of his anxiety. He was the cause of all this, both good and bad. What had been started, he'd put an end to. The man without a name wouldn't walk free anymore—he would answer for the crimes he'd committed, just like Garrison. Gabriel didn't care how many interviews and interrogations it took. The man without a name would not walk free. He would not let his fear or his inferior genetics stop him from seeing that man suffer.

It didn't matter so much that he'd hurt Gabriel, but the second he'd pointed that gun at Sir, Gabriel knew there was no way he could forgive him. No one would hurt the man who'd been so kind to him, even when he didn't deserve kindness. No one.

"Gabriel?" Adrian asked in awe. "Is it true?"

"No." Gabriel glanced at Sir. "I did what I had to do. That man... that man was the one who kept me, after the police raided The White Lotus. He took me from the room he was using me in and escaped with me through a back door, and he kept me in his house against my will. The things he did to me..." Gabriel closed his eyes and ended that thought. "He deserves to be in jail for the rest of his life, just like Garrison."

There was silence. When Gabriel opened his eyes again, he saw why. Adrian was staring at him like he'd seen a ghost, his eyes intense with confusion and his mouth open. Nothing more was said until an officer stepped forward.

"Sir," he said, speaking to Adrian. "I have to ask you to leave. This is a crime scene and you're not allowed to be here."

"I'm his brother." Adrian turned to face the officer, rigidity returning to his posture. "I need to be here for him."

"No." Gabriel couldn't stop, now that he'd started. It wasn't that he didn't want Adrian there, but he knew that all Adrian would do was worry, and that was pointless. There was nothing to worry about. The man without a name was being apprehended, and he would face the consequences of his actions. "I love you, but I can take care of myself. I promise."

Adrian didn't argue like Gabriel thought he might. He didn't even hum in disappointment. The officer gestured to the side, inviting Adrian to step away, but Gabriel shook his head.

"He doesn't have to leave if he doesn't want to. He's not disturbing me. But... but he needs to know he doesn't need to be here for me. I know that I haven't really been the most... I know that I've been through a lot, but I'm okay. I'm okay as long as I'm with Sir."

"If he starts bothering you, let one of us know," the officer said in parting. Then, just as quickly as he'd appeared, he disappeared into the chaos of the night.

Adrian sat at Gabriel's side, and for a little while, all three of them were silent. Gabriel leaned against Sir, and Sir kept the heavy blanket wrapped around their shoulders. Dry leaves skittered across the street, stirred by the wind. Officers barked at each other, and Gabriel was vaguely aware that an ambulance had arrived. A little more chaos meant nothing at this point. He was numb to it.

"I want to be with Sir," Gabriel said into the night. He didn't care who was listening. Whether anyone listened or not, he needed to get what he was feeling off his chest. "I know that I said I loved Garrison, but I never did. I know that now, because I know what love really is."

No one spoke. Leaves caught on the ridge by the sidewalk noisily. A stretcher was rushed into Sir's house.

"I know that I'm not normal." Gabriel let his eyes adjust to the flashing red and blue lights. It was hard to admit that there was something broken inside of him, but he couldn't keep burying his head in the sand. Denial was easy, but the truth? If Gabriel ever wanted a shot at the happiness he'd found, he'd have to embrace it. "I don't know if I can ever be normal like you want me to be. I'm not... I don't know if I can think that way. I might not ever be able to change, but that doesn't mean that I can't try."

Adrian set a hand on his knee, but it was Sir who Gabriel was focused on. The arm wrapped around Gabriel's shoulders tugged him closer, then abandoned his shoulder to run fingers through his hair. Gabriel held back a sigh of contentment and cuddled closer. It was a silent sign from Sir that everything was okay.

"So this is me trying," Gabriel said. "I know you don't think it, but I've changed so much since I came to be with Sir. I want to be good, but I don't want to be good in the way Garrison taught me to be. Not anymore. All this time I've been learning and listening, and even when it's too much and I'm too weak to do what's right, it's inside of me. All of it is inside of me. And maybe one day, when it all builds up, I can be more like who you want me to be. I can be someone who makes you proud."

"You already make me proud," Sir whispered. It was a simple statement, but it lit up Gabriel's world. The smile it produced was radiant, and Gabriel tried to hide it by burying his face against Sir's arm. To be praised like that by someone he loved made him want to be strong again and again.

"You've made me proud, too," Adrian said. His hand squeezed, then parted from Gabriel's knee. "Even if the police let you back in the house tonight, you're not going to want to stay there after what happened. Once you're released, come with me back to the penthouse. Stay the night, both of you. We have a guest bed."

"There's only one bed." Gabriel lifted his head from Sir's shoulder, frowning. Adrian had made it clear he wasn't supposed to touch Sir intimately. "The guest room was taken out for Lilian, remember?"

"I know." Adrian got up from the sidewalk and brushed off the back of his pants. "It's cold out here. I'm going to go sit in my car and call Sterling to let him know what's going on, and to expect guests. If you need me, you know where to find me."

"Okay." Gabriel bit the inside of his lip, equal parts excited by the prospect of sharing a bed with Sir, and dreading it. He knew the last time that had happened, he'd been bad, and he didn't want to disappoint anyone else. "I love you, Adrian. I'm sorry for making you scared."

"Scared?" Adrian shook his head and laughed a coarse, exhausted kind of laugh that made Gabriel regret the pain he'd caused him. "That's an understatement. But you know what?" Adrian's gaze softened. "I can take being scared, if this is what comes of it. I'm going to need a monster of a martini when we get home, though. You want the olive?"

Gabriel closed his eyes. "Yes, please."

With nothing more said, Adrian wandered back to his car, his hands dug into the pockets of his coat, leaving Gabriel to wonder what he meant. He didn't have long to think before Sir kissed the side of his head and sucked him back into the moment. The kiss melted Gabriel's heart and did away with the remnants of his panic. He opened his eyes again and lifted his head to look at Sir, only to find Sir looking at him with tender affection and kindness.

There was nothing said. There didn't need to be. Beneath flashing lights, they held each other. The look Sir gave him was enough to tell him everything he needed to know.

Whatever hurt Gabriel had inflicted onto him, and whatever emotional suffering he'd caused, it had been forgiven. In Sir's eyes was forgiveness and an eagerness to make things right. Gabriel had set out into the world on his own not to suit another man's agenda, but to do what his heart told him needed to be done. It had landed him in danger, and he knew that next time he needed to be more cautious, but at the same time, it had set him free.

He was worthwhile. He was important. He was able.

And now, he was Sir's.

It didn't matter how dangerous it was. To Gabriel, the risk was worth it.

41

CEDRIC

The house was quiet and the room was dark. It had to be closing in on four in the morning, but Cedric couldn't sleep. Not only was he wired from the confrontation with the intruder, but his mind raced with what had happened afterward.

The image of Gabriel, furious and panting as he stood over his abuser and took control of the situation, was etched into his mind. Cedric didn't think he'd ever forget it. And now, that same young man was curled beside him beneath the blankets they shared, looking at him through the dark.

"Sir?" Gabriel asked.

"Yes, Gabriel?"

"You're not angry about what I did, are you? Or the things I said? I'm sorry that I spoke like that. It's—"

"No." Cedric shifted closer. The sleeper sofa they shared was small enough that it didn't take much until they were chest to chest. Gabriel adjusted his position so their bodies were flush. "Don't be sorry about anything. I should be upset that you put yourself in danger like you did, but the truth is, without you, both of us would have been in even more danger. If you hadn't stepped in, bad things would have happened."

"He would have taken us," Gabriel murmured. His hand traced down Cedric's side, and just like that, the air thickened with the chemistry they shared. It hit Cedric right away, filling his lungs and plunging to his groin. He might have wanted to go to sleep, but his cock had other ideas. "I heard him. I heard all the things he said to you. I was hiding in the kitchen while he spoke, waiting for a chance to creep closer without being heard so I could help you. I'm sorry I took so long."

"No. I told you, don't be sorry about anything." Cedric traced his fingers over Gabriel's cheek, aching to kiss him. "What you did was perfect. I'm okay, and you're okay, and he's going to jail, and that's all that matters."

"I should have told you about him." Gabriel lowered his gaze. "From the very first day I came to your house, I picked up on his scent. You... you don't forget something like that, after you spend so long living in a nightmare. I don't think I'll forget it for as long as I'm alive."

"I won't forget it, either." Cedric's fingers traced down Gabriel's neck, then under his jaw along his chin. Stubble pricked his skin.

"I didn't want to tell you about what happened to me because..." Gabriel hesitated, but his gaze flicked upward. His eyes were partially lidded, and his face relaxed. Physical contact had always been an excellent way to soothe him, and tonight it did the trick just fine. "Because everyone treats me like I'm broken, and I didn't want to think it was true. I thought I was in love with Garrison, and that if I could trick you into thinking I was okay, that maybe you'd let your guard down and I could escape and find him. All I wanted to do was get back to him because I didn't know how to be on my own. I still don't, but the difference now is that I understand it."

All the times he'd run away, and all the times he'd clung to

Cedric seeking comfort. Over the years, Garrison had turned Gabriel from an impressionable teen into a subservient young man who couldn't function on his own.

Subservient, not submissive.

Cedric understood the difference better than ever now that he had confronted the truth.

"And I didn't talk to you about the man without a name because I was ashamed of what I'd let him do to me. I didn't try to fight when he took me out of The White Lotus. I didn't even scream. I was scared by what was happening, and I wasn't thinking straight, and... and so he took me, and he kept me in his house, and I hated it. I got out as soon as I could. I wish I would have told you. All of this could have been avoided if I was honest with you from the start."

Cedric's hand cupped Gabriel's cheek, and he waited until Gabriel was focused on him before he spoke. "If you were listening that whole time, then you know it wasn't you who was responsible for what happened tonight. You didn't cause any of this, and you don't have to blame yourself. Whether you were in the picture or not, that man would have come for me."

"But—"

"Shh." Cedric whispered. He let his hand wander back to stroke the short hairs on Gabriel's nape. "I won't argue with you, Rabbit. I'm here for you, remember?"

Gabriel was quiet, his lips parted the slightest bit, like he was waiting for a kiss. What he wouldn't give to make that happen...

"Let go of your pain," Cedric whispered. His fingers caressed, teasing Gabriel's hair. "Let me take your pain and make it my own. Let me shoulder it for you. I don't ever want you to feel like you belong to me, but I want you to know that I'm here to bear the weight of your world alongside you. When it feels like it's too much and you're afraid of falling apart, entrust your struggles to me, and let me chase them away."

The Gabriel Cedric had thought he knew wasn't the Gabriel who laid in bed beside him now. The meek, frightened creature he'd been told to dominate was gone, and in his place was a young man who'd started to find his footing in the world.

Cedric wasn't delusional—he knew that Gabriel wasn't cured. The warped mindset Garrison had instilled in him couldn't be undone so easily, and there was a chance he would never fully recover. But the initiative Gabriel had taken proved that all hope wasn't lost. Consent wasn't impossible. If Gabriel had the force of will to stand up for himself and subdue the alpha who'd done him wrong, and if he had the presence of mind to admit that he was broken, they had a chance.

The young man Cedric had fallen for had grown bolder, and the more confident he grew, the more Cedric wanted him.

"Adrian says we can't be together anymore," Gabriel whispered. He came a little closer, the tips of their noses so close, they brushed. "He says that after what happened, we have to live apart... and I think he's right."

Cedric's heart skipped a beat. "You do?"

"Yeah." Gabriel's hand rested on Cedric's hip, the contact between them electric. Sparks raced up Cedric's arm and invaded his chest. He couldn't hold them off if he tried. "I know that I'm not okay, and I don't want that to... I don't want that to come between us. I want to work on getting better, and to do that, I think we have to live apart. I don't know how to be on my own, so... so I need to be on my own in order to get better. Does that make sense?"

"Yes." Cedric wanted to kiss him more than ever. The confession was beautiful, and it reaffirmed his belief that a future between them was possible.

"I love you, Sir," Gabriel whispered, so small and so timid that the sound almost didn't make it to Cedric's ears. "I love you, and I need your help. Will you help me be strong for you? I don't know a lot of things, but I know that I want you. Even if it's hard, I'm going to do what it takes to make sure we can be together."

"I'll help you," Cedric whispered back. He lifted his head only enough so he could bring their lips closer, and when he spoke next, he let the words find their home on Gabriel's skin. "I love you, Gabriel."

The shiver he felt in response to his confession was innocent instead of frightened, and the kiss that followed it was sweeter yet. Gabriel initiated it, lifting his head to press their lips together. He took the lead, letting himself explore Cedric's lips while Cedric played the passive role and returned his passion, but never pushed for more. The kiss continued, uncontaminated by the aching need between Cedric's legs or his urge to mark the omega he loved as his. It was exploratory and cautious. Perfect.

"I don't want to go any further than kissing," Gabriel whispered against Cedric's lips. "Is that... is that okay? I know we're sharing a bed..."

"No, it's fine. It's better than fine." Cedric smiled. "I want you to always tell me what your limits are. I won't take anything from you that you're not willing to give, even if you've given it to me before. If, ten minutes from now, you decide kissing is too much, I'll stop. I won't ask for it again."

"You'd do that?"

"I *love* you." Cedric grinned, holding back a laugh. After all this time, after fighting with himself for so long, he was able to acknowledge what he felt out loud. There was no more shame. The past was the past, and he let it go. Gabriel was capable of consent, and the choices he made were rational instead of based in fear or desperation. Cedric couldn't ask for more. "You've given me your body and your mind, but you can always take them back. *Always.* My commitment is to serve you and to respect you... to bring you pleasure however you want. If you ever don't want something, all you need to do is tell me, and I'll stop."

"Then... then I want you to kiss me." Gabriel brushed their lips together to mark his statement. "I want to kiss until our lips are sore and we're too tired to go on."

"What you give me, I will take," Cedric whispered. He pressed a chaste, exploratory kiss to Gabriel's lips that made Gabriel moan. "And what I'm asked, I will perform. I'm yours, Gabriel. *Yours*. And no matter how long it takes, I will wait for you."

GABRIEL

"**O**pen your mouth, Gabriel."

Rabbit was gone, and Gabriel didn't miss it. He opened his mouth, eyes closed, and allowed Sir to place the pinhead-sized pill on his tongue. The box of prescription contraceptives sat on the bathroom counter within arm's reach, the packaging torn and the first pill popped out of its blister pack.

"Swallow."

Gabriel closed his mouth, and Sir pressed a glass of water into his hand. He raised it to his lips and did as he was told. The pill traveled with the water down his throat and entered his system. He welcomed it.

"Good boy." Sir took the water from him and set it by the remaining pills. "How does that make you feel?"

Gabriel knew better than to lie. He sucked in a breath and readied his response, considering it before he spoke, just like Sir wanted. "Good and bad. Good, because I know that I'm not ready to have a family, even though I want one with you so badly. Bad, because it makes me remember all the times in the past when... when he would tell me I just had to wait a little longer, and then he'd give me what I wanted."

"But was it ever what you wanted?"

The question was difficult. "... No."

"Justify." Sir took another box from the small pharmacy bag in the sink and opened the side flap.

Justification was difficult when Gabriel's thoughts were scattered. He closed his eyes and did his best to align what he thought was true, and what he knew was true. "It was true in the sense that I wanted stability and love, but... but a family doesn't always mean that. A baby doesn't guarantee that. I linked love to having a baby and it doesn't work that way. Having a baby won't make anyone love me more."

"Good boy." Sir kissed his forehead. The praise was simple, but Gabriel craved it. He smiled and opened his eyes to watch as Sir prepared the next pill. It snapped free from its blister pack and landed on Sir's palm. "Open."

Gabriel opened his mouth, and Sir placed the pill on his tongue. Heat preventatives were bigger than contraceptives, and if taken mindlessly, could have detrimental effects on the body. With his spring heat about to manifest, Gabriel knew that it was time. He trusted Sir's judgment entirely.

"Swallow."

The glass of water met his palm again, and Gabriel took a sip. The pill passed down his throat.

This time, he wouldn't go into heat. He wouldn't try to ensnare Sir. When they decided to start a family, they would make that decision together.

"Let me see," Sir said. Gabriel opened his mouth, then lifted his tongue. The pill was gone from his mouth. "Good boy. You can close it."

The release was appreciated. Gabriel closed his mouth and beamed, then looked up at Sir to search for further guidance. The tiny smile on Sir's face—almost unnoticeable—let Gabriel know there was nothing more he needed to do. He relaxed his shoulders and let himself rest. He'd been *good*.

Half a year had evaporated faster than a drop of water on a hot frying pan. During the hard times, when Gabriel had done everything he could to win Garrison's favor, time had come to a standstill, and six months had stretched into infinity. Not so anymore. Hours passed like seconds, and days like hours. Even the days when Sir was unable to attend their afternoon sessions didn't drag out—Gabriel was kept sane by the knowledge that soon, they'd be reunited, and that if he waited patiently, Sir would reward him.

Most days, Sir picked Gabriel up from the penthouse after waking up. Sir's new position in Sterling's club meant that their sleep schedules didn't match, but Gabriel took comfort in knowing that one day, when he was a little better, Sir would take him home for good.

One day, because Gabriel knew that he wasn't ready yet. Not now. The instability in his core was still too prominent, and his destructive thoughts still sometimes refused to leave him alone. When he was ready, he would give himself to Sir—but it was his choice to make, and he didn't mistake it. No matter what anyone else wanted, whether it was Adrian, or Sterling, or Sir himself, Gabriel would not give in.

Before he could let himself live with anyone else, he had to learn to live with himself.

"I want to take you to dinner on Monday night," Sir announced. He took Gabriel's hand, and Gabriel followed him from the bathroom. "There's a restaurant not far from The Shepherd I've been meaning to try that Sterling's recommended. Would you prefer to wear your blue tie, or your gray tie with your suit?"

A decision. It was small, but sometimes, even the smallest choices left him paralyzed. Gabriel bit down on his lip and quashed the voice inside that panicked about making the wrong choice. Sir had never punished him for making a choice before—in fact, Gabriel was pretty sure there never *was* a wrong option. The purpose of Sir's questions wasn't to get him into trouble. Sir was never cruel to him.

Never.

What he did, he did with love.

I want to see you grow, Gabriel. When I give you pain, I don't do it out of anger, but out of love. I want you to understand the difference. There is so much more potential in you, but if you aren't corrected and set on the right path, you'll never know it.

"Gabriel?" Sir asked again, the question firmer. "Blue or gray?"

"Blue." Blue, because Sir had mentioned before how the color brought out his eyes, and Gabriel wanted nothing more than to look good for him. "Thank you, Sir."

"You're welcome." They exited the bathroom, but they did not head to the living room like Gabriel anticipated. Instead, Cedric brought Gabriel to a door down the hallway that Gabriel had always assumed led to a closet. "Today, I want to offer you the chance to do something out of the ordinary. Are you interested?"

"Yes." Gabriel studied the door. There was nothing special about it. The color was plain, and the doorknob was simple and unremarkable. The bottom of the door was chipped, revealing the light-colored wood pulp inside.

Sir turned the handle and opened the door. Inside was a small, dark, windowless room. It was little bigger than a closet. Dark, blobby shapes in the distance suggested that it was used for storage. Sir pulled a metal ball chain dangling overhead, and a satisfying *click-click* woke the light the chain was attached to. Gabriel blinked twice to allow his eyes to adjust to the change in lighting, but even when his eyes focused, he wasn't sure what he was looking at.

At the very back of the room, positioned on a shelf high enough from the ground that it could be used as a table, was what appeared to be a microwave without a window panel. It was reinforced with matte white plastic siding and had buttons neatly assembled on the right-hand side. Six of those buttons were circular, two were triangular—one pointing up and one pointing down—and two were rectangular and color coded in green and red. Start and stop.

280

Gabriel squinted at it, but no matter how hard he looked, he couldn't figure it out. If it really was a microwave, shouldn't there have been nine round buttons?

"Sir?"

"It's okay, Gabriel." Sir stepped into the room. There were shelves to the left and the right as well, some stacked with linens, others holding boxes marked with post-it notes in Sir's sensible handwriting. Gabriel supposed it was a storage room, although the ample space at the back and the strange microwave led him to believe the room had other purposes. "I've been holding on to all of this for a little too long, and I decided that maybe it was time to see if I could put it to use again."

"I'm sorry, Sir." Gabriel followed Sir into the room. "I'm not sure what this is."

"This?" Sir gestured to the not-a-microwave. "This is an autoclave."

Gabriel made no comment and did his best to decipher what an autoclave was by examining it in closer detail. The round buttons weren't numbered—they bore symbols and words.

Optional cycle. Liquids. Wrapped...

He had no clue what he was looking at.

Sir twisted open a lock on the front of the door, then lifted the handle in a deliberate way. The machine gave, and the door opened. Inside, to Gabriel's surprise, was a round metal compartment with perforated metal shelves. The chamber was round, and reminded him of a tiny washing machine. On the inside, sitting on one of the perforated shelves, were flat plastic coverings that Gabriel only knew from the doctor's office—the kind that kept a doctor's tools sterile.

"Sir?" Gabriel asked again, more uncertain than ever. "What is all of that?"

Sir turned to look at him, kindness in his eyes. Gabriel took it into himself and breathed out slowly. What might have been panic dulled to nothingness.

"Once upon a time," Sir said, "I asked you what you thought of body modification."

The conversation in their first car ride together. The memories of Sir, nude, his tattoos vibrant and the shiny barbells through his nipples glinting beneath his bedroom light...

"When I asked you the first time, you didn't seem overly interested, but I thought that after our time together, that may have changed."

The snakebite piercings beneath Sir's lip, and the impressive geometric patterns that decorated his arm...

Sir pulled a stool out from beneath the shelf the autoclave rested on and sat. Gabriel didn't approach. He assessed the situation and tried to figure out what was going on.

"When I was younger, the woman I shared my life with was the one who tattooed me. I've told you that before." Sitting on the stool like he was, there was something about Sir that made it hard to look away. The casual nature of his posture was breathtaking, and paired with the way he clasped his hands between his legs, the stunning color of his tattoo sleeve vibrant against his pale skin, he looked so good Gabriel wasn't sure he wasn't dreaming. "But she did more than that. While I was with her, she taught me about what body modification is all about—the ins and the outs of the industry, how to pierce skin, and how to lay ink."

Gabriel's gaze swept back to the autoclave and all the carefully laid wrapping inside of it.

"I thought that I'd make a career out of it—work in her shop and serve beneath her." Sir glanced down for only a second, but Gabriel's heart skipped a beat regardless. He saw the hurt inside Sir, and it made him want to push himself into Sir's arms and do anything he could to make him forget his pain. "I was good at it. For a month or two, I apprenticed beneath her. I performed piercings while she watched from the side, and I observed as she made art from ink and skin. But when she died, that part of me died, too. I inherited her tools, but I couldn't ever bring myself to use them."

"Sir?" Gabriel asked, breathless. A tingling sensation ran down his spine, not unpleasant, but certainly not typical. Anticipation built. If Sir was telling him all this, then...

"Healing is a complicated process." Sir threaded his fingers together, his thumbs resting against one another, pointed at the floor. "I don't think it's the same for any one person, and I know that for me, it was a long and difficult journey... but I think, six months ago, that journey came to an end."

Gabriel's pulse thudded in his throat, and his body wanted to respond, but his feet were glued to the floor. In times like these, when the tension built in his chest and static-like anticipation raced down his spine, he was used to running. The feeling needed to get out somehow, and Gabriel knew no other way to express himself. Strong, confrontational emotions weren't encouraged. Garrison had taught him to be pleasant at all times, no matter how he felt inside.

But this? Here? Now?

Gabriel refused to run. Anticipation wasn't always a bad thing, and it didn't always lead to hurt. It wasn't fear that made his pulse race, but excitement. He would be a fool to run from that.

There was a moment where nothing was said. Sir met Gabriel's gaze, and Gabriel held it. He did not dip his chin. He did not look away.

"I'm ready to embrace who I was," Sir admitted. "After she died, I shut off that part of me, like I was wrapping a tourniquet above a wound in the hopes it wouldn't bleed out. But it's been a long time now, and I'm not bleeding anymore. I'm ready to take the tourniquet off."

The profound tone Sir used struck Gabriel in the chest, and it stirred his anticipation further. Staying still was difficult, and keeping himself collected even harder. The stimulation was too much.

"Today, I want to offer you a gift." Sir glanced at the autoclave, then looked back to Gabriel. "You told me you're not interested in body modification, but those words are cold and clinical, and they're not what I want to offer you. What I want to share today is a piece of who I am and who I was—a reminder of the power *you* hold over me, and the way you've pieced me back together when I was broken and ignorant of it."

The feeling in his chest twisted, and Gabriel tried his best to hold back tears. A facet of Sir he'd never known—a delicate piece of his past that Sir had hidden away for so long—opened up to him now. Gabriel had always been the broken one—the one who was never enough, who needed to get better. To realize that Sir thought the same negative things of himself dismantled his world in ways he hadn't anticipated. Affection and pity rose to fill the empty spaces inside.

"The choice is yours, Gabriel," Sir told him. "I want to pierce you—to share a piece of myself with you that you will always remember. I want you to remember every time you look in the mirror and see the glint of metal against your skin that not only are you loved, valued, and cherished, but that no matter how worthless you feel, you are *important*. You took a broken man and made him whole again by being nothing more than yourself. I never want you to forget it."

The tears Gabriel had tried so hard to hold off came all at once. He blinked rapidly to try to stop them, but it was no use. They streamed down his cheeks, and he brushed them away clumsily with the back of his hand.

"All I did was love you, Sir," Gabriel whispered, already hoarse.

"Loving me was enough."

All his life, Gabriel had run. From obligations. From problems. From family. From home. Crippling emotional vulnerability made him want to find a quiet place he could process his thoughts uninterrupted—somewhere he wouldn't be hurt.

But he'd told himself months ago that he was done with running away—so Gabriel ran forward instead.

Tears in his eyes, overwhelmed by the intensity of his thoughts, he closed the distance between himself and Sir and buried his face against Sir's chest. Sir's arms wrapped around him, and he stroked Gabriel's hair in slow, reassuring, and predictable ways.

"It's your choice," Sir reminded him in a whisper. "It's my gift to give, but it's up to you whether you take it or refuse it. I won't be mad, no matter what you decide. All I want is for you to do what brings you the most joy."

The thought that he could feel any happier than when he was with Sir was outrageous. Gabriel pulled back and smiled, meeting Sir's gaze without fear.

"I want you to pierce me, Sir," Gabriel whispered. "I want to remember that you belong to me, just as much as I belong to you."

4 3

CEDRIC

The backing of the sterilization pouch tore away from the transparent window, and Cedric's gloved hand freed the hollow needle from inside. Gabriel sat beside him on a stool in front of the autoclave, his shoulders relaxed and his cheeks still glossy from tears.

"Where on your ear would you like to be pierced, Gabriel?" Cedric carefully tore the packaging on the simple jewelry he'd prepared, careful not to contaminate the hollow needle.

"Anywhere, Sir," Gabriel whispered back. "I'd like for you to decide."

Cedric took a moment to consider Gabriel's face. The piercing needed to be subtle—a lobe piercing was too loud, and it wouldn't complement Gabriel's docile personality. What he chose needed to be understated and overlooked, but radiantly beautiful when it was noticed. The shape of Gabriel's ear made the choice clear.

"It's going to look elegant when it's healed," Cedric told him in a low, reassuring voice. He freed one of the sterilizing wipes from its packaging and ran it over Gabriel's skin to disinfect the area. Gabriel shivered. "When it's healed, I want it threaded with white gold and capped with a seed pearl."

287

Gabriel's eyes closed and his lips parted, but he didn't make a sound.

"The piercing won't be overly noticeable," Cedric explained. He discarded the wipe and assessed the part of Gabriel's ear he was about to pierce. All the while, he spoke to keep Gabriel's mind occupied. "It'll be subtle and gorgeous in an unexpected way."

He'd brought out Brittany's fine-tip surgical marker, but it wasn't going to be necessary. The piercing was Cedric's choice, and he trusted his hand. His heart knew where it needed to go.

"I need you to breathe with me," Cedric instructed, his tone even. "We're going to breathe in on a count of three, and then we're going to breathe out slowly until all the air is out of our lungs. Can you do that for me?"

"Yes," Gabriel promised. He'd yet to open his eyes, but his body language read as relaxed. Not only were his shoulders slumped, but his hands were open and loosely capped his knees. He bore no doubt, and trust like that spoke more to Cedric than words.

"Then let's breathe in together deeply. One. Two. Three." Cedric readied the needle. Memories returned. The sunny studio that had once been his every day, and the way Brittany had led his hand, reassuring and sure of herself. What he'd learned from her, he now offered to Gabriel. "And exhale slowly all the way until you empty your lungs..."

As Gabriel let go of his breath, Cedric pushed the needle through. The movement was seamless, and the positioning was exact. As Gabriel continued to exhale, no more bothered by the pain than the sound of Cedric's voice, Cedric freed the jewelry from its packaging and threaded it through the hollow needle. In one smooth movement he pulled the needle all the way through, leaving the jewelry in Gabriel's ear. He held it in place with a gloved finger and capped it, then sat back on his stool to examine his work.

The tasteful rook piercing, tucked near the fold of Gabriel's ridge, was beautifully set. When it healed and Cedric swapped out the post for one a little shorter and the head for the pearl he imagined, it would blend in against Gabriel's fair skin and only some-times catch the light. It was feminine and uncomplicated, made more unique by the absence of any other piercing.

On Gabriel, it was magical—a single mark, rich with meaning.

It was Cedric's gift to him, and in it, Gabriel's commitment to their future.

"You'll be away from me in the evening, so I'll have to teach you about aftercare." Cedric stripped the gloves from his hands and disposed of them. The piercing didn't bleed, and for a moment, Cedric allowed himself to entertain the notion that it was because it was fated for Gabriel's ear. He abandoned the stool to stand in front of Gabriel and slid his hands along the outsides of his thighs. Then, he leaned forward so that his lips were near Gabriel's unpierced ear. "Will you learn it all for me?"

Excitement swirled in Cedric's chest, starting between his lungs and racing downward like a tornado descending from the heavens. The chemistry between them ignited in the gale and rushed down Cedric's arms, raising all the small hairs there along the way.

Aftercare.

What would he give to see Gabriel with that faraway look, his body so strung out and yet so relaxed as he released himself to subspace? His bare chest would rise and fall as he struggled to catch his breath, and Cedric would wrap him up tight in his arms and hold him close so he could whisper beautiful things in his ear.

"Please, Sir." The arousal in Gabriel's voice barely broke through the storm going on inside of Cedric. "Please, teach me. I'll learn. I promise."

For six months, he'd guided Gabriel through the hell Garrison had left him stranded in. For six months, they'd touched each other in small, increasingly bold ways that only ever titillated, and never amounted to anything more. Heated make-out sessions on the couch and clothed groping was as far as Gabriel would allow him to go before he made it clear that he wasn't comfortable with more, and Cedric respected that. Simple pleasure would nurture Gabriel in the ways he needed. If he had to cast his own desires aside for Gabriel's sake, he would do so.

Sex would come. Consent had been established. All Cedric was waiting for was a sign that Gabriel's needs had evolved beyond the innocent.

And as Gabriel wrapped his arms around Cedric's neck loosely and let his eyes beg Cedric for more, he got the feeling he didn't need to wait much longer.

Cedric's hands trailed along Gabriel's thighs to his ass, and he locked his arms around Gabriel's frame. Gabriel's arms tightened in anticipation, and when they did, Cedric lifted him from the stool and carried him from the storage room. His bedroom was right across the hall.

"Never," Cedric uttered as he nudged the door open with his foot and carried Gabriel through the threshold, "try to clean your piercing with rubbing alcohol. Never."

"Never," Gabriel agreed, the breathy inflection of his reply making it anything but casual.

Cedric lowered Gabriel to the bed and took hold of his shoulder, pushing Gabriel back as he lifted a knee and climbed up onto the bed over him. "Never touch your piercing during the day. No one is allowed to touch it. Only me. And only I will give you permission each day before you leave me to clean it. You will not lay a finger on what I've given you until I tell you that you can."

Gabriel's back met the blankets, and Cedric moved him farther up onto the bed and kissed him, choking out Gabriel's reply. Whatever words Gabriel had prepared for him manifested as a hum that Cedric swallowed. Their lips locked, and the tornado inside Cedric went wild.

"Never," Cedric said, barely separating his lips from Gabriel's in order to speak. He kissed Gabriel again, long and hard, too attracted to him to hold back. When the kiss broke, he was breathless, and his cock ached for more. "Attempt to change the jewelry I put in. Only I will change it, and only when I see fit to do it."

There was no audible response from Gabriel this time around, but his tongue knew how to say yes. They kissed deeply, and as they did, Gabriel traced his tongue along Cedric's. Cedric accepted it gladly.

"Never," Cedric uttered when the kiss broke. His lungs were starved for air, but the burning only fed into the storm and added to its magnificence. "Pick at any scabs that form, or scratch at your injury. Leave your ear alone."

"What if Adrian tries to make me take it out?" Gabriel's eyes were glossed over with lust, different from any other time they'd made out like this.

Cedric smoothed a hand through his hair and looked down into the ocean-blue eyes that had stolen his heart from the very start. "You tell him that it isn't his choice to make, and if he tries to argue, then you tell him to come to me."

"I love you, Sir," Gabriel whispered. "I'm ready."

"I know." Cedric silenced him with a kiss, and the fire inside sparked and danced as it was set free on the winds of Cedric's desire. "And I'm ready, too."

44

GABRIEL

S ubmission was not mindless. Gabriel let his head roll back, the dull pain now throbbing in his ear secondary to the feel of Sir's lips on his neck and the way the smooth balls of his snakebite piercings grazed across his skin. To give himself to a man did not mean to turn his brain off, and to allow another to own him did not mean that he was no longer in control of himself. The power Gabriel lost, he entrusted to a man he knew would give back to him a thousandfold more pleasurable.

The choice was his when it had never been before, and Gabriel would never have it any other way again.

Fabric trailed across Gabriel's cheek, and he didn't realize until it passed over the bridge of his nose what it was—Sir had brought out a silk scarf, and he secured that scarf over Gabriel's eyes to deprive him of his vision. Gabriel let out a puff of air and squirmed, his body made more sensitive as his sight was taken from him.

"Sir?" he gasped.

Sir chuckled and kissed him, and the kiss was fire. Gabriel gasped into his mouth and returned Sir's passion with his own. Each touch was now a surprise, and Gabriel's body reacted to them that much more strongly for it.

Sir's teeth grazed along his neck, the promise of pain never far, but the delivery of pleasure constant. Gabriel took in a needy breath, and as he did, Sir bit down. The flat tips of his teeth pinched Gabriel's skin, and he tugged, but even as Gabriel cried out in surprise, he lifted his hips to seek friction against Sir's body.

In deprivation, he found bliss.

Sir's hips met his, and their rhythm forced Gabriel back down against the bed. The steady rise and fall stole Gabriel's senses, and he invested his trust in Sir to direct his pleasure. No matter what happened, Gabriel was ready for it.

"If I push you too far, and if you want me to stop, I need you to tell me." Sir's command ghosted across Gabriel's neck. "One word is all it takes. I want you to repeat it. *Revoke.*"

"Revoke." Gabriel's mouth worked independently of his head, and the word tumbled from his lips. "*Revoke.*"

"That's all. One word and I stop. Your command over me is absolute, Gabriel. Everything I am is yours."

Power. Once, he'd signed it away to a man who'd misused it—who'd told him that everything about him was worthless, and that he was lucky to have found someone to take care of him. Now, Gabriel knew better. Sir took his power, too, but what he left in its place was distilled and potent. Even as he nipped and commanded, he made Gabriel the god of his world—one he made offerings to in sensation, both pleasure and pain.

Now that he understood it, Gabriel would be benevolent.

Sir nipped again, the pain sharper this time. It radiated through Gabriel's neck in hot shockwaves of sensation, and he squirmed in an attempt to end the feeling—but Sir's offering wasn't complete. With a growl, Sir collected his wrists and pinned them over his head with a single hand. The other found the hem of Gabriel's shirt and ran up over his stomach. Compared to Gabriel's skin, Sir's fingers were cold, and the contrast made Gabriel tremble in delight.

Another unexpected nip. Another lofty peak of pain. The world was dark, and all Gabriel could do was trust that Sir wouldn't steer him wrong.

He trusted Sir with all his heart.

A kiss. A nip. A hand pulling his hair. Pleasure and pain stacked one atop the other until Gabriel struggled to tell the difference between them. What pain he did feel was beginning to build toward something different—a state of being that made Gabriel's toes curl and sent his heart racing.

"All of this for you," Sir promised, his words a secret only Gabriel's skin knew. "Let me make you feel like you deserve to feel. Let me prove to you that pain is worthwhile."

He was broken, brittle plastic snapped in ways that could never be slotted back together again. For so long, he'd denied it, but the truth had finally set in, and Gabriel embraced it. As pain washed over him, his body took it and transformed it. Rippling heat lost its scorching touch, and as it did, Gabriel vibrated to it.

Throbbing.

Swelling.

Expanding.

For that moment of time, driven into another headspace by Sir's worship, he was aware of every inch of himself in ways he'd never been before.

"Sir," Gabriel rasped. His voice was foreign to him, like his vocal cords had been rearranged since he'd last spoken. "*Sir!*"

The hand beneath Sir's shirt found his nipple, and Gabriel was shocked at how it stood erect. Flushed with blood and vulnerable, he *knew* it should have stung when Sir pinched it and pulled, but there was no pain. The pulsing pleasure he felt in his neck was mimicked in his nipple, and it washed through his chest and left him desperate for more.

It was only when Sir's hips pressed into him again that Gabriel realized he was hard. The throbbing wasn't only coming from his chest and neck—it came from his groin as well. Arousal spiraled through him, leaving him in a heightened state of numbness. Every touch spread across him like menthol, tingling, cooling, and addictive.

"Sir," Gabriel gasped. He rolled his head to the side and buried his face against his arm. Each breath he took came too quickly, and he couldn't regulate them. "*Sir!*"

They weren't having sex—they weren't even nude. All Sir did was nip, lick, and pinch, and yet Gabriel had never felt so good. His hips pushed upward to seek friction against Sir's body, and Sir rewarded him by thrusting down and pushing him into the bedding.

"Breed me." Old habits died hard, and Gabriel's body was ready for a heat he'd already medicated against. He parted his thighs farther and pressed up against Sir. "Sir, *please*, breed me."

Sir's finger pulled, and Gabriel cried out as his nipple was twisted. No matter what Sir did to him, there was no pain, and Gabriel was beginning to think there never would be again.

"Every day, I want to see a pill on your tongue, Gabriel." Sir's teeth grazed the edge of Gabriel's jaw until his lips met the corners of Gabriel's. "Every day, I want to see you swallow it. Someday, we will have a family, but not now. Not until we're *both* ready."

"Yes, Sir." The promise was hot on his tongue, but it was truthful. Gabriel didn't want a baby anymore—not for now. All he wanted was to know Sir's body, and for Sir to know his in return. "I understand, Sir."

Sir's kiss was sizzling, and when it broke, the darkness Gabriel saw shimmered and shifted like it had been licked by flames. There was a release of pressure from his wrists, and then the sound of fabric hitting Sir's bedroom floor. Gabriel imagined that it was Sir's shirt, and that Sir's chest was now bare, the ink he so often hid from the world on display, and the barbells through his nipples glinting in the light.

"Now you," Sir uttered, and the image in Gabriel's head disappeared in a flurry of activity.

The shirt Gabriel wore was tugged from his body, but he didn't notice the change in temperature—his skin was chilled from the strange heights Sir had already driven him to. No sooner was the shirt stripped from his torso than Sir's hands were on his chest, forcing him back onto the bed with controlled savagery that made Gabriel want more. With his hands now free of Sir's control, Gabriel found Sir's thigh and trailed along it to grope Sir through his jeans, squeezing the bulge he found there. It was hard for him —*because* of him—but Sir didn't let him take pride in it for long. In the next second, Gabriel's hands were pinned above his head once more. Sir moved on the bed—Gabriel felt the shift in the distribution of weight on the mattress—and undid the front of Gabriel's pants. He guided them from his body.

Gabriel lifted his hips, and Sir made quick work of his briefs.

It wasn't like it had been before. Gabriel *wanted* it.

Action was never so easy to take. He opened his thighs and let Sir have his way.

45

CEDRIC

Heat.

Medicated, but irrefutable. It made Gabriel smell sweet, and it drew Cedric to him. The heat blockers he'd introduced to Gabriel's system would stunt the symptoms before they became unruly, but the tantalizing scent of fertile omega reached Cedric's nose regardless. He ran his fingers between Gabriel's cheeks to find them slick.

His omega.

His.

Blindfolded and beautiful, his cheeks were flushed and his hard cock bobbed over his stomach. The desire that arced through Cedric was all because of him. Gabriel was the one he'd wanted since the beginning, and to have him now, six long months since they'd first met, confirmed what Cedric had known all along.

Gabriel was worth the wait.

Cedric tugged at his belt and undid his fly. He kicked his pants off and pulled down the boxers he wore beneath. Foreplay had left him aching for Gabriel's body, and he would not deny himself any longer. What Gabriel asked, he would provide. Gabriel's word was his command, and Cedric was bound to it.

He released Gabriel's wrists only so he could sink to his groin and run his tongue along the cock Gabriel had kept hidden from him for so long. Six months together, yet it was the first time Cedric had tasted him like this. The wait was worth it—Gabriel was delicious.

"*Sir!*" Gabriel cried with lofty delight. He arched his back, and Cedric let him into his mouth. His tongue lavished Gabriel's body with the attention he knew it needed. Before sex, before anything else, Cedric would prove to him that he was worthy of pleasure. For as long as it took to get the message into his head, Cedric would made him come again, and again, and again.

Gabriel's delicate fingers pulled Cedric's hair as he sucked, and Cedric looked up over the smooth planes of Gabriel's body to the blindfolded head that had lifted itself up as if to watch him. Gabriel's lips were red and glossy from kissing, and they were parted slightly as he drew in desperate breaths. The color in his cheeks betrayed his excitement as much as his stiffened cock did. Cedric committed the image of him to memory, then lowered his gaze and bobbed his head, letting Gabriel farther into his mouth.

"S-Sir!" Gabriel panted, voice almost squeaky from how desperate it was. He lifted his hips and pushed himself the rest of the way into Cedric's mouth. The tension in his body built—Cedric felt it in his trembling thighs. "Sir, you're gonna make me... make me..."

Come.

Cedric's tongue ran along the underside of Gabriel's cock, and he bobbed his head again to set up a steady pace. Gabriel gasped and dropped back onto the bed, going rigid. The muscles in his thighs tightened, and his legs stretched out as his toes curled. If he pushed himself any further, he would snap. Still, Cedric worked his tongue and lips, sweetening each bob of his head. To please his partner was what he was born to do—Dom or sub. Cedric wouldn't let his talents go to waste.

The bed went still when Gabriel came, and a scream pierced

the bedroom that Cedric was sure his neighbors would have heard, had they been home. Cum, thick and alkaline, introduced itself to Cedric's tongue, and he pulled back only so he could swallow. The taste partnered with the scent of omega in heat and left him wanting more.

Gabriel, panting for breath, lay spent on the bed. Both of his arms stretched away from him, his fingers curled loosely against his palm. The silk scarf remained in place, its dark fibers beautiful against Gabriel's pale skin. "Y-you didn't breed me, Sir."

"I know." Cedric wiped his lips on the back of his arm and climbed back up Gabriel's body. When he spoke next, his nose brushed the tip of Gabriel's, and Gabriel sucked in a tiny breath that made what Cedric had to say even sweeter yet. "I'm not finished with you yet."

GABRIEL

There was no need for lube. Gabriel's heat arrived without any of its usual cruelty to slick his ass and coat his thighs. But heat or not, sex wasn't supposed to feel this way. Sex wasn't supposed to be good. And more than that, orgasm was never supposed to happen with a partner.

One by one, Sir plucked all the little lies from Gabriel's head and taught him the truth.

And oh, what a truth it was.

I'm not finished with you yet.

The statement echoed in Gabriel's mind as Sir's lips met his, the slightest taste of himself present in his kiss. Gabriel closed his eyes and let the power of his taste sink in—he was the one who'd claimed Sir's mouth, and who'd used it shamelessly. In small ways, Sir proved that nothing divided them. Alpha and omega were biological concepts, not limiting agents. Just as Gabriel had been used for pleasure, now he used his alpha in the same way. The fluidity in their relationship opened his eyes to what he'd missed—and what he'd willfully ignored.

Sir flipped Gabriel onto his stomach, and soon enough, Gabriel felt Sir's thick cock run its course along his soaked taint. Fireworks exploded behind Gabriel's eyes, and he tossed his head back. The desire he felt for Sir wasn't a product of his heat—the medication suppressed his instincts and granted him clarity. What he felt for Sir was rooted in truth.

He needed Sir, and Sir needed him. They would never be apart again.

"I love you, Gabriel." Sir ran a hand across his hip, the head of his cock nuzzling Gabriel's hole, but not yet pressing inward. The delay left Gabriel squirming. "Any time it gets to be too much, or any time you feel uncomfortable, all you have to do is speak the word, and I will stop."

Gabriel nodded. He didn't trust his voice. The sounds that came from his mouth weren't familiar to his ear, and it was frightening to think that Sir's hold on him had such an effect. The numbness raced through his body, but now that the pain had stopped, a new sensation had taken its place. Every gentle caress allowed Gabriel to feel himself from the outside, like he was in Sir's position instead of his own. Slender thighs he'd never appreciated before blinked into focus, and narrow hips he'd regretted were redeemed. Every place Sir's fingers traced over with wonder alerted Gabriel to the beauty of his body—something he'd never seen before, and that he doubted he would have noticed if it weren't for Sir's guidance.

Another offering. Another revelation.

It took darkness to bring what was truly beautiful to light.

And then, just like that, there was nothing separating them anymore.

The stretch was sudden, but it wasn't unanticipated. Gabriel's body parted as Sir pushed inward, and Gabriel cried out in delirious pleasure as he stretched to accept his lover's cock. The slick he produced eased penetration, and Sir pushed in farther and farther, until something else entered Gabriel that made him gasp and squirm.

Two smooth parallel balls.

And then another set.

And another.

Gabriel struggled for breath. He'd never felt anything like that before, and as another set of smooth intrusions entered his body alongside Sir's cock, he struggled to make sense of what he was feeling. The silk scarf kept him from seeing anything.

But it didn't take him long to figure out what was going on.

Are you interested in body modification, Gabriel?

Sir's shaft was pierced all along the underside, five sets of piercings stacked one after another, their smooth balls stretching Gabriel even farther and changing what it felt like to be stuffed with a cock. Sir's frenum ladder piercings were inside of him now, the rounded heads of the barbells rubbing against him as Sir's cock stretched him full. And when Sir drew back, each of those balls dragged against Gabriel's insides and increased the friction as they left his body one by one. With his sight robbed from him, Gabriel was even more highly attuned to them than he otherwise would have been.

He felt himself stretch as Sir pushed them back in.

A moan rolled from Gabriel's lips, and he took Sir's pierced cock in full.

Pleasure exploded inside of him as the first of the balls rubbed against his prostate, leading the way for the others to follow. Gabriel threw himself down onto the bed and arched so his ass pushed up into Sir's body, howling with pleasure as bump after bump rubbed him exactly where he needed it. He'd come just minutes before, but he was already hard again. His body wanted more.

Would every time they had sex be like this? As the balls of Sir's piercing rolled over his prostate in ways that drove Gabriel to delirious pleasure, Gabriel couldn't help but think so. His eyes rolled back, and when Sir's grip loosened on his hips, he bucked blindly against him to regain some of the pleasure.

This was what it was like to want sex. This was what it was like to be cherished by a partner.

Gabriel would never let the feeling go.

"I'm going to knot you," Sir uttered, voice lost to lust like Gabriel had never heard it before, yet still firmly established in control. "I'm going to fill you up with me until you forget that there was ever anyone else. Your past doesn't matter anymore, Gabriel—only your future does. *Our* future."

"Our future." Gabriel spoke through a moan, rolling his hips as the pleasure built. The pressure on his prostate threatened to push his cum out from the inside, and there was nothing Gabriel could do to stop it. "*Y-yes!*"

Sir's lips were on him again, peppering the back of his neck with affection. Tears streaked down Gabriel's cheeks, and he worked his hips in time to Sir's thrusts. It shouldn't have felt so good. Sex *never* felt good.

But with Sir, the world was different.

Sir's truth painted a kinder, safer world—one Gabriel wanted to cling to for the rest of his life.

"Knot me." Gabriel's voice shook, and his hands locked into the pillows before him as Sir worked their bodies toward orgasm. "Want to feel you. Want to know you. *Knot me.*"

A tiny grunt and a change in the rhythm of Sir's hips was all the warning he got before the swelling began. The pressure inside Gabriel increased as Sir's knot inflated and Sir's orgasm flooded him with seed. With a cry, Gabriel buried his head into the pillows and rocked against him. The knot grew, stuffing his body right behind Gabriel's tight ring. Sir filled him, and Gabriel took everything he had to offer as his own orgasm threatened to arrive.

The knot put pressure in places Gabriel was no longer used to. Sir worked his cum deeper into Gabriel's body with short, instinctive thrusts designed to help Gabriel conceive, and the combined pressure of his knot and the sensation of his piercings rubbing Gabriel's prostate pushed him over the edge. For the second time that hour, Gabriel let loose with a hollow cry and came, decorating his belly with glossy white seed.

Sir took the silk scarf away from Gabriel's eyes, then directed his head to the side so they looked eye to eye. Gabriel allowed his head to be turned. He looked up at Sir as his eyelids drooped and he fought off sleep. One orgasm was rare, but two was unheard of. Gabriel didn't have much left.

"Every day, I want to see that pill on your tongue, Gabriel," Sir said. "I want to see you swallow it. I want you to be good."

"I can be good," Gabriel whispered, his voice robbed of volume by his breathlessness. "I *will* be good."

"And I'll be good to you in return." Sir caressed Gabriel's cheek, and Gabriel allowed himself to close his eyes. "I want to prove that I can care for you, body and soul. As long as you take those pills, whenever you want me, I'll be yours."

"We'll never get out of bed, then," Gabriel murmured, already half asleep.

Sir's laughter was the good dream he'd been waiting for all his life.

GABRIEL

Three rhythmic knocks on the club-side door brought Gabriel to lift his head. Lilian, who'd been lying on her back while she waved a teddy bear in the air, sat up and looked, too. No matter how often he babysat, Gabriel still found it hard to believe that Lilian was eighteen months old. Time flew, and her growth was remarkable—she'd gone from a tiny swaddled baby to a mini replica of Adrian in the blink of an eye.

"Ceddik." She dropped the bear onto the couch and jumped down, clumsy on her feet, but too full of energy to care. One of her pigtails had started to fall—the no-tears elastic had been pulled down by the couch cushion from when she'd been lying on her back. Gabriel was always afraid to tie the hair bands too tight in case he hurt her.

Before he could so much as rise to his feet, Lilian scampered off in the direction of the club-side door. The door was too heavy for her to open, and the knob was too far above her head for her to reach, so he had no qualms about letting her go first. And even if she did get through the door on a fluke, Sir would be there to catch her.

Gabriel's cheeks warmed, and he folded his arms across his chest to hold himself as he followed Lilian to the door.

"Hi Ceddik," Lilian said through the door. She twisted at the hips back and forth, spinning the tiered skirt she wore over her leggings so that it fanned out around her. "Hi!"

Gabriel picked her up and tucked her against his hip. She squealed with delight and latched onto him, burying her face against the side of his chest.

"Will you be nice to Cedric?" Gabriel asked. Even now, it was strange to say Sir's real name, but around Lilian, Sir had asked him to use it. "He's had a long day at work and he's going to be tired."

"Yes!" Lilian agreed.

"Then let's give him a nice hello."

The door was heavy, but Gabriel was used to its weight by now. He balanced Lilian on his hip and held the door open with his foot, smiling for Sir not because Sir asked, but because Gabriel wanted to. It was unusual that Sir worked later than four in the morning, but with Sterling gone on a business trip with several close associates, he'd taken on additional responsibilities to make sure The Shepherd ran smoothly.

That was fine for Gabriel, because it let him stay with Adrian while Sterling was out of town, looking after Lilian during the evening and early morning hours so Adrian could get some sleep. It was a little after seven now, and Adrian would be climbing out of the shower any minute to take over for Gabriel so Gabriel could go home.

"Hi Ceddik!" Lilian repeated, her grin wide and enthusiastic in the way only a toddler's could be.

"Hello, Ms. Lilian," Sir replied, bowing low the way he always did. Lilian laughed and clutched Gabriel's shirt tightly at the show. "You look lovely this morning."

Lilian buried her face against Gabriel's chest all over again. Gabriel kissed the top of her head. "Adrian has good taste."

"If I had to guess, Adrian's not the one who dressed her this morning. I feel like a certain uncle is to be acknowledged for putting together his fashion-forward niece." Sir winked and stepped into the hall. Even after a year together, small gestures like those made Gabriel's heart flutter. "Speaking of Adrian, are we waiting for him?"

"Yes. He's awake, but he's in the shower. Once he's dressed, we should be ready to go." Gabriel's tongue longed to tack on a "Sir" to his response, but he respected Sir's command. In front of Lilian, they kept their play subtle. "Did you have a good time at work?"

"I did." Sir kissed Gabriel's cheek, and Gabriel melted against him. Their relationship was no longer new, but it had not lost its luster. Even the simplest touch sent pinpricks across Gabriel's skin. "What have you been working on tonight?"

"Solving linear equations." Gabriel scrunched his nose and grimaced. "I don't like it."

"Then I suppose we'll have to work on it together this afternoon, won't we?" Sir leaned in and brushed his nose along Gabriel's ear, snagging his lobe with his teeth on the way down. The nip happened so quickly that even had Lilian been in a position where she could see, she likely wouldn't have noticed it. "You're going to need to know how to solve equations like those for your GED."

A shiver of excitement swept through Gabriel as Sir nipped him. Maybe, if he was good, when they got home they could play before they fell asleep.

"I know," Gabriel said. "I'm trying."

"I know you are, and I appreciate it."

Now that the attention wasn't on her, Lilian pushed at Gabriel's chest and started to squirm. Gabriel set her down, and she took off down the hall.

Sir chuckled. "That girl only has two modes, doesn't she? Run and sleep."

"Have you seen who her fathers are, Sir?" Gabriel gave Sir a half-smile. "If Adrian isn't doing something, it's because he's passed out, and you know Sterling..."

"By now? Yes, I do."

Sir wrapped an arm around Gabriel's waist, and they moved as one to follow Lilian. She'd run straight across the living room to the hall with the bedrooms—right to Adrian, whose hair was still dripping, but who was otherwise dressed and ready to start his day.

"Daddy!" Lilian lifted her arms, and Adrian lifted her up and kissed her cheek. Parenthood had mellowed him significantly, although Gabriel knew that his brother would never really lose his edge—not that it was necessarily a bad thing. Adrian's lashing tongue and sharp wit helped him stay on top of his game in the business world while Sterling stayed home and looked after their daughter. "Mornin'!"

"Good morning, Princess. Were you good for Uncle Gabriel this morning?"

"Yes!"

Adrian lifted a brow and met Gabriel's eyes as he approached. "Well, he doesn't look like he was thrown to finger-paint-obsessed wolves, so I'm going to go ahead and say that you've been a very good girl this morning. Thank you, Lilian."

"Love you, Daddy."

"I love you, too."

Gabriel leaned into Sir, letting his brother's joy bolster his own. One day, if he and Sir decided it was right, that would be him—but not now, and maybe not for a long time still. Gabriel was young, and there was plenty of time to have a child. When the time was right, it would happen. He wouldn't rush things anymore.

"Thanks for looking after her this morning," Adrian said. His gaze met Gabriel's, and he held it. "I've got it covered from here. You guys must be tired."

"I just came upstairs from doing admin work in the club, so it's not such a big deal." Sir's hand stroked Gabriel's hip, and Gabriel's body started to wake to his advances. The arousal was low-burning, but it wouldn't take much for Sir to work those embers into an inferno. "Sterling's back tonight?"

"Right. He'll be back sometime this afternoon. If there's a change in his travel plans, I'll get in touch with Gabriel to let him know. If you could keep his schedule open, I'd appreciate it."

"Of course." Sir offered Adrian an easy smile, the kind that made Gabriel's heart flutter. No matter how long he lived or how often he saw it, he thought that smile would always get to him. "He'll be available. I'll make sure of it."

Theirs was an unconventional relationship, Gabriel had learned, but that didn't make it bad. The truth was, Gabriel needed Sir. That didn't mean that he was worthless—all it meant was that his normal was different from everyone else's, and that was okay. With Sir there to guide him, Gabriel was happy, and every small revelation or breakthrough he made along the way was a perk instead of a requirement.

Broken was beautiful.

Sir loved him, scars and all.

They said their goodbyes. Lilian latched onto Sir's leg like she usually did to beg him not to go, and Adrian had to wrangle her so Gabriel and Sir could leave. The way Sir doted on her, and the way she loved him so unendingly, made Gabriel think that one day, Sir would make an outstanding father.

"Ceddik!" Lilian called in utmost despair from the metal platform outside the penthouse's back door. She gripped tightly to Adrian's chest as he held her. Sir and Gabriel had arrived in the alley below, and Sir lifted a hand high over his head to wave at her.

"Until we meet again, Ms. Lilian," he called. "Remember to be a proper young lady. Be good for your fathers."

Gabriel smiled and slipped his hand into Sir's. Their fingers wove together, and Sir lowered his arm and turned away from the building. Winter was coming, and it chilled the air and froze Gabriel's breath as it left his nostrils.

313

"I was thinking," Sir murmured as they walked. The sound of the penthouse door closing marked the end of his sentence—Adrian and Lilian had gone back inside. "It's almost our anniversary, and—"

A noise stopped Sir in his tracks, and Gabriel came to an abrupt stop beside him. A cardboard box toppled from a nearby dumpster and rolled several times until it came to a stop right-side up.

"Gabriel?" Cedric said in a soft, but stern voice. "I want you to stay here. Don't move."

Gabriel's pulse kicked into overdrive, and the familiar urge to run threatened to overtake him. For the last year, he'd worked hard to overcome it, but it would be a struggle he'd need to put up with for the rest of his life. "Yes, Sir."

As he remained glued to the spot, watching as Sir cautiously approached the box, Gabriel went through his breathing exercises to work himself down from his panic. Each long exhalation froze in the air on the way out, and he let the mist direct his focus away from the abstract. It was only a box. There was nothing to fear. All he needed to do was keep breathing.

Sir reached the box. He squatted in front of it, but as he reached out to move the top flap aside, Gabriel had to squeeze his eyes shut. The anticipation was starting to eat at him, and he had to cut it out of his mind before it riled him any further.

"Oh," Sir murmured. Then he laughed. The tension broke, and Gabriel opened his eyes to find Sir on his way back from the box. He had his coat tucked tightly around his frame, his crossed arms holding it in place. There was a bulge beneath it that hadn't been there before. "I'm going to take what just happened as a sign from above that what I was about to ask was meant to be."

What Sir was about to ask? Gabriel blinked and stood a little more rigidly, panic shifting into excitement. "What were you about to ask, Sir?"

"Our anniversary is coming up," Sir restated. "You moved in with me four months ago, and now that we're settled, I was thinking that maybe we should talk about making things a little more serious..."

Sir's coat *moved*. Gabriel's eyes went wide, and he took a small step back and pointed, hand trembling. All Sir did was laugh.

"You know that we're a family, Gabriel." Sir's words were kind, and as he spoke, he looked into Gabriel's eyes. "Two people are all it takes—but I know you want more. The truth is, right now I'm not ready to have kids, but that doesn't mean I want to be childless forever. One day, I want us to have a baby, but until then, I want to make a promise to you that it will happen—I want to give you something to prove that I want our family to grow."

The coat was still moving, and Gabriel had a hard time keeping his attention on Sir's face. He didn't need to for long—the blob behind Sir's coat moved upward, and suddenly, a small, gray tabby kitten with stunning green eyes popped its head free. Gabriel gasped and jumped backward a half-step. The kitten mewed, revealing a row of sharp, tiny teeth.

"I was going to ask if you would consider adopting a pet with me, but I think one may have fallen into our laps." Sir moved his arms to free one hand, and he petted the kitten's head with a single finger. "Would you like that?"

"Yes," Gabriel said without thinking. He stepped forward and held his hand out for the kitten to sniff. It leaned forward and licked the side of his finger with its sandpaper tongue, and just like that, Gabriel fell in love. "Do you think it's a her? She has a sweet face. I love her, Sir. She's perfect."

"I think so, too." Sir freed the kitten from his coat and held her out for Gabriel. She fit in a single hand, but Gabriel kept her cradled against his chest as a strange, protective joy spread through him. Was this what it meant to feel paternal? He smiled and stood close to Sir, allowing Sir to lead him to the parking garage a few blocks away. "I love you, Gabriel, and I never want you to forget it."

"I won't," Gabriel said, not because it was expected, but because it was true. It didn't matter what kind of a family Sir did or didn't give him, or what path life led them down—Gabriel had found the man he wanted to spend the rest of his days with, and they would make it a happy life together whether they had children or not. "I love you, too, Sir."

They left the alley and faced the day together.

EPILOGUE

GABRIEL

The dreams always started the same.

Sir's smiling face looked him over, one eyebrow hitched playfully, as Gabriel lazed in bed. Sun streamed through the open blinds to streak the bed in ribbons of light. It was warm. Always so warm.

"You feeling better today?" Sir asked. He leaned over to kiss Gabriel's forehead, and Gabriel closed his eyes and enjoyed the touch of his lover's lips. The simplest joys always left him the most satisfied. "I made you breakfast, if you want it. It's in the kitchen."

Breakfast sounded wonderful, but the space beneath the blankets was warm, and Gabriel's body was weightless. The "thank you" he wanted to say died before it reached his tongue, and he could only hum in appreciation as he closed his eyes again and melted into the bed.

Everything in the world was right, and there was nothing he had to fear anymore. Sir was there, and he would protect their life together fiercely. Nothing was so scary anymore.

"You know, if you don't get up soon, I have a feeling that breakfast is going to disappear." Sir's voice was equal parts playful and warm. "We've got kitchen thieves in this house, you know."

"Mm," Gabriel murmured, because he both did and didn't know. Kitchen thieves *did* sound like a big deal, but Sir's exact meaning was obscured to him by foggy, comfortable thoughts.

The giggle from the foot of the bed reminded him of everything he'd forgotten.

Gabriel lifted his head to spot the boy lying there, his elbows on the mattress and his chin cupped in his hands. Five years old and beautifully blond, he looked like Gabriel had when he was little. His green eyes were like Sir's, and Gabriel got the impression that when he grew older, he'd share all of Sir's most handsome traits.

"Oh, a kitchen thief," Gabriel said with a laugh. He pulled the blankets back, and the son he knew was his scurried up the bed on his hands and knees and slipped beneath the sheets to curl up against his side. He was in his pajamas, but his hair was recently washed, and Gabriel breathed it in as he wrapped his arms around him. "Well, I don't know if I have to worry. I'm sure that no kitchen thieves would be so heartless as to steal from a poor, sleepy dad like me."

The boy giggled again. His identity wasn't linked to a name, but to feelings—pride, adoration, endless love, and happiness. His small hands found their way to Gabriel's rounded stomach, and he stroked the taut skin there as the newest Langston woke up, too.

"Do you feel him kicking?" Gabriel asked. The bed shifted, and Sir joined them. He slid a hand over Gabriel's hip to caress his baby bump, joining their son's exploration. "He's waking up, too. He must be hungry. It's hard work, to be a growing baby."

Bright green eyes looked up at him with wonder, and Gabriel was struck with such love that he was certain he would cry. His son's small hands searched his belly until the baby kicked directly against him, and he gasped and rolled away. The cat was quick to take his place, her gray tail swishing as she jumped onto the bed from the floor and curled up where the boy had been moments before.

Sir laughed. "Get back here, Monkey. The baby's only trying to say hello."

Their son returned. He took the cat into his arms and curled up against Gabriel's chest, then became still. For a while, they laid together in bed as a family and let the lazy morning pass them by.

It was bliss.

The dreams always started the same, and they always ended the same, too—with Gabriel opening his eyes to find Sir at his side and their cat at the foot of the bed, renewed in his faith that even if his dreams never came true, the feeling of love in his heart for Sir—for his family—would always stay the same.

ABOUT THE AUTHOR

Piper Scott debuted as a trio of authors looking to write together for fun. Their collaboration led to three novella-length books (Love Me, Save Me, and Keep Me,) before life sent them in different directions, leaving just one author with an omegaverse plot bunny that wouldn't leave her alone. Obey was born several months later, but the plot bunny never left—it multiplied.

Left to her own devices, Piper Scott writes scorching but heartfelt contemporary omegaverse romance about men you can't help but fall in love with.

ALSO BY PIPER SCOTT

Rutledge Brothers Series

Love Me

Save Me

Keep Me

His Command Series

Obey

Beg

Stay

Heal

Breathe

Single Dad Support Group Series

The Problem

The Proposal

The Solution

The Decision

The Promise

The Answer

Waking the Dragons Series

(with Susi Hawke)

Alpha Awakened

Alpha Ablaze

Alpha Deceived

Alpha Victorious

Rent-a-Dom Series

(with Susi Hawke)

Daddy Wanted

Master Wanted

Teacher Wanted

Beard Wanted

Redneck Unicorns Series

(with Susi Hawke)

Seriously H*rny

Dangerously H*rny

Forbidden Desires Series

(with Lynn Van Dorn, writing as Virginia Kelly)

Clutch

Bond

Mate

Forbidden Desires Spin-Off Series

(with Lynn Van Dorn, writing as Virginia Kelly)

Swallow

Audio addict? See which of Piper's books are available on Audible. New titles are always always being added.

Check Them Out Here!

AS EMMA ALCOTT

Small Town Hearts Series:

After the Crash

.

MORE FROM LOVELIGHT PRESS

Share Your Thoughts
Thank you for reading Heal by Piper Scott.
If you enjoyed this book, please consider leaving a review on
Amazon or on Goodreads.
Your support means the world to our authors!

More from LoveLight Press
LoveLight Press is a small independent publisher specialising in
LGBT Romance. Why not visit our website or join our mailing list
to see our latest titles?

Printed in Great Britain
by Amazon

78870520R00189